The New V

Table of Contents

The New Viking Gold Mine
Bjorn Amundson in the Gold Rush
Clifford Farris
Desert Coyote Press LLC
Littleton, Colorado USA

ISBN: 1-7332512-3-5

Any references to historical events, real people, or real places are used fictitiously. Other names, characters, places and events are products of the author's imagination, and any resemblance to actual events or places or persons, living or dead, is entirely coincidental.

Cover design by CBF.

Book design by CBF.

Front image: 1866 miner and rocker box

Back image: *Norsemen at sea following their raven pilot* (c) North Wind Picture Archives from an illustration by Frank Thayer Merrill.

Printed by Desert Coyote Press LLC in the United States of America.

Desert Coyote Press LLC
Desertcoyotepress.com
CliffordFarris@Desertcoyotepress.com

Dedication

For Ann, my wife, who has tolerated an AWOL husband at home for over a year and a half during the authorship of this story.

The New Viking Gold Mine

Clifford Farris

1 - Amundson and Murrieta

Zing—a bullet from the haze on the right hillside shattered a branch over Bjorn's head and ricocheted to his left.

Flash—a revolver returned fire from the bushes near the impact.

"There he is," said a voice on the hillside. "Come out with your hands up, Murrieta,"

"*Bésame el culo*," shouted a man's voice in the bushes.

"Kiss my ass too, dammit."

Bjorn Amundson tumbled off the right side of his horse in the middle of the trail and gripped the ground in a spreadeagle.

"Yo . . . !"

With a cough to clear the dust from his lungs he sucked in the smoky sage-scented air.

"Hold your fire. I'm down here and I'm not Murrieta."

For cover he crawled under his other horse that was hitched to a wagon.

" . . . and I talk English."

The dismount on the wrong side and gunfire spooked the horse and it trampled Bjorn's ash-blonde hair into the sand on his way to parts unknown. A rattlesnake sound of "pssst" upped the tension and Bjorn rolled aside to avoid the snake bite and the hooves.

There it was again, "Pssst . . . ,"

"Hide me, *Amigo*, they're after me."

"You again." Bjorn lifted a mining apparatus in the wagon bed, "Get in here."

The whisperer curled under it with only a few splinters in his butt.

Lowering the machine like a shell, Bjorn stared at the voices through the haze. Curses from the spine-covered shrubs marked their progress.

"Can't see a damned thing in this smoke from the Indian fires," cough, cough, said a man who took form from the ridge line followed by his sidekick. He hollered over Bjorn's head, "I've got you now, Joaquín Murrieta. Come out with your hands up."

Two mounted men burst onto the trail. The leader had a scar on his jaw like Bjorn did, but was missing his little finger.

Bjorn had all his fingers.

A rattlesnake skin circled the other rider's hat and the dangling tail rattled when he moved.

Bjorn didn't like snakes.

The first rider said shaking his head, "Have you seen a greaser sneaking around? Colonel Frémont captured California in 1847 but the Mexicans are still here after three years."

"I've seen bullets flying over my head." Bjorn coughed from the dust and the smoke. "I'm taking this rocker to my gold claim and you're blocking my way." He patted the dust off of his clothes except where the sweat had turned it to mud. "I'm hot and tired. Get out of my way."

The rattlesnake corporal on the multicolored pinto said to the sergeant, "Check that rocker box."

"Too damn heavy. What the hell is a rocker?"

"It's a box on curved rockers with a handle. You shovel gravel in the top and rock it like a baby. The gravel slops out and the bottom traps your gold. At least that's the idea "

"How do you know?"

"Got one on my claim."

"Do any good?"

"Sometimes, but my arms ache by the end of the day. I need a helper."

"And that's what you call this contraption?"

"Yeah."

The sergeant said to Bjorn, "Keep your eyes peeled for a dangerous bandit on the loose. He'll slit your throat faster'n he'll say good morning."

"What does he look like?"

The soldier pulled a sheet out of a saddlebag. "Here's his wanted poster. There was a hanky-panky somewhere because he has blue eyes and his hair looks like that blonde head of yours, but trust me he's a desperate scoundrel. There is a thousand-dollar reward on his head. Nail this picture to a tree somewhere."

The horsemen yanked their reins toward the bushes. "We're on your ass, Murrieta. You won't get away this time, smoke or not." Pounding hoof beats faded into the buzzing of the cicadas.

Bjorn raised the rocker, "What has the border ruffian done now?"

From under the equipment came a whisper, "Are they gone?"

"I can't hear their horses."

Jumping to the ground, the smiling Mexican looked at Bjorn's height that was a full head more than his. He retrieved a lit cigarillo from his pocket, clamped it between his teeth, and drew a puff.

With his best winning grin he said, "Good morning. I will not cut your throat today. Muchas Gracias."

Bjorn stared at the young man who was moderately tall and well built, with a smooth complexion, light hair, and fierce blue eyes. He appeared to be about twenty-two years old with a scar on his right cheek.

Towering over him Bjorn said, "Three men with scars in these California goldfields. Yours, mine, and his. You'd think we were related."

Bjorn held the wanted poster next to Joaquín's face. "Are you lost? Here's your picture and they're looking for you."

Joaquín spit on the ground and said, "A thousand dollars? I'm worth at least two don't you think?"

"You're worth more as a friend."

"A good friend is worth ten thousand kin."

"My life lacks friends, money, and kin."

"You have me, *Amigo*."

"Well, maybe one."

Joaquín read the description, "My enemies lie about me."

"How?"

He backhanded the poster, "I never stole that mule . . . and look at those crimes. I couldn't pull those off if I wanted to."

"What crimes?"

Joaquín shoved the crude piece of paper into Bjorn's face. "Read them for yourself."

Bjorn looked at the face with a scar on the wanted poster instead of the words. Joaquín sensed his hesitation. "The foreign devil can't read? I could read when I was eight down in Mexico."

The big Norwegian lowered his head, "I'm a man of action." He raised his head and flexed his massive biceps. "I don't need to read."

Joaquín looked at the miner and shook his head, "Gringos. I have to go."

"Watch yourself and good luck."

"Gracias."

Murrieta tiptoed to a little camp the sergeant and corporal had missed. He quickly packed his horse and rode back to Bjorn. "Adios," and disappeared up the path his pursuers had broken on the hillside.

The Gringo took a deep breath, coughed, and slapped his wagon horse on the rump. "Haw. Get along." They lumbered up the path that followed the American River toward Bjorn's claim. It was registered as the New Viking Gold Mine.

Bjorn talked to himself since his horse pulling the wagon didn't say much, "My rocker box will double production—if I can find help. I'll be rich."

Man and beast dripped sweat in the blazing midday sun. The horse flicked its tail to brush off the flies, but Bjorn had to let them bite since his long hair was not a tail. They came to the bottom of a rise in the trail that promised more misery.

"Dammit horse, I forgot about Cougar Hill when I loaded the wagon. Here, I'll help you." Bjorn put his shoulder against the back of the wagon and pushed it up the slope. The horse took a minor vacation that Bjorn could not see.

"I hate this mountain."

He took a breather on top, dripping wet and panting. Leaning against the wagon, he was joined by a jovial heavyset man who took shape out of the smoke. One arm led a mule and a painted mercantile wagon. The other waved a hearty greeting.

"Good morning, Mr. Amundson. How goes your day?"

"Outside of bounty hunters shooting at me and struggling up this hill, I'm fine. How about yourself? Fatty Arbuckle isn't it?"

"Glad to see you again."

"There's a steep dropoff behind me. Got good brakes?"

"Not really. There's a load of heavy merchandise in my wagon."

"I'll help you down the hill."

As they inched down the slope, Bjorn straddled the tongue on the wagon and propped his back against the front. The peddler tapped the mule to hold her back by plowing in her front hooves. This, her natural stubborn instinct, was useful for once.

With only a few slips, curses, and cracks of the whip, they eased the brightly colored mercantile wagon to the bottom.

Bjorn said, "Whew. There you are, Fatty."

Arbuckle ignored the nickname. Talking a mile a minute, he said, "I've got new wares you have to see." He opened the double doors on the decorated display chest bolted to his wagon. Shiny tools, jars of patent medicines, a harmonica, sewing supplies, playing cards, and even a cigar lighting lamp hung inside.

"You need a razor, my friend, and here is the shaving soap and aftershave lotion to go with it."

"Naw, I kind of like my beard. The ladies say it tickles."

Fatty laughed, "Just for you, here's the best cigar in the world straight from Havana. Nothing beats a smoke and a tot of rum in the evening to the serenade of crickets and coyotes."

"I'll take the rum, but I'm still working on the cigars from last time."

"Need some leather balm for your saddle or boots?"

"What I need is liniment for my sore muscles." He shrugged his shoulders to relieve the tension from his recent exertions.

The salesman pulled three bottles from their racks and showed them to Bjorn. "Take your pick."

Bjorn studied the pictures on the labels. One showed a man flanked by two snakes and labeled *Clark Stanley's Snake Oil Liniment*. He didn't like snakes. Another bottle featured a buxom woman with the words, *Mug-wump Specific*. Yet a third showed an Indian and read, *Bennett Pieters Red Jacket Stomach Bitters*. He didn't know much about the Indians.

The woman won and Bjorn picked up the middle jar, "I'll take this one."

Since he could not read, the rest of the label was a mystery. What it said was, "Cure and preventive for all venereal diseases."

He found out later it did nothing for his sore muscles, but the preparation smelled good and kept him healthy.

2 - Back at the Mine

Bjorn hummed a tune as he unloaded his new rocker mining machine in front of his placer mine. He felt it decorated the claim where he lived and worked. A quick dip in the cold flowing waters of the American River washed off the sweat, mud, and dust from the trail.

With pride, he dripped his way up the bank to the neat but compact mining camp. Two companions now gone had helped construct a cabin to live in. Alongside the cabin, they built a wooden platform as the floor of a storage and work tent. Raunchy jokes accompanied the erection of a small privy in back. Dirt from the excavation made a mound in front of the cabin. A wooden Viking ship over the doorway was a carving from his father as a parting memento on leaving Norway.

The clerk in Sacramento had registered his mining claim under the name New Viking Gold Mine but Bjorn had not found anyone to make a sign yet.

A big dog with black and tan fur sprinted across the yard to greet him. She wagged her tail so hard it threatened to break her rump.

"Boudicca! Did Sergio take good care of you while I was gone? You've gained weight," as her tail thumped his leg. The seventy-five-pound animal leaped into his arms and licked his dripping face. "Whoa. You're a lot of dog to carry around."

He carried her into his twelve by twenty-foot cabin. Together, they checked for signs of intruders while he had been away.

The little stove opposite the bed was cold. The corner cabinet was in order, and undisturbed dust around the secret compartment in the floor confirmed his Colt revolver was safe. Views out the window were unchanged.

He walked around the cabin to the privy behind the storage shed, but before he could close the door Boudicca pushed her head in. "Do you mind? We can't both fit in here." He pushed her out the door tail first and latched it.

With Boudicca standing guard, he knew no one was around so he reached under the seat to tug on three ropes dangling toward the muck. He said to himself, "My gold is still here. Hope that linseed oil keeps those sailcloth bags waterproof."

Boudicca scratched at the door until Bjorn opened it. "Good Dog. You're a year old and big enough to keep the critters away, four-legged and two-legged."

Her ears perked up and she growled toward the trail.

"Who's coming?"

A fellow miner from the Murrieta family workings upstream walked into the clearing. "Sergio. How are you?" Before they could shake hands, Boudicca erupted in circles and jumped into his arms. She barked in his face and wagged her tail. He and Bjorn shook their heads to clear their ears after her deafening outburst.

"So, you taught her to jump on people?"

"Si, Señor, I call her the jumping beast of El Dorado County, but she learned to jump on her own. It's not my fault."

"What else did you teach my dog?"

"She sniffs her territory every morning for signs of trespassers. The other day she chased some scent for a long time. Somebody was here."

"I've seen the marks myself." He scratched Boudicca behind her ears. "Why don't you bark more? Not everybody is a friend, you know." The long wet tongue licked his hand.

"She came back with her tail straight like as to say, 'I found a spy.'"

"She doesn't miss much."

"I have work to do. See you later."

"You be good," he said to Boudicca. The mutt rubbed against his leg and sat on top of the mound of dirt, her throne.

Day after day Boudicca guarded the area from atop her throne while Bjorn shoveled gravel into his new rocker from pits in the riverbed. It was hard work for Boudicca because her dog given duty was to greet every sailor who had jumped ship, every wellwisher, or every just arrived '49er who walked the trail searching for their El Dorado fortune in gold.

The throngs of visitors stopped to pet the dog but congested Bjorn's little camp of cleared brush.

Looking into the furry face of his dog with her erect ears, Bjorn said, "We need more elbow room, don't you think?"

Boudicca didn't think so because she needed only a grassy three-foot spot around a visitor. It was her job.

Bjorn disagreed and found an open meadow higher on the riverbank. The clearing was about twenty yards wide with a view of the valley below and protected uphill by trees.

Boudicca wouldn't let her master enter until she circled the clearing with her nose to the ground. The all clear woof meant it smelled clean, at least to a canine.

Bjorn marked out a fire pit in the upper slope and began digging. The dirt was soft until his shovel hit an obstruction.

"Hmm . . . is that a rock?" He tapped it several times with the shovel.

Scraping away more the dirt, he uncovered a round surface. Bjorn was a man of minerals and studied dirt, especially anything unusual. A few more scoops unearthed the top part of a skull.

"What's this?"

More digging uncovered bits of feathers and a pattern of stones over the ribs where the chest would have been. He laid them aside in the same pattern. "They must mean something to the gravedigger."

He dug up more bones. Boudicca sniffed each one and helped to dig out more. That is, some of her dirt flew into the woods and some flew back into the hole. She liked digging and was proud of herself when she uncovered a rib or two.

Bjorn stacked the remains against a tree and added new bones as they appeared. With the skull on top, he completed the skeleton. After tying a bandanna around the neck, he stepped back to admire his archaeology.

"We've found a partner. He doesn't work very hard, but he'll stand guard . . . won't you, sir?"

Bjorn enlarged the hole into a fire pit and lined it with stones. While gathering firewood a thought hit him. "What if he is a woman? Let's see."

Boudicca watched as he held an arm bone next to his own arm. "They're as long as mine. "She was one hell of a woman or a stout brave. I'll call him a warrior by the name of Henry." He saluted the skeleton with a little bow and said, "Glad to meet you, Sir Henry. I'd shake your hand but you don't have a hand."

Bjorn was heating their evening feast of beans over the new fire pit when Boudicca snarled toward the trees.

An earsplitting war cry shattered the serenity. A tall angry Nisenan Indian leaped from the shadows and confronted Bjorn. "You dare to rob the grave of my sacred ancestor. The destiny of his spirit is offended and his ghost walks the earth to haunt the living. The coyote of his soul finds no comfort."

Bjorn said, "What do you mean?"

"You defiled my ancestor and ripped his hallowed bones from the spirit world."

"They were alone."

"You mock my grandfather." He shook his fist at Bjorn and pointed to the skeleton against the tree.

Angry braves streamed out of the trees to pay homage to their great-grandfather with guttural chants.

The Indians had never seen blonde hair and were terrified of Bjorn, yet felt a superstitious sense of wonder. They were convinced the angry ghost had returned from the dead to haunt them. Merely to look upon this apparition was death.

The Nisenans implored the ancient ones to leave them in peace.

Boudicca tried to shield Bjorn from the bows and arrows in the hands of the young bucks and and even war clubs, but there were too many.

The Indian on the left shot a ritual arrow at Boudicca. She showed her reflexes by jumping over the arrow, although it grazed her belly.

The leader attacked Bjorn with a war club but was too short to fatally smash his skull. His club did crack a rib before Bjorn could wrench it out of his arms. With wild swings and Viking war cries the blonde specter panicked the Nisenans and drove them off into the woods.

Bjorn ran to check on Boudicca. She was bleeding from her belly but was cleaning the wound with her allpurpose tongue.

On the other hand, his side hurt like hell and blood spurted from a wound. Remembering his grandmother's remedy, he stuffed a handful of dried grass into the hole and staunched the flow. "I am a pretty good medicine man if I say so myself."

Boudicca was a pretty good medicine dog as well.

"We had best return Sir Henry to his eternal rest. They might aim better next time. I hope the spirits will forgive us."

A quick rest, a dinner of beans, a scraping out of the fire, and Sir Henry returned to a warm grave. His bones snuggled in and the pebbles on his chest pacified the spirits. They approved the the mound of dirt and the cairn at the head that marked the spot.

Bjorn unwrapped the sinew that secured the stones to the head of the war club. "This is the sorriest weapon I ever saw. If it had edges I would bleed more, hurt less, and be dead."

He pried out the biggest stone and washed it off. It showed as crimson as his blood when he held it up to the campfire.

"Look at that, dog." Bjorn had mined gemstones in the Otra River of Norway and knew he was holding a garnet stone.

"What a waste of a valuable gem. They were so hopping mad at me they couldn't wait for flint."

He showed the stone to Boudicca, who sucked it and went to sleep with a sore, bored sigh. She acted like she thought, "Stupid rock."

"A jeweler can make this into a ring for Maria."

"Ah, Maria . . . "

From the corner cabinet in his cabin, he retrieved a tattered, handwritten note. Maria had slipped it into his hands at the end of their voyage from Boston aboard the brig, *Agilis*. He could not read the words but remembered her name and the sentiment from a sailor who had read it to him.

The next day, Bjorn filled a pouch with gold dust, boarded Boudicca with Sergio, and took his gem to a jeweler in San Francisco.

The jeweler said, "Give me two weeks and you will have a ring."

The cool San Francisco climate was a welcome relief from the stifling American River, but Bjorn had to get back to work in his mine above Sacramento. He bought a ticket on the schooner *Swiftness*.

Complaining to his companion as he clenched the railing with his gnarled hands he said, "This country is hot in the summer and hard all year."

"Yeah."

Bjorn was a lean and large Norwegian without an ounce of fat. The Viking blood flowing in his veins gave him blonde hair and a confident bearing. But the call of the sea to many Norsemen was replaced with a love of minerals, rocks, and mining. Exploits on the ocean were not for him, although he could navigate with the best.

Being from cool Norway, the summer heat of the Valley of California melted him. The first months had passed in a flash after he staked his claim in 1849.

The fellow passenger said, "I'm suspicious of those Asian chopstick panda trainers they call the Blue Lanterns. Or maybe it was those pendejo asshole beaner nacho Mexicans, or how about the underhanded hugger-mugger fake soldiers. Those bastards should be in the jail, not guarding the outside."

Bjorn said, "We have seen the elephant of everything haven't we."

"You're not wrong, my friend."

"That Celestial on the other railing is spying on us right now. Who can read their scribbles on the paper?"

His companion responded, "Not me."

Bjorn said he enjoyed working the American River because it was cooler than the Sacramento Valley.

"That flat plain is hot as hell in the summer."

The two men watched the bow of the vessel hunt from side to side for a safe channel. Bjorn as an ex-sailor noticed the skill of the captain as they maneuvered around new sandbars, jagged roots of uprooted trees, and sunken timbers from a steamboat whose boiler exploded. They had not run aground once, yet.

The two men marveled at the amount of mud in the river that was washed down by the gold mining operations.

Their peaceful reverie was broken by a chue . . . chue . . . chue . . . chue . . . from behind. Twin columns of smoke poured from the smokestacks on a steamboat that overtook them. As the bow pulled alongside, they could hear the clanking of the steam engine, the splashing of the sidewheels, and the shriek of released steam.

The companion read the name, "It's the Pioneer . . ." His voice was drowned out by two blasts from the Pioneer's whistle. "She's signaling to pass us on her starboard." They could hear the hoots of the rowdies on deck who were impatient to reach the goldfields. A writer in the newspaper had called it "The California Gold Rush" and termed the new arrivals as the 49ers.

"They laid her keel down the river. I watched them unload that infernal steam engine from a Boston clipper. She's a fast son-of-a-bitch. I'll give her that."

Bjorn said, "I hate that noise and stinking smoke. She looks hideous and shouldn't be on my river." When the paddle wheels on either side of the vessel turned at different speeds to steer around hazards in the river, he said, "That's an advantage on a river that changes from day to day."

The other man said, "Coming back to the Asian spies, I caught one poking around my cabin the other night after I had been out fishing for rainbow trout."

"Your claim is close to my dig. What did you do?"

"Sicced my dog on him."

"You can't be too careful these days."

"I hear they eat dog meat, but mine tried to eat him instead."

"Yeah."

"That intruder dropped a sheet of paper with tally marks for every bag I loaded. He got out of there in a hurry with my dog chomping on his heels." The man spat into the river as he shook his head. "It's damn hard to get ahead these days."

"Yeah."

"Rainbow trout fishing? I'll have to wet a hook in the river."

Even though the South Fork of the American River above Sacramento was still hot, his New Viking mining camp was home. He couldn't wait to see Boudicca, but she was with Sergio. "I'll have to get her back. I miss that mongrel."

The promise of more production from the rocker machine was elusive, especially for one man working by himself. It was efficient at recovering gold dust but required standing all day, shoveling sand and gravel, sloshing water, rocking the beast, and cleaning out the riffles. Utter exhaustion capped the end of the working day, and every day was a working day.

Bjorn found that helpers were as rare in Sacramento as were outgoing sailors in San Francisco. His requests to bartenders, barbers, and men on the street came up empty. Gold nuggets, gold dust, and gold were the exclusive topics of conversation, and work was a filthy, four-letter word.

He hated to waste time for a dip in the river, but being from Norway the summertime heat of the California Valley plagued him. Each plunge put him farther behind his goal of a thousand dollars a week.

He thought he might find helpers in the village of Vallejo where the Sacramento River drained into San Pablo Bay. Possibly the farm workers out of the Sonoma valley would like a change of scenery. And it was a chance to see his vineyard near Boyes Springs that he and a friend had bought from General Vallejo a year ago.

An ounce of gold dust paid for a seat on the westbound stagecoach to Vallejo from Sacramento. He wanted to take a boat which was cheaper but it was a couple of days slower.

He leaned over the counter and whispered to the ticket agent, "Does the stagecoach carry valuables?"

"We prefer not too because of the bandits. They watch the passengers like cats watch birds in a cage. For example, that Celestial Chinese man in the corner is noting what money passengers show when they buy tickets. He's interested in gold and peers into their purses. Then there's that vagrant who is faking sleep under his hat. If you look closely at the rattlesnake hatband, you'll see little holes that look through the snake eyes. He watches everybody who gets on the stage for their valuables."

"Thanks for the warning."

Bjorn locked the door on the privy out back. He took the leather pouch of gold dust from under his shirt and patted it flat to slip inside his boot. It held two months' recovery of gold dust. He thought to himself, Secrecy beats guards when a valuable is disguised.

Returning to the ticket window, he said, "Umm . . . "

"Are you in a hurry?"

"How long does the trip take?"

"We change horses five times and make it in a day and a half. Fall is a good time because the road is dry."

"It's dry all right," said Bjorn. "My claim is thirsty and hotter than hell. Fall is when the Indians burn the parched brush to clear their meadows for hunting. I hate this smoke." He coughed a couple of times.

The ticket master said, "Those schooner boats have to contend with the sandbars and hazards and it slows them down. My stage beats them to Vallejo every time."

"The *Swiftness* ran aground on a sandbar coming up last year." He forgot to mention he was the one mucking with the sails and almost caused her to sink.

Bjorn felt good as he waited on a bench in the waiting room and talked to no one in particular, "It's been a good couple of months, and I can buy my winter supplies. I wish there was someone to share it with, preferably female."

At the word share the door to the ticket office swung open and a lady in a stylish red outfit strutted to the waiting room. She declared, "I need a passage to Vallejo." His reverie froze in its tracks.

Standing in the center of the room was a splendid woman in a fitted ensemble that complemented her black hair and sparkling eyes. She made eye contact with every man around the waiting room ending with Bjorn. "Hello. Do I know you?"

He gaped as her attendant bought their tickets. She obviously gave more attention to her appearance than her business activities. Her curvaceous body flaunted luscious perfection as she sat on the next bench. She looked familiar.

Bjorn started to say, "Hello . . ." but was cut off by hoof beats reverberating through the waiting room. The incoming stage rounded the corner in a cloud of dust with squeaks, creaks, rumbles, rattling chains, and snorting horses.

To a hearty, "Whoa," the coach stopped in front of the ticket office. The stagecoach, horses, driver, and passengers were all a dusty tan. A slab of dirt fell away from the gilded filigree on the side to reveal a deep blue door. The waiting passengers watched as the hot, stiff, and tired travelers stumbled down the steps. They shook clouds of dust out of their clothes.

Bjorn heard the lady say to her companion, "I fear this will not be a pleasant trip. I am in a hurry, or we would take the boat." She sighed as she organized her bags for the stagecoach driver to load.

Bjorn grunted with satisfaction when the stable hand hitched up four fresh horses and said to the lady, "We will make good time with these fresh horses." She smiled and lowered her eyes.

With the luggage stacked on top, the driver, shouted, "All aboard!"

After brushing as much dirt off the seat as he could, Bjorn held out his arm to the lady and escorted her up the step into the stagecoach. The driver helped the attendant into the same seat with a push to her tush. Holding the door for Bjorn, the driver motioned to the middle-aged Chinese man as the final passenger. The Asian's darting eyes missed nothing.

They were not even settled before the driver bellowed, "Walk-on, away!" and cracked his prized whip. The five-foot handle was ornamented with handcrafted silver ferrules circling a handle made of hickory. A sharp snap at the tip of the twelve-foot buckskin lashes showed the driver could expertly reach any of the four horses in the hitch.

Bellowing over the rattles of the coach, the driver said, "The rules are posted on the side post. Read them at your leisure. I do not allow exceptions."

Bjorn could not read the list so he stared out the window and tried to look wise. If he had been able to read, he would have seen these rules:

1. Abstinence from liquor is requested, but if you must drink, share the bottle. To do otherwise makes you appear selfish and unneighborly.

2. If ladies are present, gentlemen are urged to forego smoking cigars and pipes as the odor of the same is repugnant to the Gentle Sex. Chewing tobacco is permitted but spit WITH the wind, not against it.

3. Gentlemen must refrain from the use of rough language in the presence of ladies and children.

4. Buffalo robes are provided for your comfort during cold weather. Hog-ging robes will not be tolerated and the offender will be made to ride with the driver.

5. Don't snore loudly while sleeping or use your fellow passenger's shoulder for a pillow; he or she may not understand and friction may re-sult.

6. Firearms may be kept on your person for use in emergencies. Do not fire them for pleasure or shoot at wild animals as the sound riles the horses.

7. In the event of runaway horses, remain calm. Leaping from the coach in panic will leave you injured, at the mercy of the elements, hostile Indians, and hungry coyotes.

8. Forbidden topics of discussion are stagecoach robberies and Indian uprisings.

9. Gents guilty of unchivalrous behavior toward lady passengers will be put off the stage. It's a long walk back. A word to the wise is sufficient.

They departed in a billowing cloud of dust down the road that followed the Sacramento River. Almost immediately, they passed a schooner embarking at the same time.

Bjorn glanced up and down the lady's outfit and said, "That's the *Swiftness* that brought me up from 'Frisco last year."

"It's a beautiful ship. I wish we were on it."

"Me too but I have urgent business down the river."

They watched the stately schooner navigate around the sandbars before the dust cloud that followed their progress obscured everything behind them.

He adjusted his holster to a more comfortable position, lit a Cuban cigar, and said, "I hope we don't encounter any robbers today or get attacked by angry Indians."

"Whoa! Stop!" The driver leaped from his seat and faced Bjorn eyeball to eyeball. "I told you to read the rules of the road. You've already violated three of them. My last rule is gents guilty of unchivalrous behavior toward lady passengers walk. Out." He tried to pull Bjorn out of the stagecoach.

Bjorn, who could not read of course, was dumbfounded at the anger of the driver and leaned out the door. "What did I do? I had no intention of committing unchivalrous acts toward the lady." He grinned at her.

The driver shook with rage and nose-to-nose unleashed the loudest, crudest, filthiest torrent of profanity Bjorn had ever heard. "Get out of my stagecoach! There will be no guns, no cigars, no reference to lawless thieves on my run. Out!" He raised the handle of his prize whip to reinforce the command.

The lady extended her hand through the window and gently raised her finger. With a firm voice accustomed to obedience, she said, "Neither I or my companion are offended by this gentleman. I request your indulgence to permit him to continue with us." She blinked her dark seductive eyes at the driver.

The driver was defenseless in the hands of a pretty woman, especially one as elegant as Maria. Turning without a word and grumbling, he mounted his seat and whipped the poor horses to make up for lost time.

The country grew desolate and dangerous about twenty-five miles out of Sacramento. "Here we are again," the driver said to the guard riding shotgun, "We're making good time, but bandits and outlaws infest this stretch. Watch out." They approached an outcrop that cramped the road to one lane.

"Halt!" yelled the boss of three masked men on horseback as they attacked from both sides of the rock. Bjorn leaped out of the coach before it rattled to a stop and faced the desperados, gun drawn. "What's this?"

The leader shouted, "Your money and valuables. We don't mean no harm to the ladies."

Bjorn said, "Like hell—who are you? I can't hear you through your masks."

"Move it!"

One of the outlaws, which is what they were, fired his revolver into the air. Another motioned for the guard riding shotgun to drop his weapon and dismount. "Driver too."

"Everybody out."

With a flourish, the gunman helped the two ladies to the ground saying, "Sorry for the inconvenience, ma'am, but it makes up for our army pay." He dropped his firearm into its holster and reached for the lady's purse with both hands.

The beautiful young lady clutched her purse to her chest but the robber grabbed it anyway and broke the strap.

Another outlaw relieved the Chinese man of his cash and holstered his gun to frisk him. The man bent his head in helpless resignation.

The third gunman faced Bjorn. "Drop your gun where I can see it."

Bjorn did not move. He noticed the lady's eyes shot daggers at the gunmen and scrutinized their features. His eyes followed her gaze.

The mean gunman had a scar on the bottom part of his jaw and was missing the little finger on his right hand. Bjorn was caught off guard when the elegant woman said to him, "You reek to high heaven. Why don't you jump in the river along with horse you rode in on?" She pointed to the nearby water.

Bjorn took note of the second gunman's mismatched boots. The right one was a darker leather in a bigger style. It was only a small difference but was obvious to an observer. He walked with a slight limp to the side of the darker leather.

The third outlaw raised his weapon and said to Bjorn, "Drop your gun slow like. Are you deaf?"

The attendant removed her ring in terror, her necklace, a broach, and a few coins from her purse. She held them out to the first gunman. "Th . . . is . . . is all . . . I . . . have."

"Keep your tickets, lady, and don't say I never did you a favor."

Bjorn's steely blue eyes drilled down the barrel of the revolver in the hand of the third. He slowly laid his gun on the ground with the grip in easy reach. Noticing the lady's hesitation out of the corner of his eye he created a diversion. "This lady is with me and our money is in my boot. Can I get it?"

The third gunman dismounted his pinto pony that seemed better trained than the other horses. His hatband was made of an iridescent snake skin around the crown with a loose rattling tail. Words came out of his mouth with a lisp. The lady studied his appearance.

"No funny stuff now." The rattlesnake rattles buzzed while he watched Bjorn pull a pouch from his boot.

With the first gunman opening the lady's purse and the second frisking the Asian, Bjorn remembered the Viking after-dinner game where men threw bones gnawed clean at each other to injure or knock out an eyeball or two. He hurled the eleven-pound pouch into the face of the gunman and broke his nose. It was easy to grab the barrel of the revolver. Quick as a cat he flipped the firearm around to point at the highwaymen.

"First one to move gets plugged. I assure you I can shoot faster than you plug-ugly bloody rowdies can draw, and I will." The nose of the third streamed blood onto the pouch at his feet like a stuck pig. He lost interest in the contents of the leather bag.

The second one moved. Bjorn shot him in the dark foot. He hobbled away in a stream of profanity. Bjorn turned to the other two. "Where do you want it? Foot, balls, or chest." He brandished the revolver from the ground to their chests. "Makes no difference to me."

They put their hands up and joined the one writhing in pain. Bjorn retrieved the other two revolvers from their holsters. "Make yourselves scarce and we'll be on our way, if you please."

The leader said, "Give us our guns."

Bjorn said, "I'm keeping these barking-irons for safety—mine and yours." He waved the weapon at the outlaws to disappear and motioned the fare-paying passengers to the coach. "Excitements over. Let's go."

The guard and driver were used to being hijacked every few days and knew how to fade into the prudent background. When all was safe, they jumped onto the driver's bench. "Ha, yaw! We're running late." The driver flicked his whip over the backs of the team. Bjorn trotted alongside the coach ready for action until the bandits were well behind.

His chest heaving, Bjorn leaped into his seat next to the Asian and panted, "I plastered the town with help wanted posters but these lazy bastards would rather steal than work."

The beautiful woman looked to Bjorn with tingling admiration. "You are so brave. May I ask your name, sir?"

"Glad to be of service," as he tipped his hat. "Bjorn Amundson, and yours?"

"I am Maria Juana Magdalena Rojas. I remember you from the *Agilis*."

"That's me. We escorted you and your banker friend to the City Hotel, as I remember."

"That man was a rat. He abandoned me that same day."

Bjorn said, "Do you know Don Mariano Guadalupe Vallejo of Petaluma?"

"He is my uncle. Do you know him too?"

"He sold me a vineyard from the Rancho Petaluma land grant. I'm starting operations in my spare time."

Maria Magdalena clasped her hands and said, "My hero, you saved my life." She dipped her head and fluttered her eyelashes. The faint aroma of her French perfume added a touch of elegance to the rough frontier conveyance. "Did you mean it when you said we are together?"

Bjorn turned the color of the garnet in his pocket and said, "I am visiting General Vallejo tomorrow afternoon on business. Will you be there?"

She said, "I look forward to your visit."

"Me too."

Bjorn said to himself, calm down, old boy. That's the most beautiful thing you have seen in months. Beats the company of that prospector nine ways from Sunday.

3 - Maria

Monotonous debates about money the next day with clerks in the San Francisco bank frustrated the man of action to no end "I have a ship to catch. Can't we wrap this up?" The guard rattled the front door to signal closing time, and the clanging from the wharf announced the departure of the last brig of the day.

Bjorn leaped onto the moving deck because he had to see Maria. The bad luck continued the next morning when the stagecoach to Petaluma from Vallejo was delayed by a broken wheel.

"Shit, thirty miles is too far to walk, but I have to get to the Hacienda Petaluma Adobe somehow." Bjorn glanced at a river boat moored at the local wharf and thought, The gilded letters on the stern are like Maria's name on her note.

María Rojas

Rancho Petaluma

Could it be his Maria? Could he read? Yes and no, but he undersood the labor of the crew of Pomo Indians as they unloaded crates of eggs and live poultry, hogs and cattle, hops, hides, wool, and wine. The men joked and teased each other in goodnatured camaraderie just like the forecastle Bjorn had lived in at sea. His fertile brain schemed how to hire such good workers. The problem was, he only needed two or three and the entire team was a tightknit group.

After the boat was empty the men took a break and Bjorn introduced himself to the foreman. "Can I catch a ride to Rancho Petaluma with you?"

The foreman said yes but he had to sit on the cargo since the boat would be loaded to the gills.

"I'll help you with some of this stuff."

Excited to see Maria's name, the man of action pulled off his shirt and joined the crew to load a heavy piece of machinery. The hands filled the river boat with imported equipment, ammunition, cigars, liquor, fine clothes, and too many sundries to mention. The foreman motioned Bjorn to sit on the cargo and climbed alongside.

Proud to work for General Vallejo, the gregarious leader of the crew poured out the local history all the way up the Petaluma River. "Our hacienda is the headquarters of a working ranch. We have two buildings with a ground floor and a second story that guards an open courtyard. I helped build the ranch houses with adobe bricks." The foreman held out his tattooed arms. "They give it the name, Hacienda Petaluma Adobe."

Bjorn listened with interest.

"My tribe cut redwood planks for the floors and shingles for the roof to protect the adobe. We fight off attacks from the second story veranda and relax there in the evening."

Bjorn said, "Attacks? Who?"

"Well, the Russians over in Fort Ross want the vineyards back that they planted thirty-five years ago. My Pomo Indian tribe is afraid of our enemies, the Miwoks. And don't forget that Frémont's army destroyed our crops three years ago. We fought every assault from the veranda." He swept the river bank with an imaginary firearm, "Bang, bang, bang."

"I've heard about your stories. You've got to stay alert."

The historian boasted there were two thousand Indians working on the ranch. "It is hard work to make bricks, haul lumber, construct buildings, cook, farm, forge iron tools, tan hides, and tend thousands of cattle."

"You sound wealthy."

"General Vallejo is an important man."

Bjorn marveled at the lush green banks of the Petaluma River. The bow of the María Rojas nudged to the shore under the sign that read Petaluma. Eager hands lowered the gangplank and the crew unloaded the goods. Bjorn helped with the heavy machinery. After a quick dip in the river, he donned his still clean shirt and followed the workers to the front gates of the hacienda. The name on the front proclaimed the name of Rancho Petaluma Adobe.

Bjorn rang the bell and answered the gatekeeper's questions about his name and business. Satisfied, the keeper creaked open the heavy wooden gate and pointed across the courtyard to the main entrance.

Delicious smells of baking bread from the outdoor kitchen welcomed Bjorn. He caught an acrid whiff from the tannery in the back, heard the ringing of a hammer on steel from the smithy, and saw a grist mill turned by a lonesome mule grinding flour. It was easy to believe the historian's boast that the ranch ran twelve thousand head of cattle and three thousand sheep for wool.

Bjorn walked by the first floor shops and noted the products made by the hands of the native Indians. On display were saddles, candles, soap, and piles of wool blankets. Rows of boots and shoes in front of the cobbler shop waited for the military.

As Bjorn ducked under the veranda into the main reception room, he heard María call from the balcony overhead. "Welcome to Rancho Petaluma Adobe, Señor Amundson. I am so glad you could make it."

"I'm glad to see you, ma'am." The sight of Maria thrilled him and he waved like a teenager.

Ever watchful over her little sister, a regal señorita appeared from a first floor door and graciously swept up to Bjorn. "Please allow me to welcome you to our humble abode, Mr. Amundson. Don Mariano Vallejo will see you shortly. Please come with me."

"How do you know my name?"

"My sister, Maria, has spoken of you and the messenger from the boat informed us of your arrival. You befriended the boat crew, it seems." Bjorn followed her into General Vallejo's office.

He marveled at the ornate tiles framing the corner fireplace and the elegant desk in the center of the room. It showcased fine carvings inspired by generations of carvers from Mexico City. The sister proudly pointed to the orange and yellow accented squares on the floor. "This tile is imported from Saltillo, Mexico, and is their highest quality."

"It's beautiful."

"Please have a seat, Señor Amundson."

The door from the interior swung open and a smiling man entered with authority. Bjorn stood up as the man said, "Bienvenido," Señor Amundson. Welcome to my modest home."

"It is a pleasure to see you again, General Vallejo."

"Igualmente. My house is your house, or as we say in Spanish, Mi casa es tu casa."

Bjorn said, "Thank you, sir." They shook hands.

"We have many things to discuss today, but I suggest we start with a tour of your vineyard. I was pleased when you and Mr. Porter bought it last year. He has been away I understand, but I am honored to show you around. My overseer, Peter Walden, is doing a fine job at improving your operation."

After a tour and an afternoon of mundane discussions, the General invited Bjorn to dine with them and stay overnight in a guestroom. Bjorn agreed with relish.

Maria, Maria. He could not get her out of his mind. Bjorn was lonesome.

Mariano Vallejo casually remarked to Bjorn that Yankees were hostile to Spanish speaking Californians, and he believed it came from their low level of education.

Bjorn said nothing about not being able to read since he was not a Yankee.

General Vallejo was fluent in Latin and spoke several other languages. He said, "It amuses me that we Californios and Mexicans are stereotyped as less than civilized."

Walls of smooth plaster and gleaming whitewash adorned the dining room that was being prepared for the feast. Huge beams supported the ceiling and windows opened to the courtyard through stained glass panels. A long table down the center was set and waiting for a considerable company.

The Pomo Indian steward was in charge of the seating arrangements. It was a formal dinner so he placed name cards at each guest's chair. General Vallejo was at the head of the table as host, with Bjorn on his right. The elder sister sat on the other end as hostess. Maria was the first person to the General's left, across from Bjorn. Name tags identified the rest of the seating for the caballeros, señoras, señoritas, and visitors. The sister adjusted her hair in a mirror on the wall before the guests arrived.

Arrayed in their finest attire, the superbly developed caballero horsemen to a man courted María. She and the other ladies were breathtaking in their flowing floor length skirts of every color and topped by see through lace jackets from the fashion centers of Europe.

Strolling guitarists played dances and airs in the courtyard while the guests danced away the afternoon. Champagne buoyed the mood of the company. At the height of a spirited fandango, the elder sister with her castanets clacking twirled into the dining room and switched her name tag with Maria's. She was now across from Bjorn and María was the hostess at the other end. A dashing caballero bumped into the sister as he snuck into the dining hall to move his name card next to Maria's. Others moved their names away from the sister.

Clang, clang, the dinner bell sounded. Guests milled around like a herd of cattle to find their seats. The caballero two chairs down from the sister punched the one next to her with a smirking grin. Leaning away from the sister, he punched back with a frown. The sister chose to not notice the exchange and pretended to listen to the string quartet in the corner.

Bjorn said to the General, "This is a fine home, sir, and I appreciate your hospitality."

"The pleasure is mine. I hope you enjoy yourself this evening."

Anxious to divert his attention from María, the elder sister leaned toward Bjorn. But the little sister peered around the centerpiece and locked their eyes in the mirror. The elder sister thought his excitement was for her.

Bjorn smiled. María flashed a smile back and dropped her eyes. She rearranged the flower in her hair and spoke to the caballero next to her.

Bjorn summoned every ounce of willpower to avoid staring at the mirror throughout the meal. A long glance from time to time he thought was okay.

The servers loaded the table with a feast. Everything but the imported Spanish wines and silverware was from the shops of Rancho Petaluma Adobe. Plates of turkey and chicken alternated with bowls of vegetables, baskets of fruit, carne asada (meat broiled on a spit), beefsteaks with rich gravy, onions, eggs, beans, tortillas, bread, and coffee. A native waiter poured everyone their choice of Madeira or Port wine.

The sister chattered like a chipmunk about the Vallejo family, about friends, described her favorite horse. Bjorn responded with fake interest about his mine and the trip down the Sacramento River. He stopped the rush of words by raising his wine glass a little higher than necessary while stealing a glimpse of Maria in the mirror. She raised her glass and Bjorn noticed the red wine complemented her red lips. She puckered her mouth to sip the wine and Bjorn did likewise. Their eyes sparkled at each other.

The General interrupted to ask Bjorn about his plans. "Are you having the same difficulties that I have to hire workers?"

"I am. Work is a dirty word. The only interests in Sacramento are gold, gold dust, and mining claims. Everyone searches for free wealth."

Vallejo said, "I have an advantage at Rancho Petaluma because the Indians come to work for me with enthusiasm since we treat them fairly. We have two thousand of them, mainly Pomo. I only beat them for the most egregious behavior."

Bjorn said he did not beat miners at all, but sailors occasionally if they deserved it. They clinked their wineglasses in agreement. He could see Maria conversing with the caballeros on either side. A flash of jealousy shot through him and he engaged the sister, "Do you often ride through the countryside?"

"It is glorious to do so."

A manservant offered Bjorn a platter of roasted chicken pieces. Bjorn selected a wishbone and a drumstick dripping with sauce. Conspicuous in their private mirror, he licked the sauce from one end of the leg to the other with devilish enjoyment and made sure María saw him. Admiring the clean drumstick in front of him, he complemented the chef while maintaining his gaze in the mirror.

Maria delicately extended her tongue to taste the wine and took a sip. She raised her eyebrows and said, "Ooooh, that is good."

Bjorn raised his wine glass, but it slipped from his crooked fingers just as he stood up to offer a toast. The glass shattered on the tile and Bjorn turned as red as the wine. At a snap of the elder sister's fingers, two waiters cleared the broken glass and wiped up the wine while a third placed a full glass in Bjorn's hand. He took a sip with both hands and forgot the toast.

In the mirror, María slipped an oyster from its shell to her tongue. Bjorn liked seafood and slipped a companion oyster in response.

Between staring at María and conversing with General Vallejo, while yet entertaining the sister, the honored guest ignored the hunks of meat, the crab, and the mounds of delicacies.

Holding up the wishbone for all to see and especially in the mirror, he pulled the ends apart with a dramatic flourish. The gleam on his face endorsed the break. Maria's eyes sparkled too.

The end of dinner arrived too soon with bowls of strawberries floating in whipped cream. Bjorn popped the luscious berries one by one into his open mouth. They slipped around in the cream but Bjorn persevered. Maria chased hers with more success.

Bjorn ended the meal with fruit and wicked eyes. Maria and he took bites out of bright red apples from the opposite ends of the table.

A cigar server offered afterdinner choices to the men including the new El Rey del Mundo from Havana, the famous H. Upmann, and the peaceful Por Larrañaga. Behind him, a beautiful Indian maid presented a tray of digestifs with the diners' choices of Cognac, Vieux Carre, or Sloe gin.

General Vallejo stood and clinked his glass, "Your attention, please. The town of Saltillo is famous for its serapes that decorate the walls of this room. I am pleased to present to Bjorn Amundson, our honored guest, a serape with which to commemorate this evening."

He held up the rectangular garment with an opening for the head and multicolored stripes like a rainbow. "This fine wool holds heat and is natural for our cool evenings. I do not say our guest ever quarrels, but if he should find himself in that situation he would find that the serape is a shield against sharp objects."

Bjorn said, "Please accept my profound gratitude, sir. I will treasure this gift for a long time." He lowered the soft woven garment over his head and onto his shoulders. The intricate red design set off his long golden hair. Maria stared when he twirled to show off to the guests. The room erupted in applause.

Vallejo's private orchestra entertained the guests through the night with afterdinner music, dancing, and rivalry. Between the sister, the General, and the caballeros, Bjorn could scarcely get near María. He suspected this was by design and he was right.

It was during a game from Spain that he got his chance. Their custom was to break on the heads of the opposite sex, eggshells filled with scraps of silver paper or cologne water. The trick was to catch the victim unawares. A gentleman distracted Bjorn with a description of his fight in the Mexican revolution against Spain. María tapped his head with an egg and covered his hair with bright scraps of paper. They laughed together.

One of the wise old señoras slipped an egg into his hand and he retaliated at his opportune moment. That egg contained French cologne. The entire company roared with approval. The dawn arrived before anyone was ready, least of all Bjorn.

Bjorn, carrying his serape, thanked the guests for the good time. He shook General Vallejo's hand and said, "Esteemed sir, I look forward to working with you on my vineyard." He shook Maria's hand as it was the most he could do outside of a little bow.

He boarded the river boat María Rojas and watched María Juana Castañeda Rojas fade astern waving.

The memory of her cologne lingered for days afterward, but when he put his hand into his pocket, he felt a garnet ring.

"Damn."

4 - Modern and Ancient Vikings

Maria's dancing form surrounded by caballaros so distracted Bjorn's first night back at the mine that he overlooked the herd of deer grazing on his claim. His muddled dreams mingled Maria and idle attractive men in the mirror, only to be disrupted by images of the sister chaperone. The fragrance of the big sagebrush in the chaparral did not register.

Maria's big sister parted her lips to reveal fangs. Out of the mouth exploded a screech and a coyote howl. The placid night trembled, Boudicca growled, and her fur stood up like a porcupine.

Bjorn was groggy from the day of hard travel, but the snarl outside his window woke him up. "What was that?" He rolled over to look at the pale yellow sky that silhouetted the Viking ship above his door.

"The sun comes up early for me." He yawned and the dog barked. He shocked himself awake with a splash of cold water to his face.

"Let's see what's going on."

They crunched along the dry gravel bed in the gulch that ascended the foothills. Bushes with spines lined the critter highway the animals used. Warm blood dripping from scratches on the man and his animal companion filled the air with warm sweet scents that smelled too much like prey.

Boudicca's growl-bark warning was too late as four paws of claws dug into his shoulders. Their force crushed him to the ground. A stab of neck pain brought stars to his eyes when the fangs clamped his windpipe shut and stopped his breathing.

Boudicca sank her teeth into the other end of the cougar and forced the muscular cat to release Bjorn's neck with a hiss.

Bjorn pushed the animal away and yelled, "Get off," but the cougar ripped his back with sharp claws and bit into his arm to tear out a piece of flesh. In a fight for his life, Bjorn pounded the snout with his fist while Boudicca mauled the right rear flank. She shook and cracked the bone and allowed Bjorn time to attack yellow fur everywhere. The three rolled around in a three-way wrestling match.

The overpowered cougar gave a "harrisss" and limped back to her coyote carcass. She dragged it under a rock outcrop to hide it from the vultures and ravens.

Boudicca licked the bleeding wounds of her master panting on the ground. He stumbled back to his cabin and collapsed onto his cot in a bone-tired sleep. The dog howled with pride at fighting off a cougar.

Bjorn awoke in a delirious fever. He moaned and thrashed and moaned again.

Boudicca sensed his distress and ran to a rider on a passing horse for help—it happened to be Joaquín Murrieta. The faithful canine tugged on his foot but Joaquín kicked her away. She whined and kept pulling.

"Damn dog," but he knew something was wrong and followed her into the cabin. One look at Bjorn's bloody neck with teeth marks and the shredded bloody tatters of clothes on his back told him what had happened. He felt the fever on Bjorn's forehead and said, "You have met la puma, my friend. I'm sorry I cannot help you but I know a curandera who can."

Joaquín disappeared into the trees and Boudicca resumed her vigil alongside Bjorn. She licked away drops of sweat mixed with dribbles of red.

The quiet rustling of a long skirt alerted Boudicca and she ran to a quiet woman with a large pack on her back. In Spanish she said, "Where is the injured man?" Boudicca pulled her into the cabin where the curandera could examine the delirious gold miner. She could not understand his mutterings but her intuition sensed they described a hero.

Drawing on traditional healing skills learned by generations and generations of medicine man and woman, she ministered to the delirious blonde man.

After the curandera left, Bjorn lay delirious on his cot. Heavy sweat dripped from his body and hazy dreams swirled around the towering Norwegian man.

He became again the little boy who splashed in the Otra River of Norway looking for gemstones alongside his father. The father instructed him day after day with legends of their ancestor, Bjorn the Bold. At the end of every day, the little fellow carried their pouch of wet gems, the flowers of the river, back home. One of the sagas started at Chartres, Francia.

"It happened this way in the year 911 at Chartres far to the south of us in Francia.

"Bjorn the Berserker Bold called to his companions, "Vikings, we attack tomorrow."

"Eleven huge men joined him and passed a drinking horn of mead around and around. Each pass required an oath, a gulp of golden courage, a crash on a shield, and a chaser of mead.

"Sometime before dawn, the campfire heaved with clouds of red and orange smoke that roiled the night air. Twelve heroic Viking warriors jostled to inhale the fumes that they craved. The incense from the flaming henbane leaves aroused fighting passions that were stronger than their lust for women. But they still awaited an omen for the morrow.

"All eyes turned to the owl that flew from the eye in the face of the man in the moon to alight on the hazel tree. Calls of "Hoot, hoo, hoooooo," filled the night air.

"The massive tree shuddered and its branches arched and writhed and grasped at the terrified men as though to wrestle. Each leaf throbbed with colors and the trunk sang of courage. The foliage swirled into a shaman who leaped through the flames with a bag of magic mushroom. Like Odin, the soothsayer gave a portion of powder to each warrior, who swallowed the magic fruit of the earth with a horn of mead.

"Bjorn the Bold convulsed and ground his teeth. His companions' chattering transformed to howling—the sign they reached the rage. Out-of-body grappling matches with preternatural beasts erupted. Bearskins over their bare bodies bonded each berserker to his totem animal.

The shaman shapeshifted into a spider on legs taller than three men. Superstitious berserkers watched the hairy front legs stuff struggling enemy soldiers with their armor, horses, and battleaxes into its mouth amid shrieking protests.

"The shaman parted with the words, "When you were born, the three Nornar (women of destiny) chose the moment of your death. Nothing in Chartres will change that. You are immune to steel and fire. Vanquish the Franks with courage."

Bjorn the Bold and his band were berserkers ready for the dawn.

Drops of water from her twisted hands soothed the fever on Bjorn's forehead. Speaking in Spanish the curandera said, "You are broken, Chico, but I will mend you."

She chanted prayers to the wounded man's guardian saints. After the prayers, she screamed in his right ear, "Come out and do your sacred duty."

Looking at Bjorn's unconscious form, she was glad he was oblivious to the burning vinegar poured over his mutilated body. The salve of sagebrush leaves drew on her knowledge of herbs gathered in the wilds of Mexico. In her wisdom, she knew when it was rubbed in the gashes that it healed, even though she had never heard of infection. Thin sticky slices of prickly pears glued the salve in place.

"I will return this evening." To Boudicca she said, "Stand by this man."

Boudicca sweltered from Bjorn's fever as she shared his bed. The tail wagger stepped to the floor to cool off but continued to lick the beads of sweat from his face. Her natural instinct was to evade his restless thrashing until he fell into a stupor, yet be there when it rose and raged again.

Alert ears picked up horse clops on the trail and the scent of Joaquín's cigarillo. Wagging her tail but biting his pant leg, Boudicca tried to pull him off his horse a second time.

"Perro, it's me, Joaquín. Let go of my pants." Boudicca whimpered and tugged his leg as he dismounted. She jumped in a circle, whined, and dragged him to Bjorn.

Joaquín took one look and said, "You look like hell."

Bjorn groaned.

"Some animal ate a lot of you. You should eat him instead, don't you think?"

The dog didn't understand Spanish any more than English, which was not at all, but she sensed body language and knew Joaquín was concerned for his friend. She stared back and forth with the ears upright and face concerned.

Joaquin stayed until the evening when the healer returned. He left because he was afraid of Bjorn's spirits that she would summon.

Urgent care came first. She started a fire in the stove which took about forever to boil a pot of water. Bjorn moaned when the curandera touched the wounds on his arm.

"This is very bad. Red anger in the claw marks spreads to your shoulder. You will have a new scar on your face, Chico."

Ministering in harmony with the rhythm of the desert, her sacred statues on the table set the mood by staring at glowing candles. Hot yerba maté tea from leaves grown in Uruguay was ready and she poured little sips in Bjorn's mouth. He instinctively swallowed to ease his thirst.

"We are the same body as other people, like the animals, as the fish, the plants, the stones and minerals, the earth, and all life. Illness comes from lack of balance with nature. Oh spirits, grant me limpias to remove the corruption from this living flesh."

Bjorn didn't move and Boudicca's eyes drifted closed in the trance.

"Where is my sagebrush?" She pulled a bag of dried herbs from her pack. With her quick hands in a mono and metate, she pounded the fragrant leaves to a powder and made a healing poultice with water.

Hallucinations or not, Bjorn moaned when she washed out his wounds with vinegar and filled each slit with the sagebrush poultice.

"*Tranquilo*, my son. this magic draws the evil spirits out of your body."

Boudicca watched the hands of the curandera pass an egg above Bjorn's lacerated scalp without touching the claw marks. The dog helped by licking congealed red blood that glued the yellow hair into long orange sticks.

"Hi, yah, yah, eee," she said with a screech and pitched the egg with Bjorn's infection into the fire. To a rhythm on a hand drum she chanted, "Holy Spirit, born of Santa Maria, join the ghosts of healing to renew this man, your servant on this earth."

The healer greeted the ghosts of Bjorn's ancestors as they appeared in the trance, and guided their hands to his feverish flesh. Their touch calmed his troubled body.

"Out with the bad, in with the good. Sweat of the forehead draws toxins that will injure you no more. May the power of God heal the marks on this back."

The curandera said to Boudicca, "Other distressed patients call for me. Lie by this man until I return."

She waited until the faithful dog crawled into bed with healing support—not too close because he was still burning.

His delirium increased through the night and the next day as the healer fought with baths of vinegar and aloe vera juice. She ended her treatment with a paste of crushed garlic mixed with oil that she smeared on his feet.

After two more days, she raised a weak Bjorn to his feet. He stumbled from his cot and tried to work, since nothing had happened while he was sick.

He carried the ghost of the vision with him. \

Where the words came from, Bjorn had no idea, yet there they were.

> But the wicked
> Are like the troubled sea,

When it cannot rest,
Whose waters cast up mire and dirt.

Standing alone in the middle of the sunny shimmering river and weak after two days of recovery, the miner wobbled on shaky legs. He felt the wounds from the cougar attack, "I don't think I'm wicked, but you can call me sore and troubled. I have to work for me and my dog."

He worked his way from hollow to hopeful hollow across the stream. From each one he tilted a half shovel of gravel into the rocker box. It was an aching arm he rowed the rocker with. It was a gnarled tired hand that scooped a dab of sand with a speck of gold from the riffles. The cold water made him shiver.

Another shovelful, disappointment.

Another hopeful handful, a rock, a swish. More disappointment.

Again, and again.

"What is this, my dog?"

He picked a pebble out of the debris the size of his big toe. "Boudicca!" He held it next to the red welt on his forearm. "They are the same color. This is a giant garnet stone. It's worth more than all the gold I got this month."

Boudicca broke her nap as Bjorn splashed to shore and laid the stone in front of her. Rocks are rocks to a dog and you cannot eat them, but she seemed to trust that her master liked this one.

"Guard this with your life. This is better than anything my father snatched from the Otra River."

A shovelful. A swish. Were there more garnets with a little gold tossed in?

No such luck.

Trembling arms shook so hard he missed the pan on the next shovelful.

"What's wrong? Damn, I'm tired. I need a . . . a . . . nap," he chattered through his teeth.

He barely made it to his cot before he collapsed.

"How can I run a fever and shiver at the same time?"

Boudicca dropped the red pebble by her food dish and rubbed his welts with her fur and body heat. The best treatment she knew was to lick the sagebrush salve off his wounds.

5 - Berserker

Like a ghost his father reappeared in Bjorn's troubled dreams to resume the legend of their ancestor, Bjorn the Bold. The heroic namesake strode through the story.

"Bjorn the Bold led the force of Berserkers under Rollo, the son of Ketill Flatnose, the Norseman. He watched Rollo swell with pride at the Viking longboats anchored in the river, Eure. It was the summer of AD 911 and his army carpeted the plains around the fortress of Chartres. They were fifty-six miles southwest of the great Frankish city of Paris.

"Rollo said to the assembled chieftains, 'The walls of Chartres are strong but we are stronger.'

"One of the men said, "You say 'Chartres' like the Franks do. Are you going over to the other side?" Several laughed.

"'We have laid siege for months and I am tired of waiting. Bjorn's Berserkers will lead the assault at dawn. What do you say?'

"Bjorn the Bold stepped forward, 'There are two outcomes to every danger. Either I will live or I will die.'

"The chieftains roared, 'Bjorn the Bold!'

"The immense rage of the beserkergang was poised for battle. Rollo said, "Our plan is to gather loot and capture slaves.'

"The chieftains roared their hearty approval and passed around a drinking horn of mead. 'Huh, huh, huh! Yeah!'

"'An enemy of thousands waits for us in the field and more defenders lurk inside the walls. They are brave and fight well with their axes and swords. Check your weapons.'

"The chieftains returned to their units scattered across the plain to sharpen their axes and await the first light.

"Rollo did not mention his men had stripped the countryside of food during the siege. The starving peasants were forced to join the opposing army for something to eat. The lonesome, starving women left behind offered their favors to any roving Viking for a morsel or two.

"Many Norsemen grew thin from giving away their food. You see many blonde, blueeyed people in northern France even today."

The old prospector leading his trusted mule, Jasper, rambled into the New Viking Gold Camp. He said to Jasper, "Our friend Amundson has built himself a mighty fancy operation. There is a log cabin with a carved ship over the door. Look at that work tent with a wooden floor. And around back he has got a proper privy shitter with a halfmoon vent." Jasper's long ears twisted as he complained, "Folks is getting overcivilized these days."

The sourdough was on his monthly round to pick up free staples. He had saved Bjorn's life from a bear attack and Bjorn vowed to supply him with tobacco and grub for the rest of his life. That animal's pelt was now a bear rug in the San Francisco apartment.

They were natural companions because the prospector knew where the gold was and Bjorn had the vigor to dig it. Together they filed a claim on the rich deposit that was now the famous New Viking Gold Mine.

Jasper was a silent partner and the prospector was lonesome. He got no response when he greeted the unconscious form on the bed. One look told him Bjorn had tangled with another animal.

"Can't you leave the wildlife alone? First, it was a bear and now a cougar. When will you learn?"

The man of nature rubbed Boudicca's fur. After checking out the dressings over the healing punctures and gashes, he dribbled a little water over Bjorn's feverish forehead.

"It appears you're in safe hands but, whew, that garlic on your feet stinks so bad it must be doing something."

The prospector said, "You're getting the best care in these whereabouts. Looks like that curandera is been here. Watch out for the wild animals. I'll be back in a month or so."

He and Jasper loaded up their tobacco and foodstuffs and he thought to himself, I don't know about that lad. Can't save him from everything, but I'll do what I can. He's a good man.

Drops of water on his forehead stirred Bjorn's turmoil after the prospector left. He could see a corner of the Viking ship over his doorway when he looked out his window. The prow of the ship reminded him of exploits of the Norsemen on the Viking raids. After a thousand years, chaos in the legend of the berserkergang spawned a major rage in the miner's shack.

The modern Bjorn as a berserker churned with delirious frenzy. He stumbled around the cabin. He gnawed on the table. He punched his fist through the lone window. He collapsed on his bed in weak exhaustion. Boudicca cowered in terror under the cot.

The father's voice reverberated as real as a ghost. The spirit continued the story of Bjorn the Bold Berserker.

"That Saturday in July of the year 911 dawned clear. Birds tweeted to their mates across the fields. The fields were barren and scavenged clean of every edible sprig of wheat.

"A phalanx of men from a neighboring clan approached the Norse command center. Their intent was unknown. They looked friendly, but it was good to be wary. Each knife was poised for an instant draw and the axes hung within easy reach. The leader said, "You are surrounded. We demand a piece of silver ransom from each man."

"The unintimidated chieftain said, 'Huh? Join us instead to harvest the hordes of silver from the fortress.' With a cheer, the friendly forces whooped at the prank. They rejoined their units that were scattered across the fields leading to the fortifications of Chartres. Paris was fifty-six miles northeast down the Eure River.

"Rollo addressed the enemy at first light. "You girls of the houses (wives) scare us not at all. We make water on you."

"Each man dropped his leggings or raised his pelt and pissed a mighty stream toward Chartres.

The opposing armies of Dukes Richard and Robert yelled back, "Here is the river of salt that washes you to hell," and they pissed in retaliation.

"The golden streams of used mead and whatever the Franks drank drained into a puddle on the battleground.

Not to waste a valuable resource, several dogs lapped at the little lake.

"The frontline of Norsemen mocked the Franks. 'Winners are the wolves of the camp.' Their companion army behind them lusted for battle. "Smoothing their elegant tunics, the grouped nobles of Francia countered, 'We drowned you in the flood. Go home.' The nobles rallied their aristocratic and peasant forces in formations to engage the Viking forces.

"The moment of assault focused the Viking chieftains on the fortress of Chartres. Unruly berserkers shouted profane encouragements and bashed into each other in their fervor.

"Rollo turned to Bjorn and his mad bold berserkers and signaled for them to storm the walls.

"The enraged berserkers chewed the edges of their shields coated with dried blood and boasted to the defenders lining the ramparts, 'This blood is from the soldiers of Paris. I will drink yours today.'

"Naked under their pelts, Bjorn and the eleven splashed through the moat to the grim stone wall of the castle. Equipment brigades raced alongside to throw grappling hooks onto the ramparts and raise ladders that reached the top. There were fewer defenders here than above the raised drawbridge that protected the gates to the city. Bjorn's men climbed with screamed curses of destruction.

"The first enraged man to top the ladder was Bjorn the Bold. One swipe of his battleaxe dispatched the archer on the summit who could not shoot an arrow straight down between his feet. Wild men on Bjorn's flanks reached the top and fought hand-to-hand. Every encounter was theirs and they prevailed by dispatching the furious attackers over their heads.

"Replacement defenders on the ramparts were shaken by the naked berserkers clad in bear pelts. Huge, crazed Vikings scaled the ladders like gods of decayed slaughter from Hel. The Franks poured molten pitch down the walls and threw rocks at the ascending, frothing hoard. Roared calls to their totem animals of the forest drowned out commands from the defenders whose coordination dissolved. The heavy bear pelts rejected the pitch and boiling water. Rocks bounced off. The Vikings surged relentlessly upward despite the defenses.

"The thrust of the attackers was interrupted by the deafening rumble of the loosened drawbridge at the center of the fortress. The massive wooden bridge crashed down over the moat, exposing the venerable city gates. Bjorn commanded his group to abandon the vertical assault and attack the bridge.

"The gates swung open before the berserkers could reach them. Mounted knights two abreast galloped out at full speed to engage the intruders with lances, swords, and battleaxes.

Bjorn lunged between the leading horsemen with a mighty battlecry. He wrenched the lance aimed at him away from the armed knight. It broke in half and Bjorn thrust the iron tip into the throat of the horse that was running him down. The injured horse threw the rider into the moat where his glistening armor dragged him screaming beneath the surface.

"The next rider bounced his axe on the planks of the drawbridge. He intended it to rebound under Bjorn's shield and slash his guts, but the spinning axe only clipped his left foot and severed his two smallest toes. Bjorn snatched the flying axe on the rebound and with one swing severed the rider's leg at the hip. The wicked-sharp cutting edge killed its owner on the followup blow.

"Enemies to the right of him, enemies on the left. Bjorn's berserker skills served him well. He slaughtered many foes that day, some in their armor and more without. His valor flaunted the Norsemen's deadly hand-to-hand skills and inspired the combatants around him.

"The demoralized amateur forces of Dukes Richard and Robert weakened and gave way. In desperation, the Bishop Gantelme, who was leading the defense, brought out his secret weapon, a relic kept at Chartres in those days. Unmistakable in his Episcopal miter, he exposed the tunic of the Blessed Virgin Mary and prayed, 'I implore you, Lord God, to grant everlasting mercy to your servants in Chartres. Deliver us from these pagan heathens. In Jesus' name, we pray.'

"A swell of religious zeal swept the ranks of the peasant defenders in the Dukes' armies. They rallied to overwhelm the Vikings with slings, axes, and seax knives. Their skills were honed from a lifetime of killing wild animals face-to-face. Led by Duke Richard, the knights penetrated the Viking center and divided Rollo's forces. The Norsemen were trapped between their opposing flanks.

"Despite the weak field position, Bjorn the Berserker Bold vanquished many soldiers that day in the fields of Chartres. Nevertheless, the forces under Rollo did not prevail, and the Vikings suffered a very great slaughter.

"Bjorn's father hesitated with shame before he could continue describing the loss.

"The father whispered with his head down that Rollo's forces were smitten with blindness when their heroic commander panicked and issued the order, 'Regroup for another day.' Bjorn's father fell silent.

"Never corner a desperate man without hope. See what happened when the peasants were left to starve when the Vikings stole their food. They were forced to join the Duke's armies to eat.

"More than one Viking traded his food for favors from a peasant woman left behind. You find many Frenchmen with the Viking disease of permanently bent fingers even today.

Bjorn tried to call out but could not utter a sound from within his dream. "Do not give up. Keep fighting." Boudicca trembled as he swung his hatchet against the wall and punched the air.
"No!"
"Cowards."
"Go back."

He smashed his little table to firewood and kicked the door closed. He banged his head on the wall and left marks of fresh blood. That wasn't how to fight. His hatchet slipped from his contracted fingers.

"The Duke's cavalrymen pursued Rollo's army to their longboats. Rollo improvised a defensive wall by slaughtering his livestock and spilling the guts to the enemy. He did not have time to board his longboats.

"It was a pampered mare that panicked at the smell of the livestock corpses and disintegrated the Frankish charge. The rest of the horses followed and their hysterical riders were unable to stop them.

?The Vikings escaped down the Eure river, leaving six thousand brave Danes dead on the plains of Chartres in the year of our Lord 911."

Bjorn Amundson lay on his cot drained and disappointed and despondent.

Bjorn closed his eyes in delirious exhaustion while the curandera rubbed another egg over his body to withdraw more fever. She cracked the egg into a glass of water where the white appeared cooked. "Bueno. I see a change for the better."
"Bjorn fumed at the legend of the defeat.

"But worse was the dastard character flaw Rollo showed when he attempted to hide his strategic mistake.

He secretly asked Kolfinnur, one of his sergeants, to accuse Bjorn the Bold of cowardice—the greatest of all Norse insults. The reason he gave was, 'He is the most convenient scapegoat. I have nothing against the Bold One directly.'

"Rollo gave a passionate speech to the beaten men as they disembarked from their longboats to their camp. 'You showed honor and luck today. Nothing can stop a lucky man but anything will stop an unlucky one. Sadly, one of us displayed shame by using an axe from a dead enemy. It was unlucky for the owner and unlucky for us.'

"The sergeant's eyes drilled into Bjorn. 'With Odin as my witness, I accuse Bjorn the Old of shame. You are not the man I knew.'

"Bjorn was muddled coming off his berserker high. Several warriors pushed him to the front of Rollo, who shouted to the assembly, 'This man is unlucky. Who will duel this coward?'

"The largest man in the assembly who was Kolfinnur himself said, 'I hate cowards.' He pointed his finger at Bjorn. 'You ran from the battle. Your countrymen were your shield.'

"Bjorn stood silent.

"'Look at your hands. You took a bloody axe from a fallen Frank and that was unlucky. Your axe hanging at your waist never tasted foreign blood.'

"Bjorn looked down at his clean axe.

"Kolfinnur stomped throughout the embattled army and ranted, 'All of you, look at his battleaxe. There is no sign of battle sweat (blood). I charge him of cowardice before the enemy.'

"Bjorn noticed his death grip on the battleaxe that had cut his foot off. He could not open his clenched hand enough to release it.

"He said, 'Umm . . . , I gave to many men the sleep of the sword (death),' but Kolfinnur signaled to the warriors to throw dirt on Bjorn and tear his pelt off his body.

"The ringleaders of ridicule tried to anger Bjorn with taunts and insults into making a dishonorable mistake, but he had the selfcontrol to avoid anger.

"He calmly said, 'I am a man like you. I am Bjorn the Bold who sailed to Paris on your ships. I won every single battle until today—when our forces divided with fatal results,' and glared into Rollo's face

"Rollo continued talking to someone behind him and ignored Bjorn.

'I was late because I fought three warriors with swords in gleaming armor. I was a feeder of ravens (slayer) to them and yet gain no credit . . . '

"Kolfinnur the Huge interrupted, 'You are spear shy (a coward), a dung bearer (low man), cattle kin. Your northern kiss (cold wind) chills us. I challenge you to dual tomorrow morning. That is if your mare's heart can withstand a Going-to-the-Island. Your corpse will destroy the Eagle's hunger.'

"Rollo seized the opening and said, 'We will settle this dispute in the morning.'

"Bjorn was coming off his berserk ecstasy and forgot to invoke the customary three days' preparations for a dual. There was no way he could be ready, but the arrangement was cast in stone."

Bjorn drifted into the hinterlands of his hallucinations. The specter of his father chased him through dark forests over root tangled paths to complete the shame of Bjorn the Bold Berserker.

"In the owl hours of the night after the loss but before the coming Going-to-the-Island dual, Rollo the Great summoned his chieftains into a circle. Each of the commanders' forces spread over the plains behind him. Bjorn the Bold Berserker stood in the center, solitary, desolate, naked, alone. Rollo with his back toward a raised platform said, 'I summon the Seer of Seidr magic to curse this sordid heap of shit.'

"He gestured to the chiefs to open a break in the circle. Through the gap appeared a long -aired woman pulling a creaking cart. It was known that Odin the Furious, greatest of all Norse gods, consulted the practitioner of Seidr to learn the fates of lesser gods, but also Rollo? The superstitious Norsemen were terrified because the power of her spells was final. In stages, the seer in a dark foot-length cloak mounted the platform and loomed over

Bjorn's head. With a grunt, she sat on the cushion of chicken feathers.

"Glass beads encircled the neck and a black hood of lambskin lined with ermine fur hid the head. Gnarled fingers on her left hand held the magic staff. It was ornamented with brass, inlaid with gems, and topped with a knob. Around her waist hung a girdle of soft hair clutching a skin bag.

"From deep within the black hood, her piercing eyes glowered at Bjorn. They neither blinked nor flinched until he looked down in bewildered shame. Nervous throbbing rhythms spoken by the drum of the seer matched Bjorn's racing heart. Resonating beats rose and fell, sped and slowed, and awoke the ghost world. The shaman evoked a trance over the hushed throng.

"'Many are the phantoms who come to reveal what is concealed. Evil exists in our presence. The spirits in the nine worlds of the gods fill my vision. Dishonorable coward!' The lance of her finger landed on Bjorn.

"His rage as a berserker had run its course and he was drained. Pointing crooked fingers at Bjorn's heart, she screamed, 'The Gods sentence you to the wild hunt to pursue forever the supernatural beasts of the dead across the sky. The wordfame of your life is despair.'

"A black raven landed on her left shoulder. 'Hugin, thou art thought.' A companion lit on the other shoulder. 'Munin, thou art memory.' The birds of doom stared at the outcast in the center of the circle with crawr, crawr.

"'These ravens of revenge are the flesh of Odin. They will follow your hunt evermore.' The black hooded seer descended the platform to face the spent Viking.

"At a sign from Rollo, Sergeant Kolfinnur jerked the magic staff out of the shaman's hand and swung it against the back of Bjorn's head. Blond hair in abundance mitigated the first blow, but hits against his naked body were full force from his shoulders to his feet. The foot with three toes got extra strikes for good measure. Somehow, he managed to remain standing.

"The magic staff back in the hands of the shaman dribbled red essence over the carved runes. Bejeweled fingers ripped a handful of hair from Bjorn's head to block the blood, and to the assembled multitude she said, 'A curse sealed by his own hair.' Holding the staff over Bjorn's head, she called for all to hear,

'I curse you

Who soils our glorious land.

'Hear my curse

O God of the Norse.

'Trolls, ghosts, and beasts haunt you

Serpents gnaw your heart

'Your ears never hear

Your eyes never see.

'Your penis pains when you make love

May you be weak as the fiend, Loki

'who was snared by the gods

May the gods reject your sons.

'And their sons after them

For all time past, present, future

'The gods are with me.

The spirits make this curse

'Only spirits may lift it.

Across all your generations.

'Your luck forsakes you.'

"The seer said in a crackling voice, 'We reject you. Never shall you escape the runes on this shaft.' She displayed it to terrify every Norseman.

"It worked.

"The practitioner of Seidr, her drum, and her shaft, faded into the mist but the creak of the cart endured.

"Bjorn's father shuddered and ended the ancestral story looking into the ash-yellow hair of his son.

"Rollo rose to became the high Duke of Normandy and forgot our family. His curse even yet burdens every Amundson.

"But we Norsemen are strong. We rise above that ancient malediction. Odin, himself, gives us the wisdom is that everything fades except the wordfame, and that never dies.

"With a commanding voice, the father said, 'I charge you to clear the Amundson name. Where I failed, you must succeed.' "

Bjorn sank into the sleep of the damned.

6 - Viking Curse

Late in the owl hours after midnight, the patient's Norwegian father came back.

"There is more.

"The next morning, the owner of the stable saw a new hazelwood post planted in his front yard. Trembling, he stumbled about the house. His wife said, 'What is wrong?'

" 'Lo . . .ook in . . .the . . .ya . . .rd.' She gave an earsplitting scream, 'The *Nidstang* shamepost. What have you done? It is that man in the stable, I know it.' He said, 'That stable boy tending our horses is a fearless warrior.'

"The mare's head impaled on the top of the nine-foot pole stared down at the man shaking his fist. Blood flowed down the shaft over carved runes that attested to insults and curses he did not understand. They petrified him as did the sun's sparkling reflections from tiny runic messages carved into the mare's teeth.

"He said, 'What have I done?'

"The horse's head faced the stable where Bjorn lived with the horses.

"A shaman squatting at the bottom intoned a low chant. 'Thor, the earth giant, channels the forces of Hel from the earth through the hazelwood. He smites the doomed through the eyes of the horse. Ancient runes mark the character of lewdness and rage and impotence. I place this shame pole against Bjorn the Old. May the earth sprites of the land be lost until this scum is banned forever.'

" 'I have spoken.'"

"The father's image dissolved."
Bjorn dreamed regular nightmares the rest of the night.

Reflections of bright sunlight from the waves in the river danced across the front wall of the cabin at the Viking mine. The carved Viking ship over the doorway appeared to be sailing on the open sea following its raven pilot. A flock of swifts in the trees by the cabin chattered to welcome the new day.

The Curandera entered the cabin wearing a big smile. Speaking Spanish she said, "How are you, Chico? Better I think. Let me look at you."

She studied his wounds with satisfaction and hummed a happy tune. Over a small fire in the stove, she roasted five chili peppers.

Bjorn's mind rambled as the aroma of the roasted chilies invigorated his system and the healer massaged the juice of aloe vera into his scabs. She finished with a layer of natural honey. Placing a meal of fruit, vegetable, bread, and beans on the table she said, "Eat."

The Curandera left that day confident that she had healed Bjorn. He thought so too.

Healing herbs of the Curandera had worked their magic and Bjorn stood on wobbly legs. He said to the dog, "I feel like a new man, not where I was but okay." Boudicca wagged her tail and looked at her owner with happy bright eyes. "I'll move that rocker box to the next deposit upstream.

He barely made it out of the cabin before his knees collapsed and he hit his head on the ground. Boudicca's medical tongue was not as good as the Curandera's treatments and he passed back to the spirit world.

The vision of his father was disgusted at having to reappear.

" 'Can't you take care of yourself? I'm tired of this tale and not coming back.'

"Old Bjorn the slave liked to wander along the Otra River in his free time. The flash of fishes' scales in the water interested him as they swam over the multicolored stones. He stepped in to snag a fish and slipped on a bright red pebble.

"Out of the water the dripping rock was beautiful. He hid it under his pad of sleeping straw. From then on he gathered pretty minerals every time he went out. Curious about their origin, he discovered outcrops of native gemstones along the banks. Bjorn soon had a collection of rough gems under his straw, that made a lumpy pillow to sleep on.

"Wearing a hood for disguise at the edge of town, he heard one elegantly dressed merchant say to another, "Those nobles in Francia are obsessed with luxury. They eat from fine dishes and wash their food down with magnificent wines grown in the Loire valley. Their avarice is unlimited for jewels of no productive value."

"Bjorn was an uneducated slave in the eyes of the wealthy traders who treated him like he was invisible. "I will not complain because they pay handsomely for such baubles."

" 'Where do you get your gems?'

" 'I'm always looking for new sources.'

"Bjorn with a sparkle in his eye trotted to his stable and selected a single red stone. He returned the waterfront just as the first merchant stepped into his boat.

"Bjorn's background as an elite member of the Norse community, even though he was now a nonperson and treated as a slave, maintained the manners of a high level person. He approached the merchant.

" 'Sir, you said your clients love gemstones. Such as this one?'

"The merchant looked at the ragged man with disgust but held up the red stone to the sun. When he turned it around to judge the transparency, his eyes betrayed a serious interest that Bjorn, who could read a man like a book, noticed.

" 'Where did you get this?'

" 'The river.'

" 'You stole it. I can tell.'

" 'I have more.'

" 'You have others? Show me.'

"Bjorn ran back to his pallet of straw by a devious route through town to evade anyone following him. On the return, he presented three perfect but rough gems for their approval.

"The merchant's eyes opened wide and he was speechless. Regaining his composure he said, 'I might have a buyer for one or two of these, even with the flaws. They are not top quality and suitable for a king, but possibly might interest a Duke.'

" 'I will take those, and ask around.' He snatched the gems from the outstretched hands.

"Bjorn was reluctant to release the samples but had no choice. He said, 'Please let your buyer see them. When will you come back?'

" 'The buyer is in a distant country, Francia. You are ignorant of the personage of Rollo, Duke of Normandy, but he could have a minor interest.'

"Bjorn said out loud, 'The name of Rollo is strange on my ears,' but inside he screamed to himself, 'That treacherous and vindictive Rollo is the most ruthless fiend you will ever find. The value of my gems has jumped by five.'

"He hung his head slightly and said, 'I await your safe return, sir, and will search for more pretty stones for your eminence.'

The vision dissolved and Bjorn slowly woke up. "I'm not as ready as I thought. Maybe I'll be stronger tomorrow and ready to harvest my metal yellow baubles."

He stumbled back to his bed in a daze.

Reality returned slowly in the clear air of the next morning when the rays of the dawn peeked over the Sierras and warmed the soil of the mining camp. The day was optimistic.

Bjorn shuffled to a stump to smoke his pipe and collect his thoughts. He felt better. The pot of black coffee revived his spirits and he said to Boudicca, "I'm back."

He reviewed his dilemma. "Collecting all the gold in California will help with the Amundson curse but I've got to rebuild my strength first. He flexed a giant bicep. Do I have to learn to read, is that it?

"Don't you agree, father?"

There was no answer, but he saw a man trudging along the trail that looked like the old prospector. The memory of his prospector friend hit him for a moment and he extended his hand.

"Hello there. How goes it?"

Boudicca greeted the man with her famous wet hospitality.

"You are Bjorn Amundson, aren't you? This must be the Viking Mine, although I don't see a sign."

"I haven't had time to make one."

The visitor rubbed his legs and said, "I've got to say that *Clark Stanley's Snake Oil Liniment* from Fatty Arbuckle helps my aches and pains, but I am still sore and worn out.

"My liniment from Arbuckle doesn't do much, but I am younger than you."

"Good seeing you, young fellow. Got to go."

"Thanks for stopping. Good luck and be careful."

Boudicca chased the old one a little way down the trail but came running back with the greeting mission accomplished.

Bjorn rubbed Boudicca's as he thought about his dilemma.

That is me in a few years. The Amundson curse will crush me and I will end up like that fellow when I'm too old to work. That Shaman of the North thwarts me at every turn. What am I to do?

Boudicca went to sleep.

Beasts haunt me at night. Serpents gnaw my heart when I think of Maria. Sons of my fathers, every one, are rejected. No luck comes to me. I cannot hear, I cannot see, I get naught but pain from my love member. The gods steal my strength, the wild hunt never ends.

He held up a crooked hand. "The Viking disease is for a thousand years." Seated on a rock with his chin resting on one hand deep in thought, Bjorn pondered his destiny.

With a sound like thunder, the words of his father commanded him to reach for the goal.

"I charge you, my son, to clear the Amundson name. Where I failed you must succeed."

Bjorn stood and slammed a fist into his hand. "I will end my family's scourge from the past, kill it, bury it, destroy it. A thousand years is too long."

He surprised the dog that leaped into his arms by slapping her side. They clenched in a firm doggy hug.

7 - Life Goes On

Bjorn's recovering arms ached and his still debilitated body swayed after a hard day of rocking the rocker. He sat on a log and rubbed liniment over his sore muscles from his bottle of Mug-wump Specific. The lady on the label was fetching and the smell was sweet, but he could not read the rest of the description which said, *Cure and Preventive for All Venereal Diseases*

He leaned against the cabin to light his pipe while Boudicca stretched across his feet. With no one else within an earshot, he talked to the dog as the only ears available.

"I've always been around people. My family in Norway collected in noisy groups throughout our house. It was the same on the *Agilis* when my mates in the forecastle lived next to me. Three of us, Richard, Kawai, and I came to Sacramento, but those two are back at sea on the *Agilis* and I'm stuck with you, Boudicca."

He rubbed the ears of the dog and fingered the scar on his jaw, the result of an encounter with a bear. He had grown a beard to hide it after seeing his reflection in the mirror behind a bar. Every puff made him feel more isolated.

"I'm tired and lonesome. I miss you, Father, even with your faults and endless stories of my great forbearers. I liked hunting gemstones in the river and showing off our baubles when we got home. There was always someone to touch or wrestle with."

He gave a long sigh and said, "Let's go to town and talk to something besides a tree."

The dog tilted her head and slobbered on his hand. Bjorn pulled a clean threadbare shirt from John John's laundry and said, "I want to see civilized people for a change."

Boudicca ran around him in circles.

"Now that I have a ditch bringing water from upstream, I need a sluice box to recover more gold dust but I cannot run it alone. Maybe we can find a helper in town."

They followed the path downstream along the rushing American River toward the distant town. The water was clear this far above the majority of the mining operations. Only the Murrieta family workings were upstream. Passing the downstream Chinese Lucky Ducky Pit, they came upon a new hole in the river. A pair of redhaired men was working the gravel with broad metal pans.

Bjorn called out to them, "Hello there. How's it going?"

"Going good. How are you?"

"I haven't seen you before. You new?"

"We just got in from Tennessee. I'm Jethro and this is my brother, Maverick. We're the Hatfield twins."

Bjorn stepped into the flowing water to shake their hands and Boudicca splashed up to slurp on each one as fast as she could.

"Don't let me stop you," he said as the twins took a quick breather.

"Where are you headed?"

"To see a man about a dog in town."

"Stop and talk a spell on your way back," said Jethro.

"I'll do it." They seemed like a robust pair and Bjorn resolved to visit them on his return.

Turning his thoughts to town, he said to Boudicca, "Are you ready for some furry companionship?"

Boudicca ran back to the twin brothers instead. That was the companionship she wanted.

Bjorn and his sidekick left the river walk to explore a grubby section of Sacramento. He wasn't familiar with that part of town, but the nature of the business was obvious from the furtive men entering and the relaxed clients leaving with happy smiles. One building stood out with red, white, and blue bunting over the door. It displayed a discrete sign,

Madam Pearl's Pleasure Palace.

He stood up straight, smoothed his hair with his fingers, and walked in like he owned the place. "Wow, this is civilized. Look at that rug on the floor."

Bjorn shifted his gaze from the rug to the furnishings of the elegant room. "Do the girls look like that painting of a naked lady? She's beautiful." While he admired the crystal chandelier in the center of the room, the dog sniffed the borders around the room. The modern Viking studied the prints of ancient murals from Pompeii—the brothels, not the luxurious villas.

A bell on the door from inside tinkled and he whispered, "Who are those creatures with smiles? Can they be women? I have forgotten how wonderful a lady can look." He noticed they gazed at him with interest when they eased into the cushions on the yellow velvet couch.

He shook his long blond hair over his shoulders and flexed his dramatic Viking body to evoke throbs from the ladies.

One of them whispered just loud enough for Bjorn to hear, "Look into those sapphire blue eyes. I am going to faint."

The other one whispered back, "All six feet of him fills the doorway. He isn't your usual grubby miner and I want him." She patted the seat for him to sit down and he happily obliged.

"He's mine and you can't have him."

Their argument stopped short when a tall lady flowed into the room wearing a rustling silk dress and a bewitching smile.

"Welcome to *Madam Pearl's Pleasure Palace*. Our goal is to provide companionship to a lonely man. We lack provisions for a lonesome animal, however," she said staring at Boudicca with disgust.

Bjorn flashed a big smile and said in his low rumbling voice, "Glad to meet you . . . but Boudicca comes with me." With calm confidence he wiggled between the ladies on the couch. "I have visited places like this before but yours is nicer," he smiled. A third woman squirmed in and the four filled up the elegant velvet covered lounge with the carved legs. Their sturdiness looked questionable for the load of writhing forms it supported.

Boudicca tried to lick the hands of the ladies, but the gorgeous Chinese woman pulled her dainty perfumed hand away and said, "Eaaauuu. Don't touch me."

The woman with the big brown eyes rubbed Boudicca behind her ears and stroked her fur. "So smooth," as she looked at Bjorn.

The third with auburn hair petted the dog as she lay on their feet. The company relaxed when they saw that Boudicca was clean and soft and friendly. They alternated between running their hands through Bjorn's golden locks and stroking the dog. Like all pets, Boudicca was determined to make friends with the Asian girl who hated her. The girl finally climbed onto the back of the sofa to escape the black and tan beast and left Bjorn to the other beauties.

Madam Pearl said, "We are dedicated to your every pleasure and wish to make you comfortable. I am sure you would appreciate a drink of the finest whiskey in Sacramento."

Bjorn said, "Bring it on." He sipped the fiery golden liquid in pleasure and smiled at the two lovelies who smooched all over him.

Boudicca had to join the action and climbed onto one corner of the couch. She laid her head against the butt of the auburn woman and stretched her long body across the other laps.

Bjorn couldn't move. He thought to himself,

This is heaven.

Jealous at the ménage à quatre with Boudicca, the beauty on the back of the couch played with whatever blonde hair she could reach. The lady with the big brown eyes said, "Never before has such a magnificent example of manhood as you come into our midst." She thought, since yesterday.

They were thrilled to rub his rippling arms and muscled back—and other parts. At least that was the impression they wanted to give.

Madam Pearl, sage Madam that she was, never allowed pleasure to interfere with business. In her most seductive tone, she came to life and said, "You will certainly find a favorite among my girls. Who shall it be this time?"

Bjorn could not think from lust. He decided to blend the lap girl's auburn hair with his golden mane on a pillow. With his huge curved hands, he gave her round voluptuous body a hug that slid down to encircle a slender waist and spread out around her glorious bottom.

From the darkhaired beauty came a whisper in Bjorn's ear, "Next time, me." The Chinese version of the Norse goddess Freyja of love, beauty, fertility and gold, bent over and kissed him on the lips.

Bjorn, the auburn lovely, and Boudicca between walked toward the stairs.

Madam Pearl turned the hourglass over. Some sailor had left it as payment years before. She thought about the endurance of the halfhour timepiece which was so much longer than the happy ending for the lonely, horny seamen.

Madam Pearl watched Bjorn and his companion mount the stairs to a private second floor room. Boudicca trotted between them.

Never one to neglect business, she watched the ship's hourglass to mark the halfhour of the tryst. The falling sand waited for no man. A half-an-hour was her rule.

The sounds of shuffling over the parlor held her attention. She kept a close eye on the safety of her girls and the conduct of their clients to avoid trouble.

The next words she heard were, "Get that dog off the bed!"

A man's voice said, "Down . . . I said, 'down!'"

She heard four paws hit the floor.

"What? Forty dollars in gold!"

"Take it or leave it."

After some grumbling and shuffling, she heard gentle, "Oooh's, aaah's. Yes . . . ,"

"Oh, you are most crooked down here."

"Umm . . ."

"Not to worry. I know the Kama Sutra from India and there is another path to pleasure."

"Ugh, ugh, ooooh."

"Woof."

Madam Pearl looked at her yellow velvet couch. "I'll never get that fur off."

She tried to scrape the fuzz off the velvet but it would not come up.

"That's the last dog I ever let in," as she called to her cleaning lady. "Clean this fur off the best you can."

Wild barking penetrated the ceiling. "Shut up! Damn dog. Shut up."

A door opened to a shouted, "Out," and slammed shut.

Boudicca jerked down the stairs. She had never seen a stairway before and was afraid of it.

Madam Pearl said, "This is your fault, you damn mongrel. Get out of here." She opened the door and kicked Boudicca into the street.

The cleaning lady said as she tried to clean the couch, "We might have to replace the velvet. This hair sticks like glue." She worked for half an hour with limited success.

Some absent minded patron had forgotten a wornout copy of a magazine The Knickerbocker and left it on a table. Watching the cleaning lady, Madam Pearl skimmed it. One verse from A Psalm of Life by Henry Wadsworth Longfellow caught her eye,

> Lives of great men all remind us
> We can make our lives sublime,
> And, departing, leave behind us
> Footprints on the sands of time;

Madam Pearl watched the hourglass sand run from the top to bottom and said, "Footprints in the sand are for others." She tapped the ceiling with a broom handle. The sound, of course, went straight through the floorboards to the room above.

"Already? We just got started."

Bjorn wore a big grin descending the stairs.

"Where's my dog?"

Madam Pearl pointed to the front door. "Outside where the brute belongs."

They were interrupted by wild howls that circled the yard.

Bjorn sprang out the front door and hollered, "What's wrong?"

He could see Boudicca was locked in a copulatory tie behind a coyote. The coyote yipped and Boudicca yelped, as they danced around the courtyard, butt end locked to butt end.

Madam Pearl put her hands on her hips and said, "Look at that, will you. You're going to have a litter of coyote-dog pups in about nine weeks. They're called coydogs."

"Coydogs? Never heard of them."

"That's what you're going to get. And you will never bring their mother or her puppies in here again. Is that clear?"

"Yes, ma'am." He muttered in a low voice, "She doesn't have any puppies."

"What did you say? Are you making fun of me?"

"No, ma'am."

The canines separated and Boudicca ran up to Bjorn. He hugged her and said, "You're going to be a mother. How about that?"

Boudicca leaned against his leg and wagged her tail.

Bjorn said, "We both had a pretty good day."

8 - The New Viking Gold Mine

The day of diversion in town sapped Bjorn's strength and left all his money back at *Madam Pearl's Pleasure Palace*. To the exhausted miner, the park bench looked comfortable, so Bjorn spent the night there. Boudicca warned off intruders but could do nothing to erase the visions of his father that were brought on by the hard wooden slats.

"Rollo rallied the troops the next morning with the order, 'Prepare the Going-to-the-Island duel.'

"Excited volunteers spread cloaks three paces square on a small island. They secured the corners with sacred hazel stakes to thwart the use of magic.

" 'Are the fighters present?'

"Kolfinnur and Bjorn said together, 'I am here.'

"To Kolfinnur Rollo said, 'The challenger will state the rules of combat.

"Kolfinnur said in a loud voice. 'Odin is my witness. Neither I nor the coward has a shield bearer. The first man whose blood falls on this cloak loses the duel.'

"He looked at Bjorn's partial foot, '. . . except, any blood from that scratch does not count, only new blood. A fighter is defeated if he steps off the cloak or loses his weapon.'

"Rollo said, 'Odin demands blood to validate the outcome. Whoever wins will perform the sacrifice . . . ,' he pointed at a bull tied at the edge of the clearing, 'to appease Odin and confirm this bout of justice.'

"The men crowded the river banks with anticipation. Many placed bets on the giant against the berserker and all drank raucously. The other eleven berserkers were sleeping off the effects of yesterday's battle and ignored the injustice to Bjorn.

"Rollo supervised the preparations in person, which lasted until the sun was high overhead. The spectators maneuvered to get clear views of the action.

"Kolfinnur as the challenger was allowed to pick his starting position. He chose the corner with his back to the sun. It forced Bjorn to stare into the glare from the opposite corner. Neither wore helmets, only normal clothes. Wicked-sharp axes glistened in their hands. Bjorn was drained coming down from his berserker high. Kolfinnur loomed clear and huge.

" 'Start the contest. We must have a clear winner.'

"Bjorn saw the silhouette of Kolfinnur raise his axe high to deliver the first and final fatal slash. Even in the glare, Bjorn instinctively blocked it.

"He circled to get the sun out of his eyes and aimed a flanking blow at Kolfinnur. It bounced off. Bjorn recovered into a smooth downward arc, but his opponent evaded it and buried his axe in the defender's shield. Bjorn hooked his axe behind Kolfinnur's right leg, but slipped when he jerked the hook because of his missing toes. The ex-berserker fell sideways onto the cape.

"By gut instinct he raised his shield for protection to block Kolfinnur's attack and swung the edge into Kolfinnur's off balance right leg. Kolfinnur tossed his shield away to regain his balance, and pulled his knife on the way down. Bjorn tried to swing his axe off the ground but the handle was too long for a good swing. He reached for his knife but his opponent's full body weight slammed into his torso. Kolfinnur's knife stabbed Bjorn's arm and blood gushed onto the cape.

"Rollo announced, 'By the Gods, Kolfinnur has defeated the coward.'

"Kolfinnur waved at the spectators. According to custom, the spectators splashed to the island and tore Bjorn's shirt from his shoulders. They as a mob wrenched away his weapons. Bjorn stood alone in the center of the capes, abandoned, confused, and naked. A shaman threw him a strip of cloth to wrap around his bleeding arm and protect the sacred cape.

"The spectators dragged him to the shore.

"Rollo said to the assembly, 'For bad luck and cowardice, I banish this failure to Norway. Dump him ashore at Tønsberg if the voyage is lucky, or into the sea lest Aegir, the God of the sea, drags you under. This man is an outlaw, a wolf, a monster, and I will not tolerate his kind in Francia.'

"He turned to Kolfinnur, 'Odin demands blood. The victor will sacrifice the bull to confirm this test of justice.'
"

Bjorn raged on his bed, "This is wrong. Bjorn the Bold is the noble Viking. This is not justice." He beat the wall.

"Several men dumped the exile into the nearest longboat. 'Stay there.' He wrapped a bloodstained wolf pelt around his throbbing arm and foot.

"The crossing to Tønsberg was calm with only ten-foot swells amidst a good breeze over the next five and a half days. Bjorn ate nothing but was occasionally could sneak a gulp of bilge water from the bottom of the boat. During times of no wind, he welcomed his stints at the oars to stop shivering.

"When they reached the dock of the trading town of Tønsberg, the men ashore and those aboard ignored him. They were too busy unloading the slaves and plunder from Francia, though not Chartres.

Bjorn limped out of sight as fast as he could to the home of a friend. In response to his knock, the door opened and the owner saw a bloodied bedraggled man standing there. 'What do you want?'

"Bjorn said, 'Remember me? I am Bjorn the Bold who went Viking to Francia last spring.'

" 'You were the leading warrior. What happened?'

" 'We won every battle but failed at Chartres. Rollo made me the scapegoat. I am an outlaw.' "

The new Bjorn moaned in his bed. The Curandera massaged aloe vera juice into his scabs. The dream continued.

"The homeowner said, 'You are a pathetic mess, but the most I can offer is for you to sleep in the stable tonight.'

"Bjorn asked in a low voice, 'Can you spare a scrap of fat and crust of bread? I have not eaten for five days.'

"The friend's heart skipped a beat. He remembered his friendship with an extraordinary Bjorn the Bold over the years. 'I don't care if you're an outlaw, there's food in the kitchen.' He returned with a piece of meat, bread, and a flagon of wine. 'Follow me.' He introduced Bjorn to the horses in the stable.

" 'Stay out of sight. I cannot be seen aiding an outlaw.'

"Bjorn curled up next to a young foal for warmth. His strength returned with a long drink from the clear sparkling waters of a nearby creek. It almost washed the foul taste of the bilge from his mouth. He discovered a small bag of grain. Eating a handful, he passed the rest to the horses.

"When the owner checked on him the next morning Bjorn said, 'Can I stay in the stable if I clean the stalls and brush the horses?'

"After deliberation with his family centering around a discussion of honor, the owner agreed to let Bjorn work as a slave. He was to do nothing honorable since outlaws were nonpersons.

"The horses liked Bjorn the slave. He cleaned their cribs every day and fed them treats. They had never had it so good.

"The winter of 911 blossomed into the spring of 912."

Bjorn in his miner's cabin finally lost the fever and slept straight through for a day and a half. Boudicca begged for food from passing travelers. Her winning tail wags got so many treats that she gained weight.

Bjorn's memory cleared while his body recuperated for the most part. Daily activity was part of the secret, but he was exhausted by the end of the day. But not too tired to talk. He said out loud to his little crew of the dog, "The Norsemen followed a set of Laws. Do you know the first one? Be brave and aggressive, that's what."

Boudicca eyed him and sighed.

"I'm brave enough. I drove off those scoundrels that attacked our stagecoach. You missed it because you were here jumping on Sergio."

Boudicca rolled flat on her side and closed her ears.

"And how aggressive was I toward that cougar? Should have killed her for dinner." He scrunched his face and added, "Boiled cat wouldn't taste good."

The wheels in Bjorn's mind slowed and he drifted asleep muttering about tomorrow's chores.

"I need to sharpen my knife because I dulled it dressing those rabbits. Got to set up that new sluice construction and train the twins to use it. I'll clean out the shed later. This Viking claim is harder work than sailing a ship." The cougar bites ached and he dozed off.

"Hello, father. I didn't expect you back so soon.

" 'You need all the guidance I can give you.'

" 'Guidance?'

" 'A good Viking is prepared.'

" 'I'm prepared.'

" 'No you are not. Your knife is dull and your Colt revolver is dirty. You are low on powder and your axe has not been sharpened in weeks. And look at your health.'

" 'What about my health?'

" 'You have not got any. Corruption flows through your veins, you are as weak as a girl, and you don't have a trained crew.'

" 'The Hatfield twins are helping me.'

" 'They don't know what they're doing and that cougar ate you.'

" 'You got me.'

" 'Think about your mine. You leave one empty pit and move to the next. Someday there won't be the next pit, or somebody will already be there.'

" 'The river goes for miles.'

" 'A long way is not forever. What's your plan after the mine?'

"Bjorn flexed his biceps and said, 'I will always have a mine.' "

The vision ended and Bjorn talked in his sleep to the empty cabin since the twins were moving the last gear from their camp. "They're my crew. I don't spend a lot of time in *Madam Pearl's Pleasure Palace*, and I save money in the bank. What makes a merchant? I can sell anything . . .."

Slow clip-clops on the trail woke him up.

Through the broken window, he could see two horses with riders leading a loaded packhorse. "I'm in here," he hollered. Boudicca welcomed the twins like long lost friends from BC—before the cougar.

Jethro Hatfield said, "What happened to you? You look like you're at death's door."

"Find the cougar that ambushed me and you'll see death's door."

"If you're the winner, I'd hate to see the loser."

"Go to hell, both of you."

Maverick Hatfield said, "We're ready to move in. Where can we put our stuff?"

Bjorn said, "You can sleep on the floor until you build some beds. It'll be a little tight with all of us but we'll fit. Don't neither of you snore do you?

"No, but how about you or the dog?'

"It'll be quiet unless something scares her. She can wake the dead with her bark."

Boudicca promptly laid down on the section of the floor right where they planned to sleep as though to say, "I'll take it here."

"Move over dog, we're coming in too."

A wide-open gate welcomed customers to Sam Brannan's store. The fortified walls of Sutter's Fort were not needed for defense with the hordes of gold seekers everywhere. Brannan clearly understood the virtues of a monopoly to sell goods to the miners and maintained the only general store in the Sacramento region. His two-level store had four windows and a central doorway on the upper level that opened into the market space. The massive adobe walls kept the interior cool in the hot Sacramento summer. It was the only store to buy supplies for the expanded crew of the New Viking Gold Mine.

Clad in his cleanest threadbare trousers and shirt, Bjorn climbed the stairs to the balcony in front of the door. He held the door open for the tall, lean gentlemen in an old fashioned black coat and white necktie who came up the opposite side. They walked into Brannan's Store together.

"Hello, Pastor Grove. Good to see you."

"Same to you, Bjorn. It has been a while."

"I finally got some helpers and I'm picking up supplies to feed them. It's been kinda busy upriver. How about you?"

"Bringing the Lord's word to ears who will listen and those that won't."

"It sounds like your doxology works are busy. Been meaning to ask, Pastor, aren't you a Lutheran yet?'"

"Aren't you a Methodist by now?"

They laughed at their running joke and shook hands.

Bjorn stacked his purchases on the wooden counter where the clerk had cleared a space; two bags of tobacco, four pounds of coffee, sugar, flour, and a tin of powdered milk for Boudicca. The proprietor left clear the slot carved into the surface to accept gold dust instead of money. Not that he needed them, but Bjorn noticed the front of the store where picks, shovels, and pans were normally displayed was empty, even at the outrageous price of fifteen dollars a shovel.

He poured a measure of gold dust into the slot and watched the clerk carefully sweep the gold to a scale. On the floor directly underneath was a cloth to catch any errant flakes."

The miner griped to the Pastor, "Can you believe that? A dollar apiece for eggs."

Pastor Grove sighed, "No omelet for breakfast, but we'll make do." He hung his head for a moment and gently laid two books by his small collection of food in front of the clerk. "Would you accept books on consignment, my good man?"

The clerk said, "We don't sell many books, but Alva Dahl might be interested."

"I heard she was starting a school and the church could use a few extra dollars," said the Pastor.

Bjorn said, "Who has time to read?"

Pastor Grove said, "Summers are so hot, people think they are beyond help in hell. And the winters are so heavenly there is no interest in church. I'm afraid Satan has more converts than the Lord, and few read whether they're saved or damned."

Bells jangling on the front door pulled their attention to the entrance. A striking young woman entered with a flourish wearing an elegant outfit and a hairdo that extended her height by several inches.

"Good morning, Miss Dahl," said the clerk.

"We were just talking about you. How are you this fine day?" said the Pastor.

"Madam Pearl . . .," said Bjorn, as he held out his hand with a grin on his face.

Alva Dahl flashed a smile to the clerk and the pastor but motioned for Bjorn to bend down where she could whisper in his ear, "My name is Alva Dahl in public. *Madam Pearl's Pleasure Palace* is my business."

Bjorn said, "OK."

Alva or Madam Pearl continued in a low voice, "You are that two-hundred pound man enslaved by a one-pound donkey dick. Show me some manners."

Bjorn studied her with his piercing blue eyes. His memories of romantic rendezvous with the beauties of Pearl's Pleasure Palace sent tremors through his body and distracted his attention. He had contributed his share to her prosperity.

She said to Pastor Grove in a happy singing voice, "It's always a pleasure to meet a fellow purveyor of love . . ."

Pastor Grove was knocked speechless for a moment, " . . . Perhaps . . . we look at love somewhat differently . . . ."

Alva laughed, " . . . Perhaps we do."

She stepped back to better eye Bjorn, "What is up, and where is that dog of yours?"

"Picking up a few supplies." The mention of his dog, Boudicca, snapped him out of his reverie and he was at a loss where to put his hands. He lifted one of Pastor Grove's books off the counter and asked the preacher, "What is this about?"

"They are written by a Presbyterian minister, William McGuffey, back in the States."

Bjorn opened it, replaced it, and resumed drooling at the overpriced goods he couldn't afford.

Alva Dahl followed Bjorn to the utensils and said, with a quizzical look on her face, "Talk to me."

"I work my mine and buy supplies in town. There is nothing more to say."

She thought for a few moments and said, "You look and sound like a Norwegian. Where are you from?" She looked straight up at Bjorn towering over her and her hair extension.

"I'm from Drammen, Norway, ma'am. I came over by way of Hawaii."

"I am from Norway, myself, by way of Christiana," she said

Bjorn thought to himself, Not many Norsemen are over here, and certainly no women.

He said, "Miss Dahl, . . . might I ask a favor from a countryman, uh woman?"

"Favor?"

"Would you read the name of this book," as he picked it up from the counter?

Alva Dahl read, "McGuffey's First Eclectic Reader. Read it yourself."

"Umm . . . you see . . . uh . . . uh . . . ," Bjorn said.

"What's wrong with you?"

"Well . . . Ma'am . . . it's this way . . . ,"

Miss Dahl said, "Why can't you read? My sister taught reading in Drammen for years and she was good."

"I hunted gems in the Otra river mineral area with my father before he sent me off to sea. I read rigging, not books."

"An illiterate Norwegian is an insult. You should be ashamed." She picked up the two books and said to the proprietor, "Put these on my account." After a nod to the pastor, she waved her finger in Bjorn's face and said, "You will come to *Madam Pearl's Pleasure Palace* this afternoon for your first reading lesson."

"Um . . . I don't know . . . ,"

"Be there—and no dallying with the ladies."

She thus enrolled Bjorn as her first pupil in the grammar school at the Pleasure Palace School. She commented out loud in a distracted voice, "He will be a hard nut to crack but he requires attention. My school will succeed if I extend it to Indians, illiterate Chinese arrivals, and children of the miners when they send for their families."

Bjorn overheard Pastor Grove say as Miss Dahl rang the bells on her way out with the McGuffey readers in her arms, "Alva's business is sinful, but she does good. Who am I to judge?"

Back at what felt like the salt mines, Bjorn looked up at the thubalup, thubalup that announced a horse was galloping into the workings. The horse twirled a circle and reared on its hind legs as Joaquín Murrieta wearing a flat-brimmed sombrero stood up in his silver spurs that matched his silver belt buckle and shouted, "Hola, señor." Joaquín fired his pistol into the air for attention.

Bjorn said, "Pretty fancy there. I've seen you show off in parades like that too."

"Si Señor."

"What are you up to this morning?"

Switching to English, Joaquín said, "Taking a day off."

Bjorn was intrigued by the show of horsemanship. He thought of the dashing attraction it would have for his lady friend, Maria Rojas, down Sonoma way. A flash of jealousy crossed his face as he remembered the throngs of skilled caballeros competing for her favors. He cleared his throat and thought about his dinner with General Vallejo at the sprawling Rancho Petaluma Adobe headquarters.

"Murrieta, show me how to ride a horse."

"What makes you think a gringo can ride a horse?"

"He can try."

"*¿Como no? Un momento, por favor,*" as he rode off in a cloud of dust and a hearty, "*Ha-yo plata!*"

He returned leading a horse by a halter. "Meet your new friend. I call him Thunderfire."

"Thunderfire? What does that mean?"

"He is a big horse for a big man. He can carry you and he talks English."

Bjorn stepped from the river and shook hands with Joaquín. "Let's get started."

Speaking in English for Thunderfire's benefit and Bjorn's, he started the lesson.

"Your horse feels like a man does. He will learn to trust you and you must learn to trust him." Joaquín dismounted and rubbed the ears of Thunderfire, who snorted and stomped his front feet. "Come and meet your new rider."

Bjorn walked up to Thunderfire and looked him in the eye.

"Hold out your hand for him to smell. That is how he knows you." Bjorn's long flowing hair looked like a yellow palomino horse's mane to Thunderfire. He immediately liked Bjorn as a friend but not necessarily as a rider. He nudged his hair and sniffed Bjorn's hand. The horse nodded his surprisingly large head and snorted with approval as he let Bjorn scratch his face, neck, and sides. Stroking so large an animal was a new experience for Bjorn, as was the pungent odor of his fur.

Thunderfire wanted to rub back but there was a problem. He stepped sideways and trapped Bjorn against the miner's shack.

Bjorn cried, "Get away from me. I'm sore enough already."

Thunderfire merely nodded his head.

Joaquín pulled a treat from his pouch and handed it to the horse. "Thunderfire, back off."

To the munching of the horse, Joaquín continued, "He likes you, but never get angry at him. He feels your every mood."

He handed the loose rein to Bjorn. "Walk Thunderfire in the sand to tire him out. Run him to the top of the hill as fast as you can. When he is tired, maybe you can ride him."

Bjorn walked the horse through the sand and the water, and up and down the hill until Bjorn was tired. He didn't know about Thunderfire.

Joaquín opened his eyes from his siesta and said, "Are you ready?"

"I think so."

"Walk up to his front but do not surprise him. After you get into the saddle keep your chin down on your chest and behind your stomach. Pull his head high."

Murrieta bowed, crossed himself and prayed, "Give B'Horny the strength and courage to ride this horse and honor the Virgin Mary and her son, Jesus, this day. Amen." He had not mastered Bjorn's name in Spanish yet.

He handed the reins to Bjorn and said, "Approach his left side and put your left foot in the loop. That is the stirrup. Throw your other leg over his back and slip your foot in the stirrup."

Bjorn was just settling into the saddle when Joaquín said, "Chuh, chuh . . ." Thunderfire bucked and Bjorn's feet jumped out of the stirrups. He pinwheeled flat on the saddle and rotated into the air like a Chinese kite. He held onto the reins with a death grip and hit the ground in a mighty thud. Thunderfire took off running.

"Let go of the reins!"

Bjorn said, "What?" as he bounced from cactus to cactus around the meadow.

"Drop the reins!"

"Okay," and he let go.

Bjorn stood up covered in dust and decorated with scratches from prickly pear cactuses. "Well, that was fun."

"Get back on and show him who is boss."

Thunderfire bucked differently the second time and Bjorn flew head over heels backward down his tail. "Huh!" as he hit the ground and couldn't breathe for a few seconds. "How . . . do you stay . . . on?"

"Get back up and let your butt move with the horse. Keep your body flexible."

Joaquín showed with a smooth Mexican dance step.

Thunderfire's third trick was to dance straight sideways, but Bjorn rode him with a sore swinging hip and stayed on.

"You look good, *Amigo*. Stay loose and practice every day. Here are some dried berries for a treat." He pulled a handful from his pouch.

Thunderfire plunged his mouth into the open palm and sucked up the berries in the twinkling of an eye.

"Hey! That's no good. I have a few left but hide these in your pocket. That horse is one sneaky animal."

Bjorn rubbed his ears and said, "Sorry friend, you'll just have to wait."

Joaquín said, "Next time we will practice with the bit."

John John the laundry man looked up from his steaming tank of clothes when his first cousin walked in. The cousin said, "Why do you work so hard? I labor in the day and sleep at night."

The sweating laundry man said, "You built a dam to bring water to our gold mine. I use water to make clothes clean."

The cousin said, "Listen to me. I dug a channel to bring water to the New Viking Mine for their new sluice and they gave me money." He held up a small heavy pouch. "But you wash clothes for free, only tips. Bad, bad business."

John John pulled a batch of shirts and pants from the tank of hot water. He squeezed the water out and hung them on a clothesline to dry.

He said, "These pants come in stiff with dirt and salt. They stand up on their own. I make them leave soft and folded. See."

He held the candle over the tank of dirty water and scooped a handful of dirt from the bottom. He showed his cousin, "What is this?"

The cousin dismissed the mud until he looked again. Hidden in the slop was a tiny nugget of gold. He stirred the sludge and saw more specks of gold.

John John put his finger to his mouth and said, "Most good business is wash clothes. The dirt is secret. Even the *Kongsi* gang of Blue Lanterns from Hong Kong do not know. I make much money."

The next morning he bowed to the line of men waiting at the counter with stiff pants in their arms. Bjorn's clothes were torn, dirty, and ripped. "Mr. John John, I need you to mend these rips after you wash the dust off." John John said, "Yes sir. Like new tomorrow. You see."

Bjorn had mixed feelings as he walked out past the column of waiting men. He knew they wanted clean clothes to make a good impression on the ladies at *Madam Pearl's Pleasure Palace*, and hopefully get a reduced price. Madam Pearl never allowed a discount but the ladies appreciated the clean clothes.

John John changed the subject. "How did it go with Sam Brannan? He stomped into the laundry yesterday and demanded we build a bridge. You can do that, I cannot."

The cousin described the visit with Sam Brannan's foreman. "The foreman said we know many Celestials and can tell them apart. But he say, 'By God, I cannot. You all look the same.' "

The cousin hung his head and said, "I think those white people all look the same. The foreman wants eighteen men at Brannan's store at sunup."

As customers laid down their rigid pants to be washed, Brandon's foreman barged in the door and threw his outfit on top of the stack. "Wash these first. And your damn people had better be at the store right now. Are they?"

The cousin asked, "How big is bridge?" The foreman said, "My bridge is none of your business, just wash my dirty pants," and turned to walk out. He stopped. "The river is as wide as two of your laundry buildings. I need eighteen workers. They better be ready.'"

"Very good sir. Men at the general store now.'" The foreman confronted the cousin and said, "There's hell to pay if they are not."

"Most good. I am honored to work for you."

"I'm coming back if they aren't ready to work, and it won't be pleasant. I'm warning you."

After the foreman left, the washerman called to his brother who was cleaning gold dust from the laundry tanks. "Chop chop. Ten men to work, start at Brannan store. Now!" The contractor ran with a group of men to the entrance of Brannan's store and arrived just before the lazy foreman did.

Brannan's foreman surveyed the group. "I'm surprised you made it, but I only see ten. Where are the others?"

"Most ready to work, sir. Workers come from a great distance. Arrive soon. Where build the bridge?"

The foreman said, "Follow me." He rode his horse at a trot ahead of the workers on foot for an hour. They stopped at a ford across the Dry Creek tributary to Mokelumne River. The water flow was about thirty feet across and meandered slowly. Pulling out a diagram of the bridge, Brannan's foreman said, "Mr. Brannan needs this bridge right now, from here to that road on the other side. Cut the trees you need. Rocks are up that hill. Who is in charge?"

The cousin called a man out and said, "Chi Long is most good engineer in China. He knows water, he knows wood, he knows to make you a bridge."

"I pay each man fifteen dollars a day on Friday. I want a list of workmen in English on Thursday. I will inspect the project every day to stop you from cheating me."

The cousin worked the crew so hard with his promises of the gold mountain that Brannan's foreman never noticed the manpower shortage. The cousin pocketed the earnings for the missing eight workers. He kept three-fourths of the other wages to pay off their passage from China.

The foreman reported to Sam Brannan that the Chinese miners only worked claims he had abandoned. He detested the newcomers with their wide hats and chopsticks.

"Remember that time your mine got robbed up in Rattlesnake Gulch? We laid the blame on some convenient Chinks and started a row in their camp. I promised to shoot them if they stole again, and we had to shoot a couple for an example. You should have seen them jump."

Bjorn and his dog left Sacramento town and snagged a wandering horse for the ride up the American River. In glowing contentment, he said "Some good time we had. Let's find those twins from Tennessee."

A twin dumped a shovel full of gravel into the pan held by the other and looked at the man and his dog on the path, "How was the town?"

"You rich yet?"

"It's all right. The water is cold and this pan is heavy by evening, buteven worse was my miserable farm back home."

Bjorn noticed their workings were neat but a little rough. The brothers worked together in a smooth rhythm. He liked that.

Boudicca splashed through the water.

"That's a good dog."

"I raised her from a pup. Boudicca! leave those men alone. They're trying to work."

The twin with the pan swished the gravel out and they splashed too shore.

Bjorn said, "Like I said earlier, haven't seen you before. New?"

"We're from Tennessee, Gatlinburg to be exact. I'm Jethro and this is Maverick. We're called the Hatfield twins."

"Don't let me stop you. I'm headed home."

Jethro wanted somebody different for conversation and said, "We had a hell of a trip across the prairie. I've never seen so much nothing in my life. They forgot the trees. Whiskey, our dog, didn't make it. He's buried in some godforsaken, windswept patch of grass. That mutt was one loyal dog. I miss him."

"Me too. He guarded my still up in Fox Hollow. "

Bjorn said, "Boudicca wants to replace Whiskey. She likes you."

"What do you mean?" said Jethro.

"I could use help at the New Viking Mine upstream? There is a new sluice box that needs more hands than mine to operate."

They agreed to try it out for a week, thinking they would never leave.

Bjorn and the twins fell into a smooth rhythm during the day and swapped tall tales through the night. Jethro scraped his fiddle and serenaded the night critters most evenings. He taught Bjorn their hillbilly songs and Bjorn taught them the sea shanties of Norway. They looked more like strolling minstrels than 49ers. Sometimes, people along the way stopped to join in or just listen. It was often their only bright spot in a grim day.

In the middle of a bull session, Bjorn said, "We work together good. Will you stay on?"

Jethro said to Maverick, "I'm sick and tired of staring at your ugly mug all day. I vote to look at Bjorn's beard and scar."

Maverick retorted, "You're uglier than sin, but I like Boudicca and Bjorn is not a bad soul, even if he talks funny."

"We like it. We'll stay on."

Bjorn said, "The worst arrangement for a team is three equal people. It's always one against two, but Boudicca gets to vote and that makes us two to two. Agree?"

They all shook hands and Boudicca sealed the agreement with a slurp of her tongue on each member of her new family.

9 - Calaveras Fair, Fiesta, and Rodeo

Zigzags of mended rips decorated Bjorn's clean outfit as he clomped along the board sidewalk. But those clean clothes were nothing compared to what happened next. The newspaper editor slammed open the front door of the Sacramento Transcript and screamed, "Extra! Extra! California is a state. General Vallejo's efforts have succeeded." He joined the cheers of the crowd, "California is legitimate at last." He passed out sheets to every hand in exchange for any amount of money they offered.

A mine owner standing next to Bjorn read the dispatch and said, "Wouldn't you know. The first thing they do is pass a tax on foreigners in Tuolumne County."

Bjorn said, "What taxes?" since he couldn't read the paper for himself.

"Every foreigner is required to pay a mining tax of twenty dollars a month."

"Who's a foreigner?"

"To their mind, a foreigner is greasers, Chinese, Irishmen, and even Frenchmen. Where did they get that last one? Hmmm . . . it seems the sheriff trying to arrest these individuals got himself killed, and two of his posse were wounded. As of press time, about a hundred have been detained."

Bjorn said, "So much for becoming a state."

The walk back to the New Viking Gold Mine passed many celebrations dotting the Sacramento Valley. They were offset by occasional wakes of dread by groups of Indians and bodega owners.

He asked a passerby, "What year is it."

"It's autumn of the year 1850. Make a note that we became a state on September 9. The good people in Angel's Camp organized the first county in the state and called it Calaveras. That's the Spanish word for the piles of Indian skulls in the area. Business owners from back east are enthusiastic, but shop owners from Mexico and savvy Indians not so much."

Bjorn walked into his workings and said to Jethro and Maverick, "Calaveras County is putting on a fiesta, fair, and rodeo this weekend to celebrate our new statehood."

Maverick said, "What is a fiesta?"

"It's a huge party. All the señoritas will be there. There's music all night, the next day, and the next night."

Jethro said, "Señoritas you say? Is there whiskey?"

"Anything you want. Whiskey, card games, contests, sales booths, dancing, and everything else. They'll kick it off with a big parade this Saturday. General Vallejo will lead it. He has worked hard to get California admitted as a state."

Maverick said, "I hate politics."

Bjorn said, "Me too, but he did one good thing."

"What was that?"

"He made our state free with no slaves allowed. You two can't be slaves."

Jethro said, "Glad to hear that. Can I make Maverick a slave?"

"No, you can't have slaves. You can be your own slave, though."

"Are you going to the fiesta?"

"We all are. Take a bath and wash your clothes."

"Do I have to?"

"Yes, you do because you will be around civilized people for a change. Vallejo is the best friend the United States has in California and the most influential man here. We will see Sam Brannan, the skunk. He prints the California Star and owns the general store. I hope General Vallejo brings his niece, Maria Rojas."

Jethro said, "What would a horny Viking like you see in Maria?"

Bjorn the Horny Viking said, "Shut your mouth. Maria is a classy woman and I won't let you talk about her that way."

Boudicca knew something was up and wagged her tail.

That weekend in Angel Camp, the miners from the New Viking Mine mingled with the crowd of spectators along the parade route. Strains of Yankee Doodle from a fife and drum corps announced the start of the procession. Their eyes were drawn to a pair of young girls carrying a banner that read,

FIRST ANNUAL CALAVERAS COUNTY
FAIR, RODEO, and FANDANGO

Behind the banner marched a cadre of vaqueros on their prize horses. Brilliant breast collars lined with silver and trimmed with a red fringe circled the front of each mount. The riders dazzled the spectators with their brilliant rope lariat tricks, gigantic sombreros, splendid white shirts, flowing red silk scarves, and boastful belts with tooled silver buckles. A row of silver buttons down the length of each leg accented the skintight pants. Fancy tooled silver stirrups accented with gold showed off their fine leather boots.

"*Olé*", said a vaquero with his lariat circling the air and roping inattentive bystanders. One settled over Boudicca from behind as she barked at the horses. She jumped four feet high with a howl and twisted. A flick of the vaquero's wrist released her, and she lay down embarrassed in a dog pout. The horse quit bucking.

Competing for attention was a marching Mariachi band with two guitars, a violin, and a trumpet. The musicians' matching black outfits were decorated with more polished silver. The bouncy rhythm of the huge bass guitar set the pace as the band passed and the spectators tapped their feet. Several danced in the street to the songs.

Flower-draped floats pulled by horses or decorated burros followed one after another.

Jethro with wide eyes said, "If this don't beat all." Maverick stared at the parade with open eyes and said, "This is beautiful. I'm glad Bjorn brought us."

"You don't see parades like this at sea," said Bjorn.

Fascinated waves of cheers followed the parade from spectator to spectator. Around the corner came four white steeds resplendent in red trailers, silver trim, and sombreros. A musician played flamenco melodies on his guitar as he stood on a horse. Bjorn was awed by the dancers who showed off their gypsy dances with sweeps of their skirts and clacking of their castanets. The audiences clapped their hands. Those of Hispanic heritage sang emotional verses.

No one had seen such silver-mounted saddles that were embroidered with silver or gold. Even the bridles were silver, and the reins were woven of the most select hair from a horse's mane. Thus mounted and equipped, the handsome men presented an imposing aspect in front of Bjorn and the twins.

Before they could catch their breath, another horse rounded the corner. It was protected by a ring of horsemen performing tricks every step or two. A little cowboy on a goat tossed a gold dragoon on the ground and watched a caballero snatch it up at full speed.

Inside the ring was the most striking horse Bjorn had ever seen, but all the eyes were on the rider. Bjorn caught his breath when he saw the most beautiful woman in the world and he knew her name even in her party dress.

"Maria!" He threw his hat into the air and waved. "Remember the stagecoach?"

"Of course I remember, Señor Amundson. You were so brave when the bandits attacked."

The dumbfounded twins looked at Bjorn with new respect. "You know her?" said Jethro.

"You really know her?"

"We go way back."

"See you at the fandango," Bjorn hollered.

She smiled and said, "Baile if you please. Hired hands have a fandango. We have a baile, or you say a dance." She laughed and waved to the crowd across the street, but sneaked a quick look back at Bjorn as she passed the reviewing stand.

Bjorn thought to himself, What am I saying? I can't dance.

Two señoritas carried another banner around the corner that read,

Don Mariano Guadalupe Vallejo

Bjorn was awed by pairs of horsemen leading a man on a fine horse fit for the king of Mexico.

Pointing a sword overhead, the man shouted, "Viva California! Viva Mexico!" The crowd punched their fists in the air and cheered, "Viva Mexico! Viva California!"

General Vallejo was dressed in great style with short breeches to his knee. Ornamented with gold lace at the bottom, he wore leggings of soft deerskin that were richly colored and tied at the knee with heavy gold tassels. On the General's head was a silver and ermine-trimmed sombrero.

An announcer brought up the end of the procession with a megaphone. "Remember the fandango tonight in the park. Visit the fairgrounds this afternoon."

"The dust bowl," someone said. "We don't have a decent fairground or a park either."

Temptations poured from the megaphone. "Eat fry bread, tacos, BBQ, and corn. Come one, come all, and have a good time. You'll find card games and wagers and competition. Cheer your favorite rodeo hand. Don't miss the action this afternoon at the fairgrounds."

The twins led by Boudicca made their way to the dusty fairgrounds in anticipation. Maverick said to Jethro, "B'jorn looks like somebody knocked in the head."

Bjorn was enthralled by the sight of Maria on her equine throne.

Bjorn expanded his cultural interests to the booths around the celebration area. One woman hawked a black patent medicine made with oil from a natural oil seep, but she never said what it was good for. It was his first visit to a fair and he stared into every shop and vendor with wide eyes.

Farmers' wagons were piled high with harvests from the central California Valley. Ripe fruits filled the air with the fragrance of oranges and grapefruit, kumquats, and a stand of avocados. Tables displayed berries that Bjorn did not recognize but tasted wonderful.

His frugal heritage from Norway was unaccustomed to such a range of goods for sale. There were stalls selling crafts. Chaps, jackets, footwear, pants, and anything else you can make from leather were for sale.

Munching on a slab of delicious-smelling fry bread, Bjorn wondered into a rowdy bar made of boards loaded with bottles of local beer, although wines were the more common beverage at the fair. He downed a shot of rotgut whiskey that contained only ten percent kerosene at a gourmet price.

"Step right up, you have to see this." hollered a traveling salesman at the back of Fatty Arbuckle's merchandise wagon just outside the bar. The huckster was a stranger with an enticing pitch.

Bjorn was lubricated by rotgut and stepped up. "What do I have to see?"

"You have to see *Bartholomew's Miraculous Elixir.*"

"Why is that?"

"It will straighten out that crooked hand of yours."

Bjorn self-consciously clasped his hands behind himself. "You leave my hands alone."

The speaker held up a jar. "Come one and all. This is *Bartholomew's BeneficialRrejuvenative Elixir*. It will cure anything that ails you and everything that doesn't. Step right up for a free sample of this amazing product."

"How do I get a sample?"

"My assistant will draw a portion so you can see the immediate beneficial effects for yourself. This giant bottle is only ten dollars in gold dust or coin or banknotes. Trust me, my friends, you will thank me for the rest of your days to have possession of such a wonderful tonic."

He looked at a young man in the crowd. "Are you a user of Bartholomew's Beneficial Restorative Elixir?

"Yes sir, I am."

"Will you kindly tell these fine people what it does for you, Joseph."

He looked around the crowd and added, "I never saw him before. Ahem, I just guessed his name."

Joe stood up and said, "I want to thank you, Mr. Peter. I have used your tonic for over twenty years and it changed my life. It was four years ago when I came to this first annual fair. I was on my last legs so to speak and it was all I could do to crawl to the table. After one serving I felt good. I drank some more and the rest is history. Would you believe I am actually fifty-eight years old?

Someone in the crowd gasped and most looked skeptically at the young fellow who appeared to be about seventeen years old at most.

"I was an old man like this fellow here," pointing to the whitehaired prospector. Bartholomew's Tonic rolled years off of my body like dead fleas. I recommend Bartholomew's Beneficial Restorative Tonic to one and all."

Bjorn took a tiny sip and said, "That tastes like oranges mixed with cheap rum and oil floating on top. He turned to the twins, "This Bartholomew guy has fruit juice and a good pitch."

The wheels in Bjorn's fertile brain clicked like a clock. I can make my own patent medicine with moonshine from Maverick's still and wine from Rancho Petaluma. My Indian friends will harvest hidden berries and herbs in the hills. I can make more money selling patent medicine than moonshine, even with the dejected alcoholics lining the streams.

Maverick said, "What are you muttering about?"

Bjorn said, "How does the name *Viking Venom* sound?"

Jethro said, "What the hell is that?"

"That's the sound of money. We'll blend happy herbs and mountain dew. Age it a week or two and sell little bottles for twenty-five dollars or two for forty dollars. Guaranteed to grow hair, attract women, and rejuvenate the torso."

He saw the Paiute Indian encampment at the edge of the field. "Wait. I've got a better name. We'll call it *Chief Winnemucca's Secret Medicine.*

"I know an Irish huckster with a magic gift of gab. We'll be rich."

Boudicca took a break from saluting every fairgoer, child, lady, and dog around the open space where the rodeo was planned. She didn't understand the words but listened as Joaquín Murrieta explained bull riding to Bjorn and the Hatfields.

"Those bulls are small and fast. We'll watch from the stands as they toss off their vaqueros one by one. Sergio calls the winner who has the best style and who stays on the longest, those animals over there are called a parada. They keep each other calm, usually."

Calm hell, Boudicca charged the nearest bull and drove it out of the group by nipping at his heels, "Arf, arf, arf."

Bjorn screamed, "Stop that! Come here."

Boudicca chased the panicked animal through the fair booths. A woman screamed and two men pulled their pistols, but it was no use. Wolves had chased down the bull's natural ancestors and Boudicca looked like a wolf. The beast looked back, redoubled his speed, and charged through a fabric booth displaying loops of brilliant red silk.

His horns hooked a loop. It waved red over his eyes and, of course, he charged, and charged, and charged.

Jethro and Maverick split their sides laughing. "Go, Mr. Bull."

Pandemonium reigned as the blinded enraged bull charged through the packed fairgrounds. Gathered vaqueros knew their duties and dashed after the loose animal. The leader's fleet horse chased the bull around the fairgrounds. By a dexterous movement, he leaned over and seized the runaway animal by the tail. He spurred his steed to an extra effort. The trained horse dashed forward before giving a sudden jerk. When the vaquero released the tail. the bovine that was pulling with all his energy rolled over and over on the ground. Back upright, he was subdued and submitted to a walk back to the parada.

Joaquín stepped to Bjorn's side, "Only a caballero with skill, strength, and real balls can do that."

"I'd say."

With the excitement over, the vaqueros prepared for the rodeo. The parada about one hundred paces away from the arena numbered six males. Off to one side of the announcer's stand sat the Irishman in a green hat and matching green vest. His smile revealed gold teeth and he checked the time on his gold watch. He sat at a little table.

"Hurry right up and place your bets. You alone know your winner so put your money where your mouth is."

The Irishman would bet on anything if he could get somebody to bet against him. If he could not, he would change sides. So long as he got a bet he was satisfied. But he was lucky and generally the winner. "Place your bets now. How long until we see our first fistfight break out?"

The announcer cried, "Let the rodeo action begin."

Bjorn held Boudicca tightly with a rope around her neck. She sat but quivered at the sight of the bulls and gave little woofs from time to time. "Easy girl. Stay."

The vaqueros rode quietly in pairs among the bulls and picked one. They approached the animal on either side and nudged him toward the rodeo arena.

The announcer continued, "The first event is called Jineteo de Toro. The goal is for the rider to stay on until the bull stops bucking. Here are the rules. The rider can use two hands on the rope around the bull. A vaquero must dismount upright. If he falls off he loses his entry fee."

"Out of the crowd, a Texas cowboy said with a drawl, "We call that bull riding down my way, mister."

"Want to fight about that?" said a vaquero next to him.

"I'm following the bull."

The announcer ignored the interruption and said, "Watch the chute. See the lead horseman from General Vallejo's Rancho Petaluma on a fresh bull. Sergio is the judge. Are you ready?"

The man seated on the animal said in Spanish, "Ready as I'll ever be."

The announcer said, "Let her rip."

A pickup man opened the corral gate to reveal a dashing vaquero seated on a motionless bull. Without warning, the beast swung his head with two gigantic horns toward the open space and made a leap that took all four hooves off the ground. He landed straight-legged with an earthshaking thud. The rider swung wildly while holding his cinch with both hands and shouted, "Ándale, ándale." He raked his spurs on the side of the animal to increase the determined bucking.

The bull acted as though he said to himself, "Enough of this," and flipped the rider off to one side. Picking himself up and retrieving his hat, he bowed to the crowd. The winning bull charged across the arena to rejoin the parada. A big cheer from the crowd approved of the performance. The announcer said, "Sergio has judged the bull was still bucking and gives the rider no score."

Bjorn clapped and glanced at Maria sitting by her uncle, General Vallejo, in the stands.

The announcer said again, "Who wants to try our bulls next?"

There were several vaqueros showing off their horsemen's skills with lariats and tricks and competing to impress María.

"Anyone else?"

His jealousy triumphed over his judgment when Bjorn saw how aroused she was. Facing the announcer, he waved his hand and yelled in a loud voice, "I'm next!"

He said to the twins, "I am going to ride that bull."

"You will break your gol'darn neck," said the twins together. Boudicca looked up with a worried face and then looked back to see that a worried Thunderfire was following them. He had broken his leash and followed his rider, Bjorn. The intelligent horse shook his head to warn Bjorn not to do it. He remembered Bjorn's experience on his back and knew he was not ready to ride a bull. He was barely ready to ride him, Thunderfire.

The same Texan said a drawl, "Down Texas way we call this a rodeo and you are called a bull rider when you're not a bullshitter. But we have years of practice behind us." Fortunately, all eyes were on the arena.

Maverick said, "Holy shit man. I'd hate to see that blonde hair of yours matted with red blood, brown mud, and bullshit. Are you crazy?"

Bjorn pushed through the crowd to the announcer's stand.

"Sign me up."

"You're a big man to be riding a bull," said the announcer looking at Bjorn's over-six-foot height.

"I'll do it anyway," said Bjorn.

The announcer held up his notebook and said, "Name and next of kin . . ."

"Bjorn Amundson, sir, and I don't have any next of kin. The closest are the Hatfield twins, Jethro and Maverick. They work with me."

"Head over to the chute and Murrieta will sign you in."

Bjorn walked up to the corral and said, "Joaquín, you show up everywhere."

"Si Señor, I ride the horses and the bulls for many years. I will explain to you how. Are you sure, *Amigo*?"

"I need to impress Maria Rojas over there in the stands."

Joaquín Murrieta and the assembled vaqueros slapped their thighs and said, "Good man."

With hoots and hollers and plain dumb luck, they maneuvered a second bull into the bucking chute. They could tell from his brand that he was the same one Boudicca had chased earlier and was still agitated.

One vaquero said to another, "That is one wild animal. He wants to get even with that hound that chased him through the arena and her owner as well. I'll bet on the bull." He walked over to the Irishman and did just that.

The pickup men held the gate on the chute closed with the bull and Bjorn inside. They could not move but the bull hated Bjorn's weight on his back. Boudicca's barking made things even more tense.

Joaquín looped a bull rope around the gigantic girth behind the front legs and gave Bjorn a riding glove. He demonstrated the proper way to hold the rope for the longest possible ride. Bjorn jammed his hat down on his head, leaving his flowing hair peeking out the back. He didn't notice how the vaqueros steadied him from both sides as he lowered himself onto the bull's back.

"This is nothing. This back is flatter than Thunderfire." He swelled with ego and the vaquero pickup man said, "Nod when you are ready."

Bjorn clenched his gnarled hands under the cinch and said, "What do they say? Let 'er rip," and nodded. His excitement knew no bounds. Neither did his confidence.

He saw the gate fade away toward the dusty arena and his world dropped down four feet when the bull jumped off the ground still in the chute. He landed solidly on his two front legs, twisted and kicked the side to smithereens with his back hooves.

This bull was not vicious but detested anything riding him, and was doubly angry from being chased by the wolf, Boudicca.

Bjorn yelled, "Yahoo!," like he heard the cowboys do. He tried to rake his heels down the side but unbalanced himself fore and aft as he raised his legs. He did not have spurs.

"Uuhhh . . ." as the bull's two front legs hit the ground together and knocked out his wind. With a twist, the back legs turned square to the front and rocked sideways. He was following his nature to pitch a predator off his back by bucking, twisting, kicking, and rolling in midair and snuff the predator before it killed him. There was no better time than right now and no better place than the chute.

The bull seemed to feel that no yellow mountain lion thing was going to ride him.

Even with his great strength, Bjorn could not hold the cinch and pitched forward over of the horns of the bull. He hit the dirt and rolled three times before the bull's tail cleared the chute. Bjorn was slightly stunned and struggled to catch his breath. The pickup man waved his arms to distract the bull away from Bjorn.

Maria leaped down from the stands and ran across the open arena to Bjorn. Joaquín and three other men pulled red scarves off their necks and waved them in the bull's face to distract him from the fallen rider, and now from Maria also.

Maverick and Jethro were two steps behind Maria to check on Bjorn's condition. She approached from the back of his head as he sat up. Jethro ran around in front. The twins looked into Bjorn's dirtcovered, manure-splattered face only to see a big wink.

Jethro slapped Maverick and they retreated into the spectators. Maria leaned into his dirty face and said, "Are you all right?"

Bjorn made an effort to slowly recover, but then he jumped to his feet renewed. "Thank you for your concern. Next time I will stay on like I was glued."

As Maria proudly walked back to her seat in the stands and the Hatfields to the sidelines, the announcer announced in a loud voice through his megaphone, "Ladies and gentlemen, we have a new champion. Bjorn Amundson has just made the shortest bull ride we have ever seen. Give him a big hand."

Bjorn took a little bow to acknowledge the applause. But when he saw Maria take her seat and watch him, he suddenly waved and limped out of the arena.

Jethro was amazed by the fairgrounds as the Hatfields and Bjorn limped by the booths. "I'd say the entire citizenry plays music one way or another. There's guitars everywhere, even in the hands of a couple of cow boys."

Maverick agreed, "Just look at the musical instruments around the rodeo grounds.

Bjorn exclaimed, "Now this is a celebration," cough, cough. "Everybody is playing music, singing, drinking, eating, and kicking up a storm. I can't play a lick of music but I like it. Where's your fiddle, Jethro?"

"In my pack."

Bjorn said, "Let's join the fun. Where to?"

Maverick said, "Over there," pointing to one of the few remaining spots of bare ground.

Jethro agreed. "I see the fandango in the barn, sailors chanting, the Irishman betting on a fight, and the pastor and his flock praising God. Halleluiah Brother!"

Boudicca pushed her nose into group after group. She licked on the sheriff and slurped his deputies. The mayor of Angel Camp rubbed her ears with no babies to kiss. County politicians patted her back between shaking loose hands and eating fry bread.

Bjorn surveyed the messy mob of 49ers, Chinese, Mexicans, Californios, and sundry flotsam and jetsam of the Pacific. "There's Joaquín dealing monte cards." He looked at his dusty shirt and pants from his bull nonride, "I can't go to the fandango like this."

He walked into a haberdashery tent where the clerk recognized him. "You're that tall drink of water whose our new champion. Let me make you presentable."

The proprietor brushed the dust from his clothes and reblocked his hat. The barber next door splashed him with aftershave lotion for a quarter. He tossed Boudicca a bite of leftover fry bread from lunch and splashed her with a dab of the same aftershave. She rubbed it off on the ground.

Bjorn and the twins gravitated toward an imposing barn to the sound of the orchestra tuning up. They sped to trotting when a group of young ladies in bright-colored Spanish skirts drove up in a surrey. They were chaperoned by the watchful eye of a matron and accompanied by splendidly-dressed gentlemen.

Bjorn said, "Maria Rojas is more beautiful than ever. Get a move on, the fandango is starting." The twins danced a jig from the Ozarks to the scales of an introductory trumpet.

Bjorn said, "My musical talents don't include dancing. I can only sing sea shanties," or so he thought.

Jethro's talents went far beyond dancing. He looked with pride at the layer of rosin on his fiddle that spoke of long vigorous use. Nodding his head in time with the melodies from the barn, he pulled the bow across his D string and followed the music with a couple of Tennessee flourishes thrown in.

"Them's mighty funny sounds but I can keep up." He danced and fiddled alongside the group of ladies as he entered the barn. The other two followed him.

The trumpet and bass guitar played a quick dance and Maria swung her skirts in a circle and tapped her shoes to a quick beat.

Jethro shook his head and said, "This ain't our celebration," and walked outside to a group of lookalike people. A quick warmup of Turkey in the Straw got his audience started. Bjorn couldn't keep his feet still. He followed Maverick's lead to Jethro's hoedown songs. A father of a southern family strolled over and said, "I haven't heard that mountain music since I left the South. Keep agoing son." He hooked arms with a friend and kicked the highest of all.

Not to be outdone, a painted Miwok Indian retrieved a drum from a saddlebag and started a thump, thump, pow, thump, thump, thump. Boom, boom, boom. He was joined by a group of dancers chanting and stomping circles.

Bjorn, lubricated with a few more sips of whiskey, discovered moves he didn't know existed between the Indian drums, the hillbilly hoedowns, and the Spanish flamencos.

Maria peeked out from a crowd of flashy vaqueros to see Bjorn's wooden steps. She said to her companions, "I need to get some air."

She wandered to Jethro's show and dipped her knees and let her long skirt trip Bjorn from behind.

He looked up from the ground and said, "You like me down here, don't you."

She laughed and twirled her skirt across his face before waltzing away with a passing caballero. Bjorn leaped up and tapped the man on the shoulder. "Do you mind?"

The man stared at the yellow bushy beard a foot above his head that concealed a ragged scar and mumbled, "Lo Siento, Jefe." He handed Maria's hand to Bjorn.

Maria said, "Faster on the violin." Jethro doubled his temple and a large collection of displaced Southerners gathered. They clapped to the music while Maria swung Bjorn in clumsy circles. They were just getting started when they were interrupted by a lady in the barn door.

"Your attention, please. We are starting the grand march."

Maria looked at the flash of Bjorn's golden beard in the setting sun and her heart skipped a beat. She had other thoughts about Bjorn's dancing skills that night. Maria dragged a shy Bjorn into the dance hall and pushed him into a line of people in pairs. "Get a partner for the march."

Bjorn looked around in embarrassed confusion until a tall beautiful woman took his hand and said, "Come with me."

A prosperous-looking miner reaching for the same woman said, "I'm tickled to see you, Madam Pearl." The woman corrected him, "My name in public is Alva Dahl if you please."

Bjorn was stunned to be partnered in public with the local Madam of *Pearl's Pleasure Palace*, and stuttered, "He..h..ello." She looked different from when she was working.

Only a few lucky couples included a man and a woman. Men outnumbered women ten to one in Calaveras County and most couples were two lonesome men ready for a rousing dance. Anything on two legs that wanted to dance had a partner.

Bjorn standing next to the orchestra leader overheard a short debate between the lead musician and the trumpeter. "What should we play for the grand march?"

The conductor said, "General Vallejo has been a bull pushing for California. We will play España Cañi, the bullfighting song, Paso Doble."

His baton signaled to the trumpeter to start the opening fanfare to the grand march. The same mighty rhythm that opened bullfights in Spain lured the crowd onto the dance floor. Everyone imagined themselves a hero to open the ceremonies at the Plaza de Toros in Mexico City.

General Vallejo and Maria strutted down the center of the dance hall. They parted at the far end with the General circling to his right and Maria to his left. They followed the outside walls and met at the starting point, but this time they were joined by a couple, Bjorn and Alva Dahl.

Only great selfcontrol of all parties prevented the outbreak of feminine combat between Maria at Bjorn's left arm and Alva Dahl holding his right.

They marched to the far end, but this time alternate couples circled to the left and right. The last pass was made of up four couples abreast in a grand climax.

The company gave a great cheer and the orchestra struck up a rousing dance tune.

Bjorn's partner, Alva, noticed that while she had seen other ladies in their finery or shabberie, he never took his eyes off Maria. Maria stole quick glances his way but turned to the dashing caballeros that surrounded her.

Maria and Alva hissed at the next encounter and fired visual daggers down their raised noses the third time they passed.

Bjorn thought to himself, What in God's name have I gotten myself into?

10 - Injustice

Still recovering from the fantastic fandango hangovers the previous night, Jethro and Maverick Hatfield sat on a log against the miner's shack smoking their pipes. Across the little campfire with his back against a tree, Joaquín Murrieta smoked a small cigarillo. Maverick looked through the flames and said, "You talk funny, Joaquín."

Joaquín said, "I no think so man. You are the stranger in my land."

Maverick said with a strong southern drawl, "Ain't nobody what can understand your lingo. Why don't y'all learn to talk American?"

Joaquín stood tall and said in a proud but offended tone, "I have the Spanish of Madrid like I was taught in Sonora, Mexico. I rode with El General López de Santa Anna in the battle for Churubusco. Unfortunately the American were victorious and put me in prison. The soldiers taught me English, but not too good. You talk different than the guards."

"Prisoner?"

Maverick said, "Fighter?"

"How did that go?"

Joaquín said, "I missed my family from Sonora but the army promised me pesos to join. Maybe the army pays me money someday."

He took a few puffs on his cigarillo before he said, "Hey-ter-o, how about you?"

Jethro said, "What did you call me? My name is Jethro."

Joaquín tried again, but in Spanish, a J sounds like an H. On the third try, he got out a semi, "Hah teh ro."

Jethro said, "It'll do. How about Bjorn?"

Murrieta said, "His name is hard. You mean Señor B'Horny?"

Bjorn's J did not work any better than Jethro's J.

Murrieta said, "I call him B'Horny because this is my land and that is his name."

The twins burst into laughter and Jethro said, "Horny it is. Bjorn, the Horny Viking. I like it."

Joaquín looked up as Bjorn and the Hatfield twins sauntered into his family camp. He said pointing to Bjorn, "Hola, Señor B'Horny. You will ride with me, no? I taught you to ride Thunderfire."

Bjorn said, "Horny who?"

Maverick said, "We've got you now, Joaquín. Say the name of this man again," pointing to Bjorn.

"Ba . . .hor . . . ney."

Bjorn said, "The clerk in the claims office called me that, too. Must be a Spanish word."

Jethro said, "You got that right. We're calling you Bjorn the Horny Spanish Viking."

Muttered Bjorn, "Bjorn the Viking is fine."

"I say Bjorn the Horny Viking."

"You men lack class."

"You do too."

Joaquín continued, "No jokes, por favor. I have an idea."

Jethro said, "Thinking again? Where's my gun?"

A dark cloud passed Joaquín's face and he drew his hand across his neck as though slitting a throat, "Todos, all of you." But then he smiled—this time.

Murrieta laid out his plan. "I, Joaquín Murrieta, hide among my countrymen on *El Camino Viejo*, I mean the old road, to Mexico because the gringos are my enemies. Do you have enemies, *Amigo*?"

Maverick said, "The miners are our friends, but not the thieves and spies that infest the river."

Bjorn said, "Fremónt's army is a friend sometimes and an enemy some times. I get along with the Indians in the hills, but the Blue Lantern Celestials are always dangerous. Worse more is the government. They steal with a lawyer or guns."

"I have enemies, you have enemies, we are brothers," Joaquín said. "You are a good shot, Jetero," only mangling his name a little bit.

Jethro puffed out his chest and said, "I can shoot the eye out of a squirrel at a hundred paces."

Joaquín said, "My banda guards me but sometimes they are not reliable. I need Señor B'Horny for protection.

Maverick said, "What's your problem?"

"Ride with us."

Bjorn was skeptical and said, "I don't think so. There is a reward on your head."

Joaquín held his head high now that he was a big man, "I am worth two thousand dollars."

"I rob mean people, but I am not bad. I only take what I need and honor the señoritas."

Maverick said, "You say highfalutin words, but you don't follow them."

Joaquín looked down, "I am El Jefe, but sometimes my men do not obey me."

Maverick said, "We have a bigger problem."

"What's that?"

Bjorn said, "Governor Peter Hardboy Burner has signed a law called the Foreign Miner's Tax. It says foreigners pay a twenty-dollar tax every month to mine gold." He handed a copy of the Sacramento Transcript dated June 1, 1850, to Joaquín who read it aloud in halting English.

"Resistance to the Tax on Foreigners in Tuolumne County.

"It is reported in this city, on authority not to be doubted, that the foreigners in Tuolumne County have presented a strong resistance to the enforcement of the late tax law. The sheriff of the county, in attempting to compel the foreigners to yield, was killed by them, and one or two of his posse wounded. This caused the American miners to turn out en masse, and at the last accounts about a hundred of the foreigners had been arrested."

Joaquín threw the newspaper on the ground and said, "See how these people treat me? Wicked soldiers chased me until Señor B'Horny hid me in his cart."

"Like the story in the newspaper?" Bjorn said.

Joaquín said, "My family has mined here for years. It is ours, not these foreign Erosh bandits who jump like rats off their stinking ships."

Maverick said, "You mean 'Irish'?"

"That is what I said, Erosh."

Jethro said, "They're as white as we are."

Bjorn said, "It doesn't matter, they're foreigners. They owe the tax if they steal our gold from our claim."

Pounding hooves announced four strange soldiers. One, whose hat rattled and rode a pinto horse, emerged from the brush dragging a line of five stumbling Chinese roped together by their necks.

The lead horsemen with four fingers yelled over his shoulder, "We got three more, a beaneater and two Irishmen. The Irishmen look to be brothers, so make that two birds with one stone. Hands up! Get over here." The soldiers drew their revolvers and prepared to shoot. Boudicca barked furiously and lunged at them.

The leader motioned to Bjorn to get back. He said, "Not you, just the foreigners, but grab your dog."

"Boudicca! Quiet!"

Jethro and Maverick said together, "We ain't foreigners and we ain't going."

Their skin was dark from the summer sun, but the words out of their mouth screamed hillbilly from Tennessee, not Hispanic or

Irish. The soldiers didn't care. One waved his gun in the air, fired a shot, and said, "Shut up. Our records show none of you paid the mining tax and you're running a mine."

Joaquín said, "I am a visitor. I do not mine here."

The soldier said, "Your operation is over the hill and you did not pay either. I almost got you the other day before you slithered away in the brush like a snake. Git over here."

With that, the soldier with mismatched boots tied the miner's wrists behind them with knots that would've done a sailor proud.

Bjorn objected even though he was outnumbered. "You're stealing my men." He walked up to a man with a pigtail who he knew spoke a little English. "Even you? You work harder than anybody."

The man looked at Bjorn helplessly and said, "I Charlie One in Lucky Ducky Mine. Make four dollar a week. Three for *Kongsi* master. One dollar for food. No money for tax."

Bjorn argued with the soldiers and Boudicca snarled and bit more holes in the mismatched boots of the one who limps. He pulled his revolver in anger, but Bjorn kept his fist on Boudicca's nap of her neck. "I'll get you for this. You haven't seen the last of me."

Joaquín's blue eyes drilled into the soldiers and he said, "I hate you."

The soldiers hitched the three from the New Viking Gold Mine to the group of Chinese. "Forward march, dammit. It's a long way to the jailhouse."

Bjorn stomped after the soldiers. "Where are you taking them?"

"Just following orders. We will lock them in the county jail until they pay their twenty dollars for this month," said the Sergeant.

The soldiers rode their horses away dragging the new arrestees tied to the five hapless Chinese miners, the Hatfield twins and Murrietta.

Bjorn hollered after them, "How can they pay their tax when they're locked up in jail?"

The chain gang of foreign miners stumbled down river to the jail in Sacramento. The guards untied the necks one by one and shoved them through an iron gate into the large common cell. The room already housed a crown of over a hundred agitated men. Jethro, Maverick, and Joaquín fit right in.

Two forlorn guards stood watch in front of the jail. They were unsure whether the prisoners inside or the angry mine owners gathering outside were the more dangerous menaces.

The lockedup mob clambered about anger, resistance, and escape. The rescue mob argued between a direct frontal charge and simply blowing up the jail with blasting powder.

The nuggets of gold lay undisturbed in the river that day.

Chaotic exchanges filled the jail as the men yelled cuss words enhanced by body language. Some interjections were for the benefit of the guards and more at each other for rebel credibility. Both were repeated with a vengeance. Usual enemies called a temporary truce against their common enemy, the jailers.

Jethro looked around and said, "This is a fine skillet of catfish and we didn't do anything to get here."

Joaquín looked at a group of Mexicans in the corner babbling in Spanish. "Hola compañeros. ¿Como están?"

"Joaquín!" one replied in Spanish. "El Jefe, we are stronger than ever. Why are you here?"

"My friend, Señor B'Horny, will break us out."

The Mexicans and several others who were listening in cheered at the thought of their release.

Joaquín said, "Who has the biggest reward on his head?" He looked at one, "How much for you?"

"Five hundred dollars."

"And you?"

"Many pesos."

Joaquín stuck his chest out and said, "The reward on my wanted poster is two thousand dollars, but it should be three. I have to work on that."

Maverick glanced sideways at the incarcerated population. Neither he nor Jethro had ever been around foreigners. They were amazed at the group of Chinese clustered in the far left corner who were accustomed to living in packed groups in Canton, China.

In the other corner were the Mexicans, originally from the silver mines in Potosí, Mexico. They held themselves apart from the Californios who had lived in Alta California for generations but appeared the same.

Joaquín greeted both groups equally. They chattered a hundred miles an hour in Spanish dialects from educated to illiterate. They were inured to discrimination, and this was one more torment but not unusual.

Milling about in the center of the room was an assortment of pissed off Irishmen, Chileans, French men, and a motley crew of undetermined origin. There were a couple of Indians who had been arrested on general principle. The loose collection of hostile humanity spread out as far apart as they could, the truce or not.

One Irishman said in a loud voice, "Dammit all to hell, I need a drink. This noise deafens me." An Indian said, "Me, Paiute man. Want a drink, too." He thumped his chest.

Maverick said, "I make the best moonshine you ever drank."

Joaquín said, "What moonshine is?"

"Alcohol like whiskey. You want some?"

Somebody said, "It beats this hell hole by a country mile. I prefer a crowded bar over a crowded lockup."

Maverick walked over to Joaquín and said, "Your men will guard my still, okay?"

Joaquín spoke to the Mexicans and Californios in Spanish. They gave a great cheer and he reported in English, "We accept. We will be tasters to check for quality and then we make guard."

Maverick thought to himself, That was a bad idea. Maybe Joaquín guards the mine and Jethro guards the still. Have to think about that.

"We will work together. It's a deal."

With a fixed resolution on his face, Bjorn said, "Come along Boudicca, we've got to get our helpers back. A little Foreign Miner's Tax can't stop us." Starting at the deserted workings of the Murrieta family, the aged grandfather wished them good luck but said he could not go. One lone cousin grabbed his pickaxe and joined Bjorn.

The next operation downstream was the Lucky Ducky pit. A Chinese man who had lost five helpers said, "I go too, Mr. Bjorn."

After several more visits, the mob of irate owners led by Bjorn arrived at the Salty Dog Mine. "Hell yes, I'll come, and I'll bring my keg." The dusty miner hoisted a little wooden keg of black powder on his shoulders like he had carried his sailor's ditty box in a previous life.

The throng of pissed off ore diggers arrived at the county jail to see the guard soldiers shoving the arrested men into the holding cell through the barred gate. Over a hundred men were crammed inside, all yelling at the smaller crowd outside behind Bjorn. The guards were not sure if the mad mob inside or the angry company outside was the worst danger

Joaquín's face appeared in the barred window in response to the voice that could command a man at the top of a mast. Both mobs fell silent and watched the familiar tall and big man with the ash-blonde beard and long flowing hair jump onto a rock.

"Shut up," said the blond giant and he held up his palms to face the mob.

"Are we going to let the bankrupt California government steal our men?"

"No!" said seventeen angry voices.

"Are you mining any gold today?"

"No!"

"Can you pay twenty dollars a month for a miner?"

"Hell no."

"Did you bring a weapon?"

"By God, yes." Several of the mine owners waved their well-used pickaxes or shovels."

One dustcovered man held up a little wooden keg and said, "I'll beat you all with my blasting powder." He was missing two fingers on his left hand.

A roar of approval swept the crowd. They chanted,

"Boom, boom, big,

Blow up the brig."

The dusty man said, "Powder River, let her buck."

"Where are you from?" said Bjorn.

"I was the champion anvil blaster in South Pass City over in Oregon territory."

"What is an anvil blaster?"

"Anvils have a hole in the base. Turn one upside down, fill the hole with black powder put another anvil on top. You light the fuse and run like hell. I blew an anvil two hundred feet high once." He pointed in the air where two hundred feet would be. The crowd was awestruck to think an anvil could shoot that high. Where it landed was anybody's guess and everybody's danger.

"I had to leave town when I blew up the stage stop but, hey, they cheated me. It wasn't my fault?"

Bjorn said, "You're the man."

Maverick waved through the bars on the window and pointed to the corner of the jail opposite from the sheriff's office.

Bjorn said, "After me."

In an ominous voice, the dusty miner said, "Men with picks and shovels, follow me."

Bjorn led the motley crew around the corner to a small back window that was blocked with rusty bars. Murrieta and the Hatfields crowded inside.

The dusty demolition expert sat the keg on the ground and said, "Keep sparks and metal away."

Maverick whispered out the window, "I've blasted anvils myself and I can use black powder. This window is a weak spot. Load your powder against the base with a fuse in it."

"Dammit man," the expert said, "I know what I'm doing and I don't want your advice." Turning to the group he said, "The blast," he emphasized the word, blast, "needs something to push against." He pointed to the men with the shovels, "Cover this with dirt and be careful, no sparks."

Bjorn said, "I've lugged my powder all the way from San Francisco. Now I'll learn how to use it."

Mr. Dusty said, "Watch me."

Tipping the little keg, he poured a heavy line of black granules against the foundation. He cut a section of fuse and curled it out from the powder. "Cover this up but watch for sparks."

Four angry but terrified miners with their shovels and their hands scooped about six inches of loose dirt over the powder. They did not tamp it for fear of setting off a premature explosion.

The two guard soldiers peeked around the corner with dread. They could not use blasting powder either but knew a bullet would set it off. One said to the other, "That wooden keg with twenty-five pounds of Laflin & Rand's Orange Express black powder outranks my smoothbore musket seven ways from Sunday. My gun has a stamp, 'Rejected by George Washington, 1774.'"

The other guard muttered, "We get the oldest weapons the Army has, don't we?"

Bjorn pointed through the cell bars to the front gate and said, "Go make a noise."

Several prisoners rattled the front iron gate and yelled, "We want out! Boom! Boom! Bang!" They beat on the grating until the guards, who ran to the front, feared it would break.

Bjorn ran around the jail and glared at the two guards. "You bastards. Let my men go."

One guard yelled, "Get back or I'll shoot."

The other guard said, "No! You'll blow us to kingdom come."

"Get back anyway."

One of the guards ran around the other side of the jail and pounded on a door. "Sheriff, you better get out here. We have trouble."

The sheriff confronted Bjorn. "What is the meaning of this, Mr. Amundson?"

Bjorn said, "Your army kidnapped my men. I want them out now, or your jail will have three walls and you will have no prisoners."

"You've made your point Mr. Amundson. It is our mistake, and I give you my word this will not happen again."

"You cost me a day's production to say nothing of these other operations."

The sheriff shrugged his shoulders and backed down. "That Foreign Miner's Tax is a stupid idea. They arrested workers on my claim too and ordered me to lock them in my own jail."

Several men rattled the wrought iron gate, "Let us out!"

The Sheriff said, "I don't see any real criminals, open the gate."

While the guard fumbled for the key, the dusty miner around the backside who could not hear the sheriff shouted, "Fire in the hole." He lit the fuse with his flint.

Bjorn cried, "Run like hell, everybody."

Men outside and inside looked confused as the sheriff said, "Open it! I'm not going to be a part . . . "

It was too late.

"Chaboooom!. Bjorn's momentary deafness gave way to the sound of rain as the loose dirt fell through the bushes thirty feet away. A rolling cloud of smoke followed the dropping debris and engulfed the jail.

Bjorn shook his head and hollered to the protesting crowd, "Grab your pickaxes men. We'll mine out the wall."

The ore diggers surged to the ruins where the window and bars were long gone. Their flying pickaxs pulled loose bricks out of the wall accompanied by cheers from within.

Joaquín Murrieta grabbed the arms of the twins and said in Spanish, "Let's get out of here." Pointing to the group of Mexicans, he added, "Vámonos." They poured through the opening.

Bjorn motioned to the Chinese man who knew a little English, "Get back to your Lucky Ducky Mine. Several men bowed slightly with their hands together as they left and said in their Chinese dialect, "Thank you." Their discrete humble smiles showed their gratitude for a little kindness. He watched their long pigtails hang down and as they shuffled away to their mine. They would remember Bjorn, even though he could not tell them apart.

Bjorn pulled the other prisoners through the breach in the wall as fast as he could.

Many hostile eyes focused on Murrieta as they left. They still didn't like Mexicans. The truce was over.

11 - Viking Enterprise

A abandoned placer mine downstream from the New Viking swarmed with activity again. It had been abandoned as depleted by earlier inpatient miners. A little Asian man stood in the center of in the Lucky Ducky Pit. Orders to the crew resifting the river sand were crisp and final. In a previous career, he had been the project leader over the Grand Canal across China. The humble workers and he dressed the same in blue loose pants and shirts. Like them, his hair was long and hung in a braided queue from under his conical bamboo hat. It was the same man Bjorn had spoken during the jailbreak. He knew a little English. But

The working overseer liked to brag, "Tin mines across all China are successful because of my waterworks. I make the the Sacramento gold mines successful the same way."

Their Lucky Ducky Gold Mine was especially lucrative, even after the Blue Lanterns spirited away two bags of gold for every five wrenched from the water and confiscated another one to repay their passages from China.

The lookout said, "A big blonde man approaches from upstream." It was Bjorn.

"Hello Mr. Bjorn. I trust you are well."

"We miners have our troubles but I am well also."

Bjorn noticed a curious contrivance at the top of their pit. An endless chain looped around two parallel shafts. One shaft was in the river and one on the bank. Four coolies rotated the upper shaft by walking on little extensions. Crosswise paddles on the submerged shaft scooped water up a trough, where it drained into the rocker equipment.

Bjorn said to the leader, "I see you're working hard after escaping through the hole in the jail."

"Thank you, Mr. Bjorn, to get us out."

"Why don't you dig a channel for water from higher up? The water ladder is hard work."

"Yes sir, most correct, sir. But we are not allowed to move water outside our claim. Only white miners can do that. We clean old claims after white man quit." He proudly showed Bjorn the details of the water ladder that fed their rocker box.

Thuds from an unusual hole on the hillside caught Bjorn's attention. "What is that?

The engineer explained, "We build a framework with a wheel over a hole. The man raises and lowers a drill with the wheel. We get mother ore of gold. Much gold."

The water engineer gave Bjorn a tour of their Chinese drilling machine. Bjorn saw the rhythmic flow was smooth but inefficient. He turned to the Chinese engineer and showed off his newfound blasting experience by asking, "It is easier to break the rock with blasting powder?"

The engineer said, "I drill wells all my life with happy outcome."

"Let me show you another way." Bjorn returned with a bag of black powder and a coil of fuse cord.

The Chinese drillers had a hole dug to break the rock. Bjorn poured six inches of powder into the ragged hole and tamped it with mud. Extending a length of a fuse several feet away, he motioned everyone to step back.

A little spark from a flintstone lit the fuse, which hissed and sputtered on its way to the powder. The curious men imitated his gesture of hands in the ears and waited. And they waited some more. And were ready to give up when a tremendous explosion belched fire and shook the ground.

A wave of astonishment swept through the men. "Ah so. Most big firecracker." Everyone gave a rousing cheer and had a drink of wine from a community jug. By the time the wine was gone, the cloud of smoke had cleared from the shallow hole. They crowded to inspect the damage.

The pile of blasted ore was bigger than three miners could dig in a strenuous day of work. They chattered over the small sizes of the rubble and the evidence of scattered gold throughout. This was not their ancestral drilling technique but they understood how to blast the rock with powder.

The engineer said to Bjorn, "I buy your keg of magic powder."

Bjorn said, "I'll keep my keg, but I can buy you one from Brannan's store. He doesn't sell blasting powder to a Chinese person."

"We invented gunpowder."

"No matter, he won't sell it to you."

Bjorn returned the next day with a keg of twenty-five pounds of Rand's Orange Powder on his shoulder.

He gave them handling precautions.

Do not hit or heat with flame.

Keep containers tightly closed when not in use.

Do not pour the black powder into a hole directly from a flask. You'll blow off your hands.

"Most good, thank you, Mr. Bjorn," the engineer said as he bowed.

Even though he was from Norway and used to drinking alcoholic spirits, Bjorn had no experience with amateur alcohol. The Squatter's meeting was a week off and the twins and he ran out of things to talk about until the subject of spirits came up. Bjorn asked Maverick, "What is this moonshine you talk about?"

"Maverick said, "Magic from the woods. You take corn, clear water, and my secret fixings. Mix them in a big pot and wait for two weeks. She bubbles and moves and puts on a show. Some say it stinks, but when it dies down, you are ready.

Bjorn said, "I toss out spoiled corn."

"Oh, hell no. That's the good stuff," said Maverick.

"Light a fire under that barrel and collect the mountain dew off the top. I make it at night by the light of the moon and calls it moonshine.

Jethro said, "Yee-haw. I got a real hankering for some about now."

Bjorn said, "It makes you feel good, does it?"

"I'd say so."

The subject came up again that evening when Bjorn, Jethro, and Maverick lay around the fire. They smoked their pipes and reminisced about times past.

Maverick blew a puff of smoke into the trees. Bjorn made a quick in and out whiff and blew a smoke ring that floated up. Boudicca slept by the fire and didn't smoke.

Knowing Jethro was a sharpshooter and hunter, Maverick gave a tiny puff to form a cloud and followed it with a long sausage. With pursed lips and four quick puffs, he made four legs. "What do you see brother?"

"I see a crippled squirrel. Damn, you're good."

Bjorn said, "Looks like a drunken rat to me."

Maverick said, "Y'all haven't seen anything yet. Watch this."

He blew a cylinder of smoke in the air and rolled his head to make a twisted collector. Ending with a little flame underneath, it looked like a rough still. Maverick was a moonshiner and loved everything about a hidden still in the hills.

Bjorn said, "What is that supposed to be?"

Maverick said, "Ain't you never seen a still?"

"Can't say as I have."

"Let me tell you. There's a hidden spring back a piece in our mountains. Just a few animal tracks around it."

Bjorn and Jethro looked at him with interest.

Bjorn said, "Go on."

"With a pot, corn, and fixings I can brew a batch right now."

Bjorn said, "How do we start?"

"We need corn to start the mash," said Maverick, "but I don't see many ears around our mine."

Bjorn thought about the supply wagons coming to Brannan's market. Being a farmer he said, "This land looks fertile and should grow corn. Let's look in the morning."

Jethro said, "I don't know how to farm, so I'll stay here and watch Boudicca."

The next morning, Bjorn and Maverick set out toward the little settlement a few miles off. They passed many miners, or at least gravel movers, on the way. Some looked unsuccessful and others looked to be abject failures. One pair was splashing around to shouts and howls in the morning air and Maverick said, "If they're this drunk this early, I'd hate to be around later. They'll buy lots of moonshine, though. Hope they ain't no guns around."

As they neared the foot of the hill overlooking the little town, Bjorn said, "What's that rattling?" They turned to the sound of a beatdown nag hitched to a wagon filled with yellow ears of corn.

"Howdy, partner. What you got in the wagon?" He could see the corn.

The driver looked around for bandits since he had suffered his daily robbery and it was not even noon. More thieves? the farmer thought to himself. They look like honest men, and I'm lonesome.

"Hello. I'm bringing my corn to town. There's a good market for it."

Maverick saw the ears had been picked for a while and were the worse for the heat. He said, "That ain't the best corn. What would you take for the load?"

They bargained for a while and agreed on a decent price.

It dawned on Maverick that he lacked a tank to hold his mash. Down in his native Tennessee, there were abandoned containers and pots scattered through the hills, but here in this wild country, there was nothing. He said to Bjorn, "I need a pot."

Bjorn said, "Hey driver, we need a big vessel. Have you seen anything in your travels?"

"Matter of fact, I have. A man is storing water in a copper vessel just over the hill. He's quitting and headed home. You might get it for a song."

Bjorn and Maverick climbed the hill to a dry gully. Sure enough, a man sat swaying back and forth with his head between his knees. He was gaunt and his eyes had no spark of life. He didn't look up when they approached.

Bjorn said, "Hey, sailor man, how is it going?"

"I can't do anything with that piss poor stream of water," said the man. "It ran full last spring, but all it's dried up now. I'm headed back to Missouri. I don't want this stuff here. It's yours if you can use it."

Bjorn said to Maverick, "Catch up with the farmer and buy his wagon if you can."

"Will do," and trotted off.

Rattle, rattle, the wagon with Maverick on top of a pile of corn rumbled into view. He said, "The driver is discouraged like this miner and I got the whole rig for fifty dollars. He threw in the horse for nothing."

Bjorn said, "Miner, I'll give you twenty-five dollars for the whole kit and caboodle of your equipment."

"You got yourself a deal."

They loaded the tank on the corn and returned to the New Viking Gold Mine with Maverick singing at the top of his voice,

My uncle Mort he's sawed off short,
and he measures 'bout four foot two
But he thinks he's a giant
When you give him a pint

Of that good old mountain dew

They call it that good ole mountain dew, Lordy, Lordy
And them that refuse it are few
I'll hush up my mug
If you'll fill up my jug
With that good ole mountain dew

Well, my brother Bill's
Got a still on the hill
Where he runs off a gallon or two
The buzzards in the sky
Get so drunk they can't fly

From smelling that good old mountain dew.

Taking a break from returning to work and leaving the Hatfield twins to continue operating the rocker, Bjorn walked upstream to check on the Murrieta family's placer diggings. Each new arrival from Mexico constructed a shanty somewhere inside the borders of the claim, or occasionally a bit beyond.

Bjorn washed down a burrito with a bottle of cervesa to be neighborly. You built instead He belched and said, "That was good as usual. I was hungry." He and Joaquin sat on a log to catch up with gossip. Stretching out to get comfortable, they were surprised when a fake deputy of the pretend sheriff burst into the compound with two accomplices, guns blazing.

High on whiskey, the alleged lawmen attacked the first structure of logs and canvas they came to. Inside, the curandera was tending to Joaquín's sick uncle. One of the semioutlaws flung the weak man sprawling in the dirt and leveled his shack with several swift kicks. Then he kicked the old man.

Bjorn wasn't fast enough to stop them. "This is a damned outrage. What are you doing?"

"Following orders. You are trespassing on Brannan's land and he wants you gone by nightfall." The one with a rattlesnake on his head whacked a couple more tents on the way out. He was disappointed that they were empty. "I'm warning you. Out by tonight." They raised a cloud of dust heading for the next mining operation.

Bjorn said to Joaquín, "I had no idea it was this bad. Have they done this before?

He looked down and said, "Si, Señor, but what can I do? They tear apart my camp many times."

Bjorn leaned the sick uncle against a tree and helped Joaquín rebuild the simple structure. They carried the uncle to his cot somewhat the worse for his experience.

Bjorn seethed with anger and said, "I have to stop this damn Brannan. This is going too far." He stomped toward his claim expecting to see the same chaos.

The farther he went the madder he got. He worked into a fighting frenzy. A right jab to the jaw. A bob, a weave, and an uppercut. He followed a cross body counterpunch with a clinch and a throw to the ground. But between the counterpunch and the clinch, his arms connected with something solid. A surprised man looked at him from three inches away.

"Whoa there, young fellow." After breaking the clinch and regaining his composure, the welldressed traveler touched said, "It's a little early in the day to engage in fisticuffs wouldn't you say, especially with strangers.?"

"Indeed it is, sir, and I mean no harm, at least to yourself." He shook hands with his opponent and said, "Bjorn Amundson."

"They call me Doc Robinson. What gets you so up in arms?"

Bjorn told him about the attack on the Murrieta camp. Robinson exploded, "That's a damned outrage. Those bastards pulled the same trick in town. I had nourished an invalid for several days when they burned his shelter. They claimed he was trespassing on the old Sutter land grant now owned by Sam Brannan."

Bjorn said before they continued their separate ways, "Let's join forces. I'll round up the miners when the time comes."

"I will remember that."

Back to shoveling gravel into his rocker box for the twins to shake and clean, Bjorn got angrier with every scoop. "Brannan did that to Joaquín. He sends is Vigilance Committee to attack anybody in a tent on his stolen land."

Maverick said, "What are you muttering about?"

"I'm so mad at Brannan I could shoot them."

"That will do some good, huh?"

"I'd feel better."

Bjorn started pitching boulders the size of his head onto the shore. "Wraaaagh!" One of them barely missed Boudicca. Another one knocked a hole in the storage tent.

Jethro said, "Take it easy, man. The river ain't going nowhere and there ain't no gold in those boulders you're heaving our way."

Bjorn splashed out of the river and said, "That settles it. I'm gonna find Doctor Robinson and do something."

He found the Doc back in town. Robinson was just getting started so Bjorn helped him post handbills that he could not read. They plastered buildings, trees, and two wagons that slowed to navigate a corner.

Bjorn said, "Those are fancy notices we're putting up. What is in them?"

Robinson said, "The people of the United States paid Mexico fair and square for this land. It is public. These lowdown land speculators take John Sutter to the bar just to get him drunk on his ass. It's not hard since that's his natural tendency. He'll sign any piece of paper they lay in front of him. Those signatures transfer the land title to the speculator. Guess who the speculators work for."

Bjorn said, "So they don't really have title to this land."

"That's what I'm saying."

"Then what?"

"Those speculators are beholden to Brannan one way or another and sign the stolen title over to him. He sends that fake Sheriff's posse to extort money and drive the workers out."

Bjorn said, "Explain this handbill."

"I am organizing a meeting at I Street and the wharf. We've stacked a cord of firewood for light. Notify the squatters and miners to come in make a big crowd when they see the smoke. There is safety in numbers. What the hell, ask the damn land speculators too. We'll show them who we are."

Bjorn said, "I'll run physical security if you point out the speculators."

"No, we are going to do this properly."

"Okay."

"See you this Saturday."

"See you there."

Bjorn ran into the cousin at the laundry when he dropped off his clothes to get ready for the Squatter's meeting. The Chinese water engineer chatted with Bjorn as they smoked their pipes on the front porch.

Bjorn said, "Damnedest thing I ever saw over in the Chinese part of town."

"What was that?"

"My curiosity got the best of me one day, and I stumbled into that oriental looking building. I was aiming for the gambling hall next door."

"Wagering will lose your money."

"I know, but it gives me a thrill."

"So?"

An offduty Chinese janitor with me called it a Joss house, but I'd call it a temple. It was thrown together from abandoned junk and stones, at least on the outside."

"Like your cabin."

"Pretty much. We snuck in out of curiosity."

The water engineer gasped and looked at Bjorn, "You didn't?"

"I saw a stream of dejected young men coming in the front door. They kept their heads down and ignored me. A big gong announced their entrance."

"What did they look like?"

Bjorn tugged at his beard and thought a minute. "Not like me for sure, more like you. We hid in a back corner behind some tall vases." A scribe made a list of the refugees.?

The janitor whispered, "This *Kongsi* club calls new members to join the fellowship of the Blue Lanterns."

"What are Blue Lanterns?"

"They are a brotherhood of low men with nonblood kin. The frontman is Mountain Master Dragon Head. He is leader."

The spies watched as the leader motioned each trembling recruit to lie on a table. A rough looking man dipped a sharpened stick into black ink and tattooed a line of five dots across his forehead. "He now Blue Lantern," he said in the Chinese language, my companion explained.

The young man was replaced by the next one. When they were all tattooed, the attendant went down the line and drew blood from each initiate. It dripped to the ground and the recruit said an oath if the janitor next to me was right, "May the Earth drink my blood if I break my silence."

After the tattooing and blood oaths, the Incense Master invoked the ancient five heroes and offered libations of tea and wine.

The janitor said, "The *Kongsi* is a partnership of protection for the gain of money. They help sworn brothers in trouble to pay their passage fee. They give an oath to join, 'If I break this oath five thunderbolts kill me. I will be cut by myriads of swords.'"

""I must never commit indecent assaults on wives, sisters, or daughters, of my sworn brothers. After entering the Hung gates I must forget any grudges against my sworn brothers. Our common aim is to avenge our Five Ancestors.'"

With the ceremony over, the hideaways ducked out the door and ran down the street away from the new Blue Lanterns.

Bjorn thought to himself, I know they will make trouble.

12 - Reading

With mixed feelings, Bjorn followed Alva Dahl into a side door. A girl approached that he recognized from an earlier encounter. She said, "Madam Pearl . . ."

Alva stopped her, "I am Alva Dahl and busy. See me later."

She held out her hand to Bjorn, "Please have a seat."

Bjorn was nervous and jabbered away, "Sailing was easier than hunting gems . . . I'm good on board the *Agilis* . . . mining is tough. I . . ."

Dahl said, " . . .was it tough on the ship?"

"I was scared shitless in the shoals and thunder and lightning and war . . .but not much."

"Others too, I should think."

"I learned sailing from my mates, and ships from the waves."

"How did you read the charts?"

" . . .wanted to, but couldn't. My Cherokee Indian friend called pages of books the talking leaves, but they didn't talk to me."

Dahl got serious, "In a business like you have, Mr. Amundson, there are agreements, newspapers, and printed pages everywhere."

Bjorn did not say anything, but thought, I navigated storms around Cape Horn and hurricanes in the Caribbean, but this reading lesson scares me worse.

He squirmed on the small round chair as he looked around the office that was furnished with an elegant French desk and a gilt carved chair. Through an open door into the parlor, he saw the velvet couch that was now clean of Boudicca's fur, but empty of females.

"The girls are off this morning."

Bjorn's face fell. He stammered and turned red under his golden locks and sunburned skin, "Yes, ma'am."

"My furniture is from the court of Louis XIV. Be careful with that chair. it doesn't look too sturdy for a man of your size."

She took the first book from the bookcase and laid it on the marble desktop. She read the title, McGuffey's First Eclectic Reader.

Bjorn stared with trepidation and interest.

She opened the book in front of Bjorn and said, "We will start with the alphabet."

"I know my letters . . . some of them, anyway."

"Show me."

"My family is Amundson that starts with A."

"Very good. Next."

"That is my name, Bjorn."

"Say it."

"B, like the bug that makes honey."

Bjorn's mind formed another word, B is for breasts.

He couldn't help himself and his eyes climbed the mother-of-pearl buttons on her shirt up to the plunging neckline that covered part of her womanhood.

"What the hell are you looking at? The tits don't teach reading and they are not for sale."

Bjorn blushed and dropped his eyes back to the First Eclectic Reader.

"What is the next letter?"

They worked down the alphabet to the letter "G".

Bjorn said, "This is a G.

"Give me a word that starts with G?"

"A gun like this one."

Bjorn pulled his revolver from its holster and displayed it on the cold white marble desktop.

Dahl turned it over and over. The dragoon was a huge weapon, far larger than the Queen Anne pocket pistol in her purse. She pointed it to the window and pulled the trigger.

The unexpected blast deafened them, the window shattered, a cloud of smoke filled the tiny room, and dust from the chandelier sprinkled the desk. Bjorn dove to the floor, while the gun jumped overhead. Dahl's involuntary twitch fired a second round into the ceiling and doubled the smoke.

"What holy damn all to hell shit was that?" Dahl yelled at the top of her voice. "Do you carry this thing around loaded? You should be ashamed of yourself."

From the floor, Bjorn said, " . . .put it down, slow like."

Dahl laid the revolver on the desk with the muzzle facing out the broken window. Bjorn waited for the clatter on the marble.

Bjorn said, " . . ..got . . .varmints in the hills," as he stood up and brushed the dust off of his clean clothes and shook his head to clear his hearing.

"There are not any varmints in here," cough cough, Dahl said, fanning the smoke out the broken window. Alva Dahl, known as Madam Pearl, grabbed a piece of paper and wrote in big, dark letters,

New Policy

CHECK ALL GUNS

Before Entering

"This is an N . . ."

Bjorn and Alva never forgot the first G.

It was a windy night under a moon at the New Viking. Bjorn and the Hatfields had put in a stout day and were soundly asleep in the sleeping cabin. Boudicca was dreaming at their feet. She was tired of chasing rabbits and visitors all day.

A scruffy young man with a limp hobbled down the trail. Every few steps he stopped to listen and look as best he could see. His partner followed. The first man motioned for the other to come up and spoke in a low voice "Where do they stash their gold?" "I couldn't see good 'cause of that damn dog they call Boudicca, but they've got a loose floorboard in the far corner of the tent's wooden floor."

"Okay."

They snuck into the storage tent through the unlocked flap and felt their way around. "Can't see a thing. Where's that corner?"

"Away from the river."

At the same time two Chinese spies, Blue Lanterns, entered from the other way, their footsteps masked by the wind. The scruffy man slid his hands along the top of a table. On the far side, he bumped an arm coming from the other way. "Watch yourself, be quiet," he whispered.

His partner said, "I'm over here."

"Who's this?"

He thrust his arm into a loose -fitting sleeve. The person inside the garment and gasped and muttered a Chinese expletive. A quiet sound of four pattering feet crossed the floor and out the front. One of the Chinese men stumbled and kicked a loose rock in the yard.

Back in the cabin Boudicca's ears jumped up and she shot out the door barking to wake the dead. Following her sense of smell in the dark, and the vision and hearing that were equally effective, she crossed the yard in two leaps and crunched the nearest leg.

The owner yelled an expletive in Mandarin Chinese, "Yaaaoou. Fuck your ancestors to the eighteenth generation. Stupid dog."

The other one kicked Boudicca through the air with his padded foot. The two were saved when Boudicca heard a sound from the storage platform. An assortment of forty-two permanent adult teeth in her snout led her body in. A vicious roar erupted.

By this time Bjorn and the Hatfields were out the door with their revolvers drawn. Bjorn fired in the air because he couldn't see in the night. Boudicca's barking pointed to the men, and one of them yelled, "Call off your dog. He's got my leg."

The scruffy man looked out the opening of the tent as Bjorn's helper lit a lantern with a coal from the stove and faced off with him in the circle of light. The scruffy man yelled again, "Call off your dog." Boudicca's teeth were still clamped on his leg.

His heart sank when Bjorn said, "You're the same bandits I have run into before. Remember what I said last time?" He said, "No. What?" and shuddered to think about the answer.

"Boudicca!" She released the leg, but barked and growled and lunged at the slightest move. The scruffy man and his partner stood stock still with their hands straight up in the air. His eyes followed Jethro as Bjorn said, "Get that coil of rope we bought last week. I'll need it right now."

Jethro and Maverick roughly grabbed the other man with two good legs. "Hands behind your back," and they lashed them securely. "Same for you," he said to the man with the bleeding leg. The trussed men listened as Bjorn said, "We'll deal with you in the morning."

Between Boudicca and the ropes, the interlopers were incapacitated but their mouths weren't and both complained loudly. It was louder still when they got tied to separate trees at the edge of the clearing.

"Damn, my leg hurts," as the miners tied them to a tree with the same lashings as used on the *Agilis* to flog the sailors. They trembled at Boudicca after Bjorn pointed and said, "Guard. Anybody moves, bite them." Boudicca lay down three feet away and batted an eye by the light of the moon.

Back in the cabin before they dropped into sleep Bjorn said to Jethro. "You've got a hell of a voice, Jay. I heard you yelling at the sailors in the bar."

Jethro said, "Ah, shucks . . . had to call my cousin over the hollow."

Bjorn continued, "In the morning . . ."

"Yeah . . . ?"

"After being out all night, our claim jumpers at the tree should be ready."

Jethro and Maverick were all ears. "Ready for what?"

"Blindfold them, spin them around so they don't know where they are and—.

"Ane butter my butt and call me a biscuit," said Maverick as the twins rubbed their hands in glee.

"String these two gentlemen to a tree . . .?" Jethro said, "And shoot apples off their heads . . .?" said Maverick.

Bjorn said, "Good ideas all, but I have a better one. Stake them to the ground where they can hear each other but not see them."

"What are you goin' to do?" said Maverick.

"Remember the honey dripping from that hive up the hill?"

"Yup."

"At first light, before the bees wake up, borrow some honey. Move slow and they won't miss it."

"What you aim to do?"

"You'll see."

The three went to sleep with dreams of the coming jest with the claim jumpers bouncing in their heads. Boudicca got up several times and sniffed the men securely tied up. They were grumpy and sore.

The next morning, the dog licked the faces of the sleepers at the first rays of the dawn. Bjorn greeted the two tied up claim jumpers. "Sleep well?"

"Go to hell."

"After you."

The slumped thief with the hole in his boot lisped, "Damn foot hurts like hell . . .." he hesitated, but his cat was out of the bag and he added, " . . .where you s.s.s..s..shot it."

Bjorn said, "First you tried to rob my stagecoach. Now you're jumping my claim and you're not even wearing masks. Serves you right."

Scar-on-his-jaw with the missing little finger growled, "Cut us down and we'll split. You took our guns."

Bjorn said, "They're mine now. You, gentlemen, need a rest. Untie 'em." Boudicca bared her teeth and rumbled as Jethro and Maverick unleashed the two from the tree. Their hands were still lashed behind their backs.

The jumpers shouted common profanity as each was wrapped in a blindfold. Jethro took Hole-in-the-Boot and Maverick took Scar-on-the-Jaw, twisted them around ten times, and led the confused pair to an open spot and threw them on their backs in the dirt.

Boudicca growled at Scar-on-the-Jaw through her forty-two teeth as they untied Hole-in-the-Boot, and staked him spread-eagled, with the blindfolded eyes up. They staked Scar-on-the-Jaw the same way.

"Let us see what you're doing."

"Oh what one man can do to another . . .. okay," and Bjorn pulled their blindfolds off. They blinked in the rising sun.

"Time for a little breakfast. Bring your pot over here, Maverick." Bjorn poured honey over the heads of the staked out intruders and anointed their arms, legs, and body, but avoided their mouths. "Breakfast for the flies and ants. Say hello to the bears for me."

"You ain't leaving us like this."

"Would I do that?"

"Help!"

"Help!"

"Aaaa . . .hhh . . ."

"No . . .!"

"Yes, I would."

They groaned in dismay, "That'll attract bears!"

"Bears? What makes you think that?" Bjorn walked away whistling. He explained to the twins as they walked to the cabin, "I am tired of messing with these two."

Jethro said, "I reckon that'll teach them a lesson . . ."

Maverick said, "And show 'em when the sun gets high and the flies cover them."

Boudicca punctuated the screams all the way to camp with barks at one and the other.

"Don't leave us here."

"Where are you going?"

"Help!"

The sun blazed hot towards midday. Yet their howling did little to drive off the carpet of flies eating the honey. It didn't knock the ants down either. Bjorn looked up from working in the cool river and said, "Its time to check on our miscreants."

"Our . . .what the hell . . ."

"Miscreants—villains so to speak. I learned that of a professor."

"If you say so . . ."

"Jethro, sneak up behind them and show us your world-famous bear roar."

"You got it."

A few silent moments later, the hills echoed with a deep bellow. It even scared Boudicca, who came running out of the woods, when she heard a hullabaloo and branches crashing. Bjorn grinned, "I want to scare the shit out of them, and I think we have."

Jethro emerged from the brush splitting his sides, "What do you think?"

"There's a bear up there for sure," said Bjorn. "I've got experience along those lines," referring to an early grizzly attack that almost killed him.

The cries from the brush degenerated into hoarse croaks. "Think they've had enough?"

" 'spect so."

He pulled his Colt revolver and fired several times into the air with a yell, "Get out of here!" Bang! Bang.

Jethro scratched and ripped strips of bark from a tree. He threw them down and made loud slurping sounds like a bear eating honey. He smacked his lips, made happy little grunts, and did it again.

He yelled, "Go away!" Screams of pure terror split the air. Maverick and Bjorn rolled on the ground laughing.

"Old Jethro can really call up a beast, can't he . . . ," said Bjorn. "I heard him in the yodeling contest at the fair."

"Like the commotion when that bear mauled our jackass?" said Maverick.

Bjorn said, "I never want to hear that ROOOAAAAARRRR!!!!! or the honk-ay-EEE-Oooo again, except for our sweet friends."

Jethro said, "Let's check the miscre . . ., what the hell were they, again? Take our weapons in case we see a real grizzly." The twin brothers were from Tennessee and stealthy in the woods. The men on the ground turned as far as they could in their panic and yelled for help, but couldn't pull their stakes out.

"Oh Jesus, help me," Hole-in-the-Boot said and began sobbing. They sweated under their honey glaze and itched so bad where they couldn't scratch that they forgot to be thirsty. Flies dived from above and ants crawled from below. The ants ate honey, not flesh, but the men didn't know that. They expected to be skeletons by nightfall.

A low menacing snort was intermingled with by the sound of more scratches on the tree bark. There was an intense roar and a banging on a tree trunk. A terrified voice yelled, "Get away."

The other stinking, helpless claim jumper, that is Scar-on-his-Jaw with the missing little finger, envisioned his leg eaten or chewed off as an appetizer for the rest of him. "I'll give you anything you want. Take what I've got, and more. Anything."

Hole-in-the-Boot stopped sobbing long enough to plead, "Take the ten dollars in my pocket. There's more on my horse. Take it, but just let us up."

Bjorn said, "Blood money for robbing the stage. I don't want it."

A furious thrashing noise came out of the countryside accompanied by earsplitting growls, threats, and pounding on the ground. A tree fell over. The fight raged back and forth and tore up the forest. "Take that . . .and that." Two pistol shots rang out to a yip and a yelp and a crashing that faded into the distance. The tiedup claim breakers screamed in terrified agony.

Jethro ran panting through the brush into the clearing. "Oh, there you are. I think he's gone, but I had to beat him off. He loves that honey, especially on people."

The staked men were speechless in misery. Bjorn sat in plain sight on a rock with his knife drawn and a whetstone in hand. He methodically sharpened the knife and muttered as though to himself,

That was wrong when the Donner party cut up Jay Fosdick to eat him a couple of years ago. I wouldn't do that. Boudicca does have to eat, though, if the bear leaves any remnants.

He threw his bandana into the air and swung his knife through it. The bandana fell into two separate parts. Bjorn took a few more passes with the whetstone and walked over to the staked men.

"What are you going to do, you crazy old coot?" Hole-in-the-Boot said as he twisted as far away as he could get.

Boudicca woofed.

Bjorn knelt down and slid his knife along Scar's forearm. "Don't move." The hair fell away leaving naked skin. "That'll do."

"Mercy man. I helped Colonel Frémont rescue the Donners from the snow. Let us up to rejoin the army and we won't never come back."

"Promise?"

"Yes."

"Yes."

"Boudicca, go." Boudicca ran to the men on the ground and licked the remaining honey off their faces and continued slurping the ants and flies. She lapped up the puddles of urine. Her tail whipped from side-to-side.

"Tell everyone you see?"

"All of them . . ., you crazy ass loon. Let us go."

Bjorn cut their bonds with his wicked sharp knife. One limped the other ran to the river and made two big splashes.

Bjorn said to the twins, "I don't think we'll see any more of them."

A week later, Bjorn heard from a traveling sergeant in Colonel Frémont's army that two deserters had turned themselves in and demanded to receive their punishment.

"Damnedest thing I ever saw. They spouted some cock-and-bull story about a miner off his rocker."

13 - The Curse

"I am plumb tuckered out," said Jethro as they wrapped up operations late that afternoon.

"Me too," said Maverick, "but it's been a good day."

Bjorn held up a sack containing their day's efforts and agreed. "This is our best showing in some time. We're a good team, don't you think?" He went to set the sack on the ground when Maverick shouted, "Stop! Don't set our poke on the ground or we'll be hard up for a year."

Bjorn placed the sack with their day's winnings on the log instead.

Jethro said, "Maybe we're a team, but don't forget Boudicca. I'm wearing that lucky foot from that rabbit she caught. Every time I rub it in my pocket, I find a nugget in the stream." Maverick retorted, "You're nuttier than a squirrel turd. But a black cat crossing your path, that's bad luck even when it has white feet."

Never one to be left out, Bjorn said, "I don't believe in superstitions like you two, but my old man knocked on wood. He said a tree connects to the lucky nature spirits of the earth. Now that works because I knocked on the tabletop before I got up this morning and look at what we found."

The twins nodded in agreement as they walked up the slope to the cabin where an evening meal of beans and rabbit stew bubbled over a fire. While they ate, the crickets came out and a distant coyote howled the approach of evening.

Bjorn puffed on his pipe. He picked up a large rock and hefted it in time over his head. "Got to keep my strength up. It brings me good things."

Jethro snorted around the pipe in his mouth and said, "You'd be better off to put your energy into the gold rocker in the river."

Bjorn laid his pipe next to the sack on the log and said, "Care to arm wrestle?"

"Sure. Come over to the stump."

They locked arms. Bjorn said, "You're stronger than you look, Mr. Jethro, but I'll take you anyway."

They wrestled back and forth with grunts and puffing. Boudicca's ears shot straight up when, with a great, "Wraaah, rrraah" from both wrestlers, Jethro's arm flopped down and Bjorn jumped up, "I'm the winner!" He looked over at Maverick, "You're ready for a go?"

"Naw. Got to save my strength to make a mash."

Bjorn waxed philosophical as they settled back and relit their tobacco pipes. He waved the stem around his little empire. "We're fortunate mates. Glad you signed on. Jethro plays the fiddle like a banshee and shot the hell outta that cougar at fifty paces. I'm adding his pelt to my bear rug collection, I mean the cougar, not Jethro."

Maverick said, "Tell us about that bear again."

"Well, you might not believe this, but I swear on my grandmother's grave it is true. When my placer mine played out to barren sand I prospected for a new claim. There were rumors of a mother lode somewhere upstream."

"What in the hell is a mother lode'?" asked Maverick

"A vein of rotten quartz with gold."

"Is that what we've got here? "

"After the quartz washes into the river and collects it, we do."

"What happened?"

"I wrapped my bandanna around a sandwich of elderberry jam on sourdough bread and threw in a can of beans. I headed upstream like a tramp and a pack."

"You're telling me you. A jam sandwich alone into bear country? Without a dog?"

"It was before I found Boudicca. I checked every naked rock for nuggets but found not a thing. Way back was a little meadow that said "Nap time." My sandwich picked up an army of ants, but despite the gnats and mosquitoes . . . ,"

Maverick said, "I'm going to bed if you don't get on with your story."

"I had a dream."

The twin's eyes got big, "My grandpappy always said, 'Dreams are the truth of a man's soul.' He gave them a lot of credence," said Maverick.

"I tried to sleep but my Viking ancestor roared like thunder through the mist and attacked a white ghost of an elk when . . . ,"

Maverick said, "White ghosts prowl the hollows of Tennessee at night. I seen them when the souls of the dead was riled up."

"My dream wasn't about bears, it was about screaming pain, the worst ever. I didn't know ghosts had eyes but that one did. Those flaming eyes glared at me above a row of fangs on my face. I was eyeball to eyeball with a grizzly."

Jethro exclaimed, "Dammit all to hell, that's dangerous."

"I had bad breath because the giant flipped me on my stomach and tore into my pack. The elderberry jam saved me. That bear ate the thing in one bite and licked the jam off her chops. She jumped on my back for the main bite of meat, me. God was that animal heavy and knocked the wind right out of me."

"Holy shit, didn't that hurt?"

"A little. I noticed real good when those teeth took a bite of my butt and lifted my ass to shake me."

"Then what?"

"What could I do? I reached down her throat to the tail and pulled that bear inside out. Want to know what a twelve-foot grizzly bear eats?"

"What?"

"Anything she wants."

"Her stomach was full of a rotted elk carcass and she wanted me. I was the best tasting bear bait on this side of the mountains, but her teeth were facing out and couldn't chew. That animal shapeshifted back with a poof and prepared to dine on my back when, 'Kaboom,' a blast of smoke shot out of the woods. The beast dropped me and charged the sound. An old prospector behind his double-barreled shotgun pulled the second trigger. The slug knocked out a front tooth and hit the spine of that bear internal like. She fell over with a snarl."

Jethro said, "You're a lucky man."

With more shots from a revolver and several hours waiting that animal finally died. She's the bear rug in my cabin with the missing front tooth and all the claws. I walk on her to show who's boss."

"Is that where you got that scar?"

"Yep. You can read the rest of the story in the scars on my body."

Boudicca walked around the team and licked each one to relieve the tension. Clouds of pipe smoke filled the air and made the crickets move to another crevice. The distant coyote trotted away too.

Bjorn turned to Jethro and said, "It's your turn. How did you get that cougar so quick?"

"Called to him."

"Don't pull my leg, do you talk cat?"

"I talk to nature. There were fresh cougar tracks where I was hunting rabbits. Them big cats are fast, agile, and dangerous and I wanted to get him. I sat by a rock outcrop to protect my back and made a sound like a trapped rabbit. 'Squeak, squeak, squeak.

"It took a long time before I could see him slinking into sight. The wind was coming uphill and I was as quiet as could be. I wished Boudicca was with me but she was in camp. The cat sniffed and I sniffed. I squealed and the thing looked at me. It didn't know what I was."

Bjorn looked at him like he had the secret to the universe.

"I sure as hell wasn't a rabbit. He checked his territory. I could tell it was his territory when he scraped dirt, grass, twigs, and leaves into a pile and pissed on it as a sign for other critters to stay away."

Maverick said, "You never told me about that."

"Got to keep a few secrets so you don't trick me."

Bjorn asked, "Why not use bait?"

"Live bait is best and I had dead meat."

"Okay. And . . ."

I whistled loud and treed that cat. The back leg was mangled from a fight. I shot him in the head from fifty paces and there she is. You and it are even steven about now."

"Thanks." Bjorn leaned back and surveyed his New Viking Gold Mine empire. "I meant to tell you, Maverick, I've got an agreement with *Madam Pearl's Pleasure Palace* in town for all the moonshine you can make. She's happy because we're giving it to her at twenty-five dollars a gallon under what Brannan charges in his store. Don't waste our profits in her establishment.

Jethro said, "Would I do that?"

"You're a man ain't you?"

"Mr. Maverick the moonshiner, how much liquor can you make in a month?"

"Some months are better than others but probably thirty gallons a run. That is thirty gallons of joy when I mix water into fifteen gallons of pure firewater."

Bjorn spread his arms wide and declared, "Life is good. I have defeated the ancient curse my dad told me about."

Jethro exclaimed in a terrified voice, "Oh no! A big black and white magpie flew onto the open door of the cabin."

"So?"

His voice shook as he said, "A magpie on an open door says death is coming."

Maverick said, "Shut your mouth. I've seen flocks of magpies and never had any kind of problem. That's an old wives' tale, and you scare the dickens out of me."

14 - The Gold Rush Beginning

"B'Horny," rang across the crowded bar tent. Bjorn looked through the smoke to see who was mangling his name and pushed his way to a card table covered with a green flannel cloth.

"Joaquín, how the hell are you?"

They shook hands.

"When are you going to learn to say my name right?"

"I Joaquín, you B'Horny. All good in Spanish."

"Aye, yeah, yeah, I guess. What are you up to?"

"Three-card Monte. It is only three cards and you follow the lady."

"That doesn't sound too hard. Show me."

"I take three cards from this deck, see?"

Joaquín pulled three cards from the deck of cards sitting on the corner of the table. He turned them over and said, "The Queen of Diamonds is red. The Nine of Clubs is black and the Ace of Spades is black."

He bent each card the long way.

"I will make it easy. I turned up the corner of the Queen of Diamonds so you can follow her."

He turned the three cards face down with the bent-corner card in the middle and the bent corner facing Bjorn.

"Where is the Queen?"

Bjorn pointed to the card with the bent corner. Joaquín turned it over. It was the red Queen.

"You follow the lady good, Mr. B'Horny."

Somebody in the bar said, "Horny B. sounds right to me." The bar erupted in laughter and they returned to their serious discussions and endeavors of drinking.

"This is easy," said Bjorn with satisfaction.

The bartender pulled a new bottle of whiskey off the shelf and hollered, "Belly up to the bar boys and B'Horny B. Too. Got a new bottle here."

Bjorn and the patrons crowded around to sample the new bottle of whiskey. Joaquín dealt a hand of Monte to a man with a hole in his boot who bet he could follow the lady. The dealer shuffled the cards on the table but Hole-In-the-Boot still picked the Queen of Diamonds.

"Hooray! I won fifty dollars."

A second man with a lisp said, "I bet seventy dollars to follow the card."

Joaquín dealt three cards and mixed them, but the sharp-eyed bettor spotted her anyway.

"Eureka! I just won seventy dollars easy."

Bjorn said, "Let me play."

"How much do you bet, *Amigo*??"

"I'll lay down one hundred dollars to follow the lady."

Three cards later with a bent queen, Bjorn pointed to a card. Joaquín flipped it over and sure enough, it was the Queen of Diamonds. Joaquín handed Bjorn two hundred dollars.

"I'll bet everything on me, one thousand dollars."

Bjorn watched Joaquín lay the three cards faceup on the table. He noted carefully the bend in each and the upraised corner on the Queen.

What Bjorn did not see was the smooth slick fingers of the dealer even out the bend on the Queen and raise the corner of the Nine of Clubs. He did notice the bent corner was turned back toward the dealer and not facing him. His eyes blurred in the rapid shuffling of the cards on the table.

"Where do you think is the Queen?"

Bjorn pointed to the card with the raised corner. Joaquín flipped over the Nine of Clubs.

"I am so sorry. You chose the wrong card."

Bjorn gulped and said, "I think I better get back to the mine. I just lost a week of production."

Joaquín said as Bjorn left, "Better luck next time. Hasta Luego."

Bjorn talked to himself on the way back to his cabin.

I am a poor gambler and cards are not my friend. I won't do that again.

When he got back to the workings, he walked up to the twins in the river and said, "I did a bad thing. I lost all our production from last week betting on a card game. Don't ever play Three-card Monte. Monte will steal everything you've got.

Maverick said, "I know. I lost the shirt off of my back once."

His father's story about smuggling gems to Francia inspired Bjorn. He swaggered down the streets of San Francisco searching for exotic mining supplies to bring to the mine.

"Good day to you, Sir."

"Top of the morning, wouldn't you say."

He dropped a coin into the outstretched hand of a beggar. "You need this worse than I do." On closer inspection, he saw it was the gaunt man who had sold Maverick the tank for his still. Bjorn said, "Aren't you on your way to Missouri?"

The beggar said, "I cannot get passage out. Ships arrive, the crew deserts, and the ship rots in the harbor. I'd be a sailor but I can't manage an entire ship alone."

Bjorn gave him a handful of nuggets, "Keep trying and good luck to you mate. Squeaks from the hinges of an overhead sign drew their attention to the picture of a colt standing over a pistol. The gaunt man read the words aloud.

Gun Shop

God made men

I make them equal

Sam Colt

A brace of shiny revolvers in the window called out, "Look at me."

The beggar said, "Maybe I should invest these nuggets in a revolver. I could rob a bank."

Bjorn was horrified. He thought about his hard-won deposits in the bank and said, "No, No, No, my friend. Keep calm and carry on."

"Okay."

The bell on the gun shop door in San Francisco jangled when Bjorn walked in. The proprietor rushed to shake his hand and said, "I remember you from last year. How can I forget your friend, Richard Porter? He shot up the bar next door and I had to teach him to handle a Colt revolver. How's yours' working out?"

"Haven't shot any grizzlies but I get a rabbit now and again. My hired hand makes mulligan stew with anything I shoot."

"What can I do for you?"

"Got any books?"

"Over here." The proprietor showed Bjorn a shelf lined with several books.

Bjorn sounded out letters in the titles but was unsure what they meant. "Which ones do you like?"

"One of my favorites is this one, Two Years Before the Mast, by Richard Dana. He was a young fellow like yourself who described his visit about ten years ago."

"I'll take it. What's that contraption on the back shelf?"

"That's an Argand lamp."

"Does it work good?"

"I'll show you. You pour whale oil in this reservoir and the wick soaks it up." He lit the wick and replaced the glass chimney.

"It lights up the whole room. I could read my lessons after dark. I'll take the book and the lamp."

"Here's a gallon of oil for the lamp."

A few days later, he carried his book and his lamp to his reading lesson with Alva Dahl.

"See what I bought. I've got a book and a lamp to read it by."

Alva was pleased and said, "I'm proud of you, Bjorn. You are doing your part." She looked at the book and said, "Oh, you will enjoy this book. But first you need to improve your reading and writing."

Bjorn beamed in the light of the uncommon praise.

"Here's a gift for you. In our next lesson, I expect you to bring this slate board with the big and little letters written on it." She handed him the slate board and a box of chalk

"All of them?"

"Yes, all of them. Look through your book and include every letter you can find. Say your alphabet for me."

"A is for Amundson, B is for Bjorn, C is for Chinaman, D is for damn, E is for . . . "

"Stop! Mr. Amundson, you must quit using foul language. You are not on a ship among sailors."

"Yes, ma'am."

He finished his alphabet with only a couple of corrections."

Bjorn's final stop before the Squatter's meeting was the barbershop. The proprietor trimmed Bjorn's beard and hair. A splash of aftershave smelled even sweeter than the *Mug-Wump Specific Liniment*.

He was ready for the meeting but made a side trip that afternoon to *Madam Pearl's Pleasure Palace*. Making good progress in his reading lessons, Bjorn proudly presented his slate board with the big letters and little sisters to his reading teacher.

"I've got all my letters, and I can say them. Numbers too." Following the numbers on the slate board with his gnarled finger, he started reciting each one.

Ms. Dahl corrected him." Do not use your finger. Remember to read with your eyes alone."

Bjorn read the alphabet through in good form.

"We are going to use those letters to read a famous Norse poem."

"What's a poem?"

"A story in short lines. The words follow a rhythm and sound the same at the end of the line."

"Remember the saga where Odin gives a speech?"

"My father told me many times."

Alva opened a book to verses from Odin's famous speech and read,

> *My garments in a field*
> *I gave away*
>
> *to two wooden men:*
> *heroes they seemed to be,*
>
> *when they got cloaks:*
> *exposed to insult is a naked man."*

"Tell me the first two letters."

"That is M for Murrieta and a little Y for yellow gold."

"Very good. Say the letters."

"Emm. Why?"

"Faster

"My."

"Who is my?"

"Me. I can read!"

Bjorn stood up and shook his hands overhead in triumph at his first official reading success.

They worked through garments as a coat. The simple words of in, a, and field were easy. By the end of the lesson, Bjorn was reading a Viking poem, although haltingly.

"I'm sweating, this is so hard, but I am reading."

"Yes, you are. That is enough for today. It is good you have a lamp. You can study your book, Two Years Before the Mast, tonight. I think you will enjoy his adventures "

Bjorn thought about his lonely insulted ancestor and shivered as he returned to his cabin.

The old prospector entered the New Viking Mine workings with his mule Jasper in tow. "I reckon to grab my monthly share of liquor, tobacco, grub and get gone." Jasper toted his total earthly possessions on her back.

He greeted Bjorn and the twins working in the river as he swung by the shack. "Howdy pards. Hard at work, I see." He added with a chuckle, "I can watch you all day."

Bjorn called up from his sluice, "You can give us a hand if you'd like."

"Nah. I'll grab my share, and get along. Me and Jasper is going to do a little exploring."

"Where to?"

"We've walked every gulch in these mountains, except one little area we ain't seen. I want to check out the river named after the Paiute Indian chief, Truckee. He guided pioneers over the Donner Pass. Them Donnor families were the ones who got snowbound four years ago. They should've had the chief instead of that halfbaked James Reed."

Bjorn said, "Some of those Indians are hostile. Be careful."

"So I've heard. But Chief Winnemucca is my friend. He told me about the Boca Springs area, the coldest place in these mountains. He claims it as theirs, but he's got his problems with it too."

"What problems?"

"Them young brave are hard to control. They're itching to fight their enemies and want to be the next chief."

Bjorn said, "I was like that until the sea beat me up."

The Hatfield twins said together, "We still are. Ain't nothing gets in our way."

The prospector continued, "Winnemucca complained to me just the other day. 'Our people are surrounded by enemies. The Washoe from the mountains and the Miwoks from the other side attack us whenever they see us. Pale faces from over the mountains cut down the trees that give us pine nuts. A white devil pissed in the spring we drink out of, and a soldier threw my baby son into the fire to kill him.' "

The miners continued to heave gravel into the sluice and hoped for a nugget or two. The prospector took a sip of whiskey from his little metal flask with a hoof print where Jasper stepped on it one night. He refilled it from Bjorn's jug.

"Much obliged for the supplies, and watch out for the grizzlies. A good thing you've got your dog, Boudicca."

The prospector and his mule headed up the American River and over the summit. They passed aging snowdrifts left over from the winter before, and circled Donner Lake to a well-traveled trail that ran along the Truckee River draining out of Lake Tahoe.

He remembered the chief's directions that Boca Spring was about a day down river from the crossroad of the mountain trail and the river trail. "You will like the area. My warriors favor Boca Springs for the good water and room to race their horses if they're not gambling."

Sure enough, as the prospector and Jasper rounded the corner, he saw a pack of five Paiutes in war paint practicing their raiding tactics on horseback. He had picked up enough of their native language to understand they were four young warriors and a teenager on his first raid. He heard a warrior say to the teenager, "Be brave, and attack with strength."

Bjorn did not see Chief Winnemucca anywhere.

The braves raced in a circle and shot their arrows into a heap of brush in the center. They practiced their war cry in high falsetto tremolo, "Eah ya ya eeeh ya ah, wah-wah."

The teenager spotted the prospector and charged toward him screaming, "I no want you here. No mules."

His first arrow missed the prospector but hit Jasper. She brayed and began pulling at her tether. The second Indian shot an arrow through her haunches and she fell in a heap unable to walk. All she could do was "yee-honk". The third Indian cut the tether and clubbed her across her head. She lay still.

The warriors circled the prospector for attack practice.

The prospector knelt behind Jasper for cover and reached for his rifle, but before he could grab it an arrow pierced his throat and pinned him to a tree. When he reached up to pull out the arrow, the five Indians aimed down on him. Their rain of arrows made him look like an aroused porcupine.

He choked three times and fell to the earth breaking the arrow shaft off the tree. Blood pouring from innumerable body wounds carried his life spirit into the ground.

The tribe dismounted their horses to steal everything of value from Jasper's fallen form. One finished the whiskey, and with a mighty yell he hurled the flask as far as he could. After they retrieved their treasure, they turned on the prospector's dead body.

The leader said, "Our shaman says clearly, 'The enemy must never enter our lands again.' " They cut slits in his legs and arms so he could not walk or throw a spear. A quick slash of the knife removed his manhood member to prevent fathering new sons. His voice was silenced by his manhood stuffed in the mouth."

A teenage brave said, "He no eat our food," and sliced open the prospector's belly to pull out his guts. Five waiting wolves downed them in a flash, their tails were tall and quivering.

With a war hoop, the leader took his knife and skinned a section of scalp with its long hair from his head. He waved the bloody trophy overhead with a whoop.

Faithful companions, he in the land he loved and Jasper with the arrow in her heart, completed their final journey together.

What a life he had led, what people had he known, what animals were his brothers? The great spirit knew.

Gray wolves as a pack approached the flesh and fed voraciously. The meat was tough from the old prospector, but there were strips enough to feed their hungry pups. The cycle of life continued.

The warm up warpath was over and the Indians were prepared to inflict revenge on a remote settlement.

A few days later, the clippity-clops of a horse on an urgent mission disturbed Bjorn. He looked up at the soldier entering his camp. Boudicca growled as the horse stopped at the riverbank with a snort and took a quick drink.

Bjorn said, "Boudicca! It's all right, he's a soldier."

The sergeant in the saddle said, "Good morning y'all. Things look peaceful here, but the Redskins across the mountains are causing trouble. I'm passing on a warning to the men working the American River. Keep your eyes open and your weapons handy."

Bjorn said, "Thanks for the news, but things are quiet around here." He noticed a little metal flask with a hoof print in the soldier's pocket. "Where did you get that flask?"

"It was abandoned on the ground over at Boca Springs. It is handy for a quick nip now and then, even with a dent in it."

"It looks like one a friend of mine carried. Did you happen to see an old prospector and a mule anywhere?"

"Can't say as I did. There was nobody around the springs but the ground was all torn up. It looked like those rampaging savages have been on a warpath. They attacked something from the pools of dried blood on the ground."

Bjorn was concerned and said, "Where are these springs you mentioned?"

The man on horseback said, "Up this river and over the summit to Donner Lake. Follow the Truckee River for a day and tou can't miss them. A lot of pioneers coming in from the east stop there. It's the best water they've had in weeks. Watch out for the gray wolves all over the place. They feed on the trash the pioneers throw out, and maybe a dog or two if the Indians don't get them first. I saw bones scattered all over the place."

"I appreciate the information."

"I've got to keep going. Watch the woods and keep your weapons handy is all I can say."

He galloped off the way he came.

Bjorn made a decision. "Maverick, keep on working and guard the place. Jethro, grab your rifle. We're going to find the prospector. This doesn't sound good."

Jethro crawled out of the river and said, "How long will we be?"

"Pack enough supplies to last a week. I'm borrowing two horses from that ranch over the hill."

They loaded the horses and rode upriver at an urgent pace. Bjorn said, "Keep your eyes open for danger in the woods. I don't want to feed another bear."

Over the summit on the shores of Donner Lake, they met up with a wagon train from Kansas. Bjorn said, "Hello travelers. Been a long trip?"

"Yes, it has. That clear water from Boca Springs was the best we had in weeks and gave us hope we were going to get to California."

"Any news about hostile natives on the way?"

"I'm afraid so," said the wagon master. "We saw signs of a significant skirmish about a day down the Truckee River near Boca Springs."

Bjorn said, "You're only about four or five days out of Sacramento. Good luck to you. We'll be on our way and thanks for the information."

Late the next day along the banks of the Truckee river, Bjorn said, "We're getting close from the looks of those bushes and the grass there."

Jethro, who was the crack shot from Tennesee, exclaimed, "What is that? That's a gray wolf if I ever saw one and it's got something in his mouth."

Bjorn said, "Get him."

Jethro raised his rifle and took one shot. The wolf looked surprised, ran about three steps, and collapsed lifelessly. Bjorn and Jethro rode up to the carcass.

Jethro said, "I'd call that a hand in his teeth."

Bjorn picked up the bloody hand and studied it. "If I didn't know any better I'd say this hand is full of arthritis. I hope I'm wrong, but he chewed it off a man."

Boudicca snapped for the bloody fingers but Bjorn said, "No dog, this might be somebody we know. Show some respect."

They tied up the horses and explored the woods. As usual, Boudicca followed her nose through the trees sniffing the ground every inch of the way.

Jethro stumbled over a bloody bone in front of what appeared to be the scene of an animal fight. What the hell is this?"

"Looks pretty fresh. What is it? You're the hunter."

"'I'd call that a leg bone from a man. I worked with a country doctor once and we had to amputate several legs that were mauled by a wild animal or in an accident."

Bjorn said, "I saw a leg in a shark's mouth this same size and shape."

Boudicca barked furiously and they ran to see what she had found. Bjorn said, "What have you got? Damn, Jethro, those wolves have been at work. Looks like the rest of our old prospector."

Jethro said, "Maybe so, but it wasn't just the wolves. The whole top of his scalp hair is gone. It looks like the knife of an Indian. Those slits on the ribs were made by arrowheads.

"You're right. There are arrow shafts all over the place. And look at that pool of dried blood. I'm afraid our friend met a bad end at the hands of these filthy Indians. He told me that Winnemucca was his friend. Some of his braves were not it seems."

He picked up the skull which had been chewed loose from the rest of the skeleton.

"Over there are the remains of the mule. Between the Indians and the wolves, there's not a whole lot left. Her skull was bashed in."

Bjorn slumped down onto a rock and said to the mutilated head, "I am sorry, Mr. Prospector, I don't even know your proper name. You saved me from a bear and made me rich, but I couldn't save you from a band of wild Indians. I am so sorry. You are my faithful friend."

Boudicca knew who the remains were and felt she had lost her first friend.

Bjorn said, "All we can do now is give him a proper burial and keep these wild animals away.

They took turns digging a shallow grave in the rocky ground. Boudicca dug as much as she could, but some of her dirt went out and some got kicked back in.

They buried the bones of the prospector alongside Jasper. "It's only right since they were together longer than most people."

They piled stones on top for protection and scratched into the top one, "1850."

He did not know enough letters to make an inscription.

15 - The Gold Rush

The New Viking crew was despondent after burying the prospector and shuffled into town to forget their sorrow. Bjorn, Maverick, and Jethro heard a roar from the outskirts of the village.

Jethro said, "I haven't heard a ruckus like that since the wake for old Peterborough down in Tennessee."

Bjorn said, "Neither have I. Let's check it out."

They joined a crowd milling around an openair bar. A live band added to the chaos. Agitated patrons demanded beers from an overworked barkeeper and hurried away with their brews.

Following their ears to the cheers, the New V crew elbowed their way to the entrance of a round makeshift structure. Intense men with knapsacks collided with others waving fists holding money. Bjorn felt trembling excitement in the sweaty bodies that stumbled against him.

Maverick said, "What's in those sacks?"

Bjorn said, "It's alive."

Jethro said, "We're at a cockfight. We had matches all over Tennessee but they were secret." He described the setup.

"There's an eleven-foot arena inside a fence as high as a rooster. Drop in any two roosters and they naturally attack each other."

Bjorn said, "What's the point?"

"You bet on the birds. They fight to the death."

Squawk! Squawk! A cloud of white and red-fringed black feathers exploded out of the ring. Spectators shouted at the birds in a deafening roar to start the bout.The miners were used to gold but not the flamboyant jewelry on the rubbernecked cockers. One man's chest was crisscrossed by a massive gold chain and a gold pendant carved into fighting gamecocks.

Over the din, a man at the scale called out, "The Whitehackle weighs in at five pounds thirteen ounces." The handler picked up his bird and paraded through the spectators holding the fowl overhead. He called out, "Who has a bird that's man enough to fight Whitehackle?"

Secure in the hands of the handler, the rooster calmly let the crowd feel his muscles and judge his temperament.

Astonishment showed on the miner's faces, and Whitehackle's owner stepped to their side. "You are new."

Bjorn said, "My first time."

"Two of my birds will fight today. First up is Whitehackle." He waved the handler over and let Bjorn stroke the feathers. "Feel those legs and wings, but watch out for the sharp metal spur on his leg. This champion has won seven fights."

Jethro said, "What's his style?"

"He is powerful and hardhitting with deliberate blows. My other bird is stronger." He opened his knapsack to reveal a rooster with a redheaded black tail and white accent feathers. The cock in the sack tried to peck Whitehackle who struck back.

"After the gentlemen bet with the Kristos, we match the gamecocks in the cockpit. They naturally go at each other in a battle royal. Whitehackle will win unless he jumps out of the ring or dies. Then he's a chicken, not a rooster."

Ready to start a new match, several spectators cheered when Whitehackle was paraded through the group. Others booed.

"Who will fight the famous Whitehackle?

"Yellow Leg Hatch will." The feeder handed his fighting bird to the man at the scale. "Five pounds and twelve ounces for the challenger."

Hatch crowed, Kuku-ru-yuk. Ru-yuk.

Bjorn smoothed the feathers of Whitehackle who was so calm and delightful it was hard to see him as a bloodthirsty killer.

Impatient bettors were anything but calm as they assaulted Kristos to place bets with hand signals.

Bjorn made eye contact with one who came over. "Want to wager?"

"I bet three hundred dollars on this bird here," pointing to Whitehackle.

"Does he have a name?"

"Jojo."

"I bet three hundred dollars on Jojo."

The Kristo said, "You are new. When Jojo is placed in the ring, point to him so I know who you are betting for. Next time hold up your fingers. Straight up is ten dollars a finger, sideways a hundred, and down for a thousand. Watch where you point."

"Will you remember?"

With a snort, the Kristo said, "I always remember."

The owner said, Next time you will be fast, no?"

Bjorn said, "Next time I will have my hands in my pockets."

Jethro's eyes gleamed and he said, "I love to gamble. When I lose I am excited. When I win the chance of big money eggs me on. Nothing matches my excitement in action. Better than a woman, better than moonshine."

Maverick grunted.

Jethro waved down a different Kristo and said, "I bet one thousand dollars on JoJo."

Bjorn said. "That's your own money, man."

Placing his bird into the arena, each feeder removed the hood over the head. Leaning down he whispered pointers to his gamecock. The handlers waved the cocks back and forth to build up energy and speed. The birds faced off a foot apart.

All eyes focused on the action in the arena. Bjorn pointed to JoJo with three fingers to the side and put his hands back in his pockets.

The fight began in a cloud of feathers and squawks colored by splashes of blood. The electrified spectators jammed chest to back, side to side and strained to track the action. Bjorn felt a tension in the sweaty bodies that crowded him from all sides. He towered over the other spectators but still stood on his tiptoes to see.

The fight went a lot faster than the betting ritual. Whitehackle tried to avoid the first shock from in the air and force Yellow Leg to meet his fighting style. His plunging spur made a deep gash in Yellow Leg's wing. He turned wildly aggressive jumped with all five pounds and twelve ounces at Whitehackle's five pounds and thirteen ounces. Grappling with Whitehackle, he gashed both legs and pecked out an eye.

A cheer rose from the assembled humanity when Yellow Leg pecked out Hackle's other eye. The onlookers might wait for the outcome but had to yell continuously. Amid calls of victory or sighs of defeat, much money changed hands.

A gap in the spectators gave the miners a quick sight of the ring. A white rooster, blind in both eyes, jumped and jerked and pecked and slashed until he could move no more. Laying on the ground with streaks of blood across his white feathers, Whitehackle took his last strained breaths and dropped his head to the sand. Within seconds he was covered with a basket and pushed from the ring

Bjorn was deeply affected and thought,

Those feathered birds showed courage like I have never seen. Fighting even after they're blind. That courageous guy on his back kept grappling— never gave up. He showed true Viking courage. Can I do less?

"No!" he exclaimed, startling the men next to him. "Never!"

"There's the parts, build us a still," said Bjorn when they arrived back at the miner's cabin from the cockfight in a well-diverted condition. Piled in front of the storage tent were pots, tanks, valves, and stirring rods. Nearby, an old crop wagon was stacked with dilapidated ears of corn.

Maverick took charge, "Load that equipment on the horse and follow me." They loaded the equipment on the back of the tired horse.

Unlike his brother, who was a rat hunter and sharpshooter, Maverick was a moonshiner and a man of special skills. The man and his horse tramped upstream to Maverick's secret spring, with Jethro and Bjorn trailing as extra hands. Boudicca plunged from side to side into the brush to ward off dangerous attack rabbits. They unloaded the equipment in a hidden clearing where a spring of cold clear water poured out of a small cave.

Maverick explained, "Somebody has been here before us. This tin cup hanging from a chain in the rock was left by some sourdough years ago. That cast iron pot is left here for a traveller or a hunter to make stew or biscuits. Who knows that food has come out of it?"

He gazed at the utensils like they were his long lost love.

"This spring water is perfect. The limestone it comes from adds minerals and makes it ferment the mash pretty as a speckled pup." He pointed as he planned the layout. "Put the fermenter by the hole in the hill where is easy to fill with water. Unload the corn in the flat space. Mount the condenser below that little waterfall."

Bjorn and Jethro worked to remove several large boulders and pack down the soil for the fermenter. The tank sat on stilts with room for a fire underneath. The twisted pipe from the top, which Maverick called the condenser, they routed under the waterfall. A flat stone at the outlet was to steady a jug and catch the moonshine when it dripped out.

Sounds of grunts, groans, and snorts came from the downstream edge of the clearing. Maverick said, "Wild pigs are watching us. They love the spent mash after you boil off the moonshine, and will come running when we dump it down the draw. Old Jethro can bag one and I'll cook the best barbecue that ever passed your lips."

Bjorn said, "I've never heard of barbecue."

"You roast a hog over a fire as the Indians did in the Caribbean. Generations ago, traders taught us hillbillies the secrets of making barbeque."

They finished the construction with soaring spirits. Maverick started his first batch.

Maverick hummed a southern love song to pass the time in the middle of the afternoon as he fired up his still.

"Dum, da dum, the Bonny Black Hare". He started singing to himself,

On the sixteenth of May, at the dawn of the day,
With my gun on my shoulder to the game field did stray,
In search of some game, if the weather proved fair,
To see if I could get a shot at the bonny black hare.

After heating the thirty-gallon vessel filled with spring water, he mixed in fifty pounds of crushed corn and laid down to wait for the mash cool. By the cool of the evening, it was time to add the old yeast from Brannan's store.

I met a fair maiden, as fair as a rose,
Her cheeks were as fair as the lilies that grow,
Says I, "My fair maiden, why ramble you so?
Can you tell me where the bonny black hare doth grow?"

He had soaked the mix called to mash for eight hours.

The answer she gave me, the answer was "No,
But under my apron, they say it doth grow,
An' if you'll not deceive me, I vow an' declare,
We'll go to yon green wood to hunt the black hare."

The mash itself was eager to ferment. Maverick did not know the difference between wild and store-bought yeast and let the mash mixture go its own natural way. The wild yeasties won while Maverick finished his song.

> *I walked on beside her an' vowed that I would,*
> *I laid there her in the green grass to see if I could,*
> *I pulled out my ramrod, my balls they played fair,*
> *Says I, "My pretty maiden, do you feel the black hare?"*

The mash was heated to a hundred and seventy degrees.

> *The answer she gave me, the answer was nay,*
> *"How often, young sportsman, do you ramble this way?*
> *If good be your powder, and your balls they play fair,*
> *Why don't you keep firing at the bonny black hare?"*

> *"My powder's all wasted, my balls are all gone,*
> *My ramrod is limber an' I cannot fire on,*
> *But I'll come back in the morning if the weather proves fair,*
> *An' I'll take another shot at the bonny black hare."*

Maverick explained to Bjorn, between verses of the Bonny Black Hare, how the moonshine was made. After two weeks, the mash is called sour. "I boil it off. The vapor condenses in the coil under the waterfall and liquor drips out. That is magic moonshine. By the sun or the moon don't make no difference. It's all good."

Silenus, the Greek God of Beer Buddies and Drinking Companions, did not smile on Maverick's first batch. Hostile yeasts from the corn farmers' cattle dung regained control over the natural ones and spoiled the mash. Maverick dumped it down the draw, washed the fermentation vessel, and started a second batch.

The spoiled mess was not a total loss, however. Its pungent fragrance lured two wild pigs from the hillside into their hog heaven. Maverick watched them slurp the remains and said to himself, "Better get Jethro's rifle up here. I can taste smoked ribs already."

The second batch resumed where the first left off. After two weeks, Maverick built a fire to boil out the alcohol. "Still has damn leaks everywhere. I'm losing my magic 'shine." He stopped the holes and loose connections one by one and recovered enough primary corn whiskey for a little celebration pick.

"Look what I've got," he shouted as he stumbled into the New Viking works with a jug. Jethro and Bjorn abandoned the rocker in midriver and splashed to shore.

Bjorn said, "We better test this for quality," and took a sip. He shook his head in wonder and drew a quick breath.

Jethro grabbed the jug and took a long drink. He waved his head and said, "You got it, man."

Bjorn retrieved the little brown jug. "Follow me." He walked to the reburied Indian and poured a bit on the earth. "Our guardian spirit is thirsty too."

Lighting their three pipes of tobacco, they blew smoke signals in the trees to celebrate Maverick's achievement. Their evening of testing approved every last drop of the jug. The three laid on the ground and giggled themselves into silly lunacy. Nightfall and sleep came together.

Dawn and agony came together the next morning.

"Oh, my head is splitting," said Bjorn. He turned the jug upside down into his mouth and nothing came out. He took a long drink from the river as the Hatfields groaned. "God, that was fun."

Bjorn was a lean young man without an ounce of fat anywhere. He especially enjoyed working in the river because it was cooler than the Sacramento Valley where summer temperatures regularly hit a hundred and ten degrees, even without a thermometer. He was vigilant for the most part. but sweat dripping from his forehead in the heat of the day sometimes obscured his eyesight.

Utter exhaustion at the end of a day led to sleep of the dead that night. The twins slept so hard they forgot to snore.

Boudicca was off hunting with Sergio and couldn't warn him about a small Chinese man stalking his property in the middle of the night. The marks he made on a piece of paper were in Chinese, but Bjorn couldn't have read them in any case. Those marks tallied the daily take from the mine. The spy was ignorant about the grade of the ore but assumed it was good enough for the mine to operate.

The Blue Lantern spy kept his regional *Kongsi* contact, Red Ghost, well informed. The leader always demanded to know everything about Alta California. Other Blue Lanterns on the ground reported on successful and unsuccessful pits. Their report confirmed that the New Viking Gold Mine was the premier pit on the American River.

Uneasy for some reason, Bjorn aroused the twins early. "Travel day. Get our stash from the privy." A pot of black sludge that mocked coffee fortified the trio. The twins hoisted heavy bags from under the seat in the outhouse. Even though the canvas sailcloth was waterproofed with linseed oil, they took care to keep each one on a short leash and well out of the muck.

"Son-of-a-bitch these things are heavy," said Maverick as he stacked the bags on the table in the cabin.

"We've done well the last six weeks," said Bjorn. He lifted the bags one by one. "We must have two thousand ounces of dust. Pack it up."

"What are those things?" asked Maverick when Bjorn threw little leather bags with no seams on the table.

"Gold pouches that a hunter makes out of elk scrotums. They have a drawstring at the top and hold two hundred ounces or twelve pounds. No seams to leak is their advantage. And don't listen to claims these are an aphrodisiac. I tried it and it doesn't work."

Artistic talent was a skill of Bjorn's that also didn't work. It did not stop him from drawing a distinctive Viking longboat under sail on each pouch. He handed them to Jethro and Maverick to fill since his crooked fingers didn't handle gold dust very well.

They loaded their pouches on the horse and walked to Sacramento. Jethro stood ready to draw his weapon on any bandits. Bjorn and Maverick treated every friend and stranger as a potential assassin.

At the ticket office, Bjorn bought tickets to San Francisco for the gold and himself on the schooner *Swiftness*. A uniformed guard whom Bjorn knew from past trips prowled the decks. "Do you keep a close eye on activities?"

"Without fail, sir."

"Here is two hundred dollars to guard those twelve pouches with my ship's marks. They're everything I own in this world." Bjorn handed him a bag with fifteen ounces of gold. The extra five were a tip." He made one last count of the dozen bags stowed away in the hold. A passing vendor sold him a quick lunch when he climbed out into the sunshine.

Moored at the new wharf in San Francisco, Bjorn watched the stevedores unload the Viking bags from below deck. Bjorn counted nine and waited for the other three. Where were they? He jumped into the hold bypassing the ladder. They weren't there. He accosted the ship's mate. He checked the passengers. He ran through the schooner, the hold, every nook, and cranny. The bags were missing. He suspected robbery by the Blue Lanterns, who would have turned the gold over to their *Kongsi* master. He didn't know they had already brewed the pouches into a tea.

"That bite of lunch was the most expensive meal I ever ate. It cost me three pouches of gold. And that crooked guard took my two hundred dollars and let it happen. So much for friends when money is involved."

Bjorn fumed but had to get on with business.

Maverick hurried to check on his beloved apparatus that was both a lucrative business and a fire in his belly. The batch of mash was mature and ready to distill off the whiskey. Starting the fire occupied his full attention and he overlooked the three deputized desperados. They had sneaked their horses through the bushes toward the rank smell.

He never saw the rattlesnake hat that parted the branches and reconnoitered the small clearing. Instead, his sharp eyes chased leaks in the coils from the tank as they cooled under a waterfall. Success was in the precious drops of whiskey that fell from the outlet into a one-gallon stoneware jug.

Hole-in-the-Boot pushed his horse past Rattlesnake but stumbled into the barrel of boiling mash on his dismount. Four-Fingers shot holes in the tank to announce the purpose of their visit and barely missed adding holes to Hole-in-the-Boot. All three cheered when the mash spurted to the ground.

Not to be outdone in the mayhem, Hole-in-the-Boot unsheathed his axe and chopped a leg out from under the bleeding tank. Hot contents from the falling tank spilled on his clumsy tender foot. With a yell, he tripped and stum-bled over his good foot, and both clumsy feet kicked a burning log into the dry grass.

The spinning log smashed an unfortunate jug of moonshine and ignited a ball of flame that erupted like a volcano. The whiskey was almost pure alcohol.

Four-Fingers yelled, "Brannon said save the moonshine. It's the best liquor for bribes. Give me a hand." He and the henchmen tried to empty the rest to douse the grass fire but the vessel was empty. The meantime, delighted wild hogs lapped and loved the spilled mash.

Raging flames raced through the grass to a hidden second jug. It exploded in a beautiful blue fireball. Beautiful except to the horses who instinctively heated fire. All three steeds bolted down the draw.

It was Maverick's scream of frustration at the loss of his moonshine that halted the chaos for a moment. Waving an unsteady revolver, he hollered at Hole-in-the-Boot. "Can you dance, you son-of-a-bitch?" He started firing at Hole's feet but was not the shot that Jethro was. His bullets went wild.

"Ou . . . oh . . uhh . . . , stop it," yelled the Boot as he jumped on his good foot, his bad foot, both feet, and backed away.

"Every one of you varmints, get out for I'll shoot your worthless carcasses and feed them to those wild hogs."

Four-Fingers said, "We can't go—ain't got horses."

The smell of the mash had attracted the horses to the drinking party along with a couple of buzzards. Just like people, the wildlife got woozy, boozy, and ready to fight.

"Your mounts are drunk on the mash you wasted."

"Horses can't get drunk, can they?"

"They already are," said Maverick. "You'd better ride 'em home while they can still see."

Rattlesnake said to Four-Fingers that Brannan wanted to confiscate the liq-uor. The grass fire got there first and another jug blew its cork into fireball.

Maverick said, "So you thugs do Brannon's dirty work. I'm not surprised."

Hole-in-the-Boot said, "What are you saying? We're here to protect public safety and stop this illegal operation."

Four-Fingers trained his firearm on the Hatfields. "Don't move." Mad Maverick and he stared eyeball to eyeball while the deputies destroyed the equipment to make sure it would never make another drop of moonshine.

"We're done. Let's go," said the leader. They ran downhill to their slurping horses and mounted the giddy equines. Only a generous application of spurs induced the horses to leave their treasure of summer mash. Mounted men and horses crashed into trees on one side and the other, hee-hawing all the way down the hill.

Maverick said, "I'll save what I can."

He stomped out the flames encroaching on a separate cache of jugs some thirty paces away. By setting up a one man fire brigade from the spring, he saved fifteen valuable jugs.

Barely were the jugs were safe when an earsplitting scream even louder than his echoed between the hills. Two drunken red-eyed pigs charged up the draw fighting and biting. They stopped slashing each other long enough to ransack the pile of useless equipment, toss the pipes in the air, and wallow in a pile of discarded trash.

Maverick dispatched the drunken swine with several shots from his revolver. "Those porkers are worse than the thugs." Rubbing his hands with glee and dressing the animals on the spot, he said aloud, "There's my barbecue, brother. Them pork shoulders make the best pulled-pork in a coon's age, and I can do it."

Barbecue turned to despair at the wreckage and the twin vowed, "I have to build a new still. Ain't no fake sheriff can stop me."

16 - Squatters or Trespassers?

Back in camp, the master distiller showed his butchered wild pigs to Bjorn and described the destruction of their still. Descriptions of the delicious pig roast that was coming help ease the pain. "Politicians back home use a free barbecue to draw people to a rally."

Bjorn said, "These beasts are huge. How do you fix them?"

Maverick cleared his throat, stood tall, and gave a lecture on how to prepare a traditional North Carolina barbecue.

"You dig a hole six feet wide and fill it with burning coals. Spin this pig on a spit over the fire and you're done."

Bjorn thought about the Squatters' Meeting planned for the next night. Grabbing Maverick, he said, "You've got to tell the good Doc Robinson about your barque."

"Barbecue."

They found Doc Robinson nailing up more flyers in town. Maverick described how politicians attracted a crowd with a pig roast when they were not kissing babies and shaking hands.

Doctor Robinson said, "Excellent idea. Who knew we had a pitmaster in our midst? I've missed that southern barbecue something fierce. Maybe folks around here don't know what a barbecue is, but they can smell a free meal."

Bjorn plastered the final notices that proclaimed FREE BARBECUE over the Squatters Meeting signs. Robinson hired men to carry walking billboards up and down I Street with barbecue slogans.

Barbecue cannot be eaten
except in the company
of family and friends.

Anyone Can Put The Heat

191

To The Meat,
But Only A Few
Can Barbeque.

Get sauced without the hangover.

Boss of the sauce

The trio of pitmaster, organizer, and enforcer prepared for the Squatter's Meeting in downtown Sacramento. A hole in the middle of Brannan's fraudulent park seemed like a good place to start. Bjorn engaged two unemployed miners with idle shovels to dig the six-foot pit and fill it with wood under Maverick's direction. The pitmaster, which is to say Maverick, lit the fire and gave lectures to the curious crowd about the virtues of barbecued wild hogs. "Good to eat and saves the hills." The rising column of smoke attracted the population of Sacramento if they were not discussing matters of gold.

Bjorn surveyed the group of sturdy curious miners and said, "I need protection from Brannan's constabulary tomorrow night. Who is in?"

The crowd roared, "We are!"

"Bring your friends."

Robinson added to the cord of firewood stacked for the ceremonial bonfire.

Hungry spectators watched Maverick skewer two pig carcasses on pipes from his wrecked still. He hung them over the coals and slowly rotated the spits to roast each side evenly. Helpers chased away stray dogs. Drunken idle patrons wandered from the circle of drinking establishments to follow the pit's progress. They formed a rowdy ring of security against Brannon's vigilantes.

It was the delicious aroma of roasting barbecue in the dawn of the next day that drew a crowd from near and far. Maverick circulated among them saying, "Good things take time, but it is worth the wait. Spareribs beat beans."

"I'll say."

"Ain't no lie there."

Bartenders rolled kegs of beer to the edge of the assembly and dispensed gallons of golden courage. Impromptu boards across barrels offered jugs of Maverick's rescued moonshine whiskey to the thirsty.

A little table appeared out of nowhere around noon. An Irishman in a green vest and gold teeth said, "Place your bets gentlemen. How long until Brannon's bastards show up? Put your money where your mouth is." A line of gamblers formed, placed bets, and argued about the arrival of the roughnecks.

Robinson and Bjorn worked the crowd. "Come tonight and support the Squatters' Meeting. Toward evening, they lit the cord of firewood to send up a massive smoke signal. It was fun but not needed since the population of the city was gathered around the barbecue pit. A handful of spies for Sam Brannan had the good sense to lay low.

Following the successful feast, the men whether drunk or sober congregated around the speaker's platform. A little man with a quiet voice stood up to start the meeting. Off to the side, Bjorn said to Robinson, "I don't think this fellow can control the meeting. You better step in."

"Let's see how it goes. I have a statement of resolutions for later."

Bjorn bellowed to the rowdy crowd, "Quiet! Let the president talk."

After introductions, the quiet man said, "A representative landowner desires to speak."

A speculator clutching a signed title from John Augustus Sutter muscled his way to the stand and said, "I would remind you illegal squatters that California has been a sovereign territory, not a state.

We adopted our constitution last year the same as the Republic of Texas did in 1836. Laws passed under that guiding document are now in effect, even though we just were admitted to the United States."

Bjorn said, "And who bribed the legislators to pass those laws?"

The speculator looked the other way and continued, "They give purchasers of lands from Colonel Sutter the full rights to the same. You can expect us to protect our rights."

One man stood up to say, "I have examined the definition of the land grant to Sutter from the governor of California. It granted permission to settle in the territory."

"You are a wolf in wolf's clothing," rang out.

"The governor allowed Sutter to establish a colony. Fort Sutter protected the citizenry, that is you I might add, against the Indians, the Russians, the Americans, and the British.

"Indians were here first and then the Spanish."

"Will you let me speak?" He glared at the anonymous speaker.

"That grant was 48,800 acres on the Sacramento River but no more. The land beyond the boundaries was not included and Sutter's signatures on those titles are invalid."

Robinson said, "You, sir, have described the situation precisely," as he and Bjorn walked to the front of the meeting. Jethro and Maverick followed for a physical back up." The claims of the speculators are null and void."

The crowd erupted in loud cheers, "Null and void! Null and void! Null and void!"

Another man stood up and said, "From the first, you stopped any legal process. You attacked the poor settler in his shanty with unknown thugs who demand possession and money."

Next to him, his companion said, "Only those with courage stood their ground. Others of limited resources left. A hardworking courageous man who stands his ground is visited by the fake sheriff and his posse."

A man with a badge shouted, "Who are you calling fake? I am the duly elected sheriff over this region and have deputies to help me. Yes, Mr. Brannan makes modest contributions to the cost of running my department, but we are independent and upholding the law."

"Your thugs beat my neighbor up one side and down the other."

"Where is your witness? I'm sure he was only doing his job. It is my job to oust the intruders as quickly as possible for the good of all concerned."

A great shout of derision arose.

One brave and educated squatter waved a document at the crowd. "Here is a true and accurate copy of the wording of the original Alvarado land grant. He read from the document the boundary descriptions from the original land grant.

The speculators as a group rushed to inflict damage on the speaker until Bjorn stepped in front as a shield. "It's me first before you assault this honest man."

Doctor Robinson stepped into the momentary hesitation and, gathering his courage as he was unaccustomed to speaking in public, made his way to the stand.

"I have a preamble and resolution. We have listened to you but it is now your turn to listen to me." He cleared his throat and pulled a sheet from his pocket.

"Whereas, the land in California is presumed to be public land, therefore,"

"Resolved, that we will protect any settler in possession of land to the extent of one's lot in the city, and one hundred and sixty acres in the country, until a valid title shall be shown for it."

The crowd received the resolution with roaring enthusiasm.

"Yes!"

"I paid good money for my land and I have a title for it."

"They promised me that a title was forthcoming, and I was free to build my cabin."

"The speculators have priced the land so dear no human being can pay for it."

"Nobody can settle in this track without being assailed by some claimant under Sutter or his minions."

Bjorn Amundson ended the evening with a loud motion. "I nominate Doc. Charles Robinson for president of our Squatters Association. He dares to act and can speak. How many of you present vote aye?"

A forest of hands reached for the sky accompanied by shouts of agreement.

"Are there any present with the courage to vote no?"

Only a few speculators' hands rose.

Bjorn announced, "With your approval, I declare Doctor Charles L. Robinson our esteemed president. Good luck to you, sir. You're going to need it."

17 - Squatters' Rights

The speculators were relentless in their campaigns of eviction. They had thousands of acres and millions of dollars on the line. Most if not all had ties to Sam Brannan. They rushed from the meeting to his home at midnight and roused him from his sleep. He set emergency messages to his advisers to be at his home early the next morning. Bottles of fine whiskey and boxes of Cuban cigars appeared out of nowhere, and the speculators enjoyed the night in rare luxury. They gave a full report on the meeting and the ringleaders, especially Bjorn Amundson and Doctor Charles L. Robinson.

Advisors crowded into the living room where Brannan addressed his henchmen, "Gentlemen, it appears there are those who dispute our land titles."

A cockroach scurried across the floor and Brannan stomped it flat.

"I want you to crush them like I did that insect. We stole the land from Sutter fair and square and that rabble is trespassing. The El Dorado County Board of Supervisors, my board of supervisors I might add, passed an ordinance last December to remove the squatters' camps. The sheriff has hired deputies to enforce that edict."

The members of the gathered assembly thought about their own lucrative deals and supported Brannan wholeheartedly. One of them said, "That giant Norwegian is a pain in the ass. I want to get him."

Brannan cleared his throat and said, "We guardians of the law are resolved to uphold the statutes of California and the ordinances of Sacramento City. Your continued support of the good fight with appropriate donations, where absolutely necessary, is welcome I assure you. We conduct our business on a handshake, and have no need to commit the proceedings to written form."

The recording secretary said, "I have nothing official to record since each of you is independent and acting solely in your own selfinterest. Mr. Brannan is offering encouragement but not participation. You must make that clear in your eviction enforcement."

Brannan's foreman asked, "Where do we start?"

"I have been told the biggest camp belongs to Joaquín Murietta's family. Start there and you'll have a good chance the Norwegian will show up to protect them. You can take him down, but be sure to have ample manpower. He's a beast."

The posse of ragtag hired desperados stormed into Murietta's family camp on the American River. For a full ten years, the Murrietas had lived and excavated on the site. Four masked cowards in a tight cluster of horses were an insult to the proud traditions of cavalry units everywhere.

As the Pinto skidded to a stop, his rider with the buzzing rattlesnake skin on his head jumped down. He kicked burning coals from the cooking fire into the nearest tent. When he heard a cry from within, he reached in and jerked an old man out onto the ground and kicked him. "Dammit, we got rid of this shack last time and here it is again."

Joaquín's wife screamed from a little cabin door. Instantly, a second masked rider dismounted and clamped a hand with four fingers around her waist. "Got a beauty for us all."

Sergio ran to get Bjorn from the New Viking Mine but they could not get back in time.

With swinging clubs, another masked man dismounted and attacked every structure and tent around the clearing. They pulled boards off, bashed in doors, kicked burning coals everywhere to ignite the buildings, and hooted in delight when they kicked and stomped the terrified Murrietas.

Joaquín and his brother dropped their rocker box in midriver and splashed to the camp. Yelling in Spanish, he said, "Stop! What is this?"

Without a word, Rattlesnake Hat lunged at the brother and pinned him to the ground with an accomplice who had an oozing wound on his foot. The Hole-in-the Boot said, "Got him. Grab the rope." The thug seized a ready made noose from his saddle and dropped it over the Mexican's neck. He tossed the loose end over a branch and lashed it to the saddle horn with a quick half hitch. With a slap on the flank, the horse bolted and jerked the brother by his head into the air. The horse came up short when the noose hit the branch and broke the neck it encircled. The ruffian retied the rope to the tree, its evil job done. The brother's body dangled without life.

Joaquín ran to support his brother's feet but a swinging club from behind knocked him to the ground. That club rained blows on every part of his body. When he tried to stand and rescue his brother, the beater tripped him and said, "This greaser doesn't even wear shoes. I'll stop him from walking anywhere." He beat the soles of Joaquin's feet to a bloody mess." You'll never walk again." Joaquín spewed hate from the stabs of pain and remained silent.

Two on one held Joaquín's wife while the third attacked. When done they rotated and continued, all of them in turn."

Four fingers surveyed the carnage and declared, "We're done here, boys. Good job."

He glared at the terrified people in the camp and confronted Joaquín to his face. "Brannan gives you trespassers until nightfall to vacate his land." He waved his club and said, "There's more of this if you're still here."

The mounted horsemen made a final round of destruction through the camp to attack anything loose and burn everything left. Yellowbellies hiding behind their masks rode away through the smoke.

When Bjorn and Sergio arrived at the destroyed camp, the first thing they saw was Joaquín's brother hanging from the tree. The sound of groaning from the prostrate grandfather in front of a smoldering tent was second. His crippled hand grasped a little white flag. He was crying and his right leg bent at an unnatural angle. Sergio gently picked him up while Bjorn stamped out the embers of the fire.

Bjorn ran over to Joaquín and said, "What happened here?"

Joaquín ignored him and ran to hold the torso of his brother. The body was still except for the slow drips of blood from many wounds. In a low voice, Joaquín shook his head and said, "They thought he was me. They thought he was me. They thought he was me."

Joaquín said, "Hold my brother," and untied the rope to let him down. Bjorn laid the brother in a comfortable spot of sand while Joaquin ran to his wife who was sobbing hysterically. "Mi bebé, Mi bebé." Her ripped clothes told of her shame from the lynch mob. Joaquín raised her in his arms and said, "Te amo. Te amo." He brushed her hair from her face and sat her down to hold her. "Tranquilo, mi amor."

In English, so Bjorn could understand, he said, "We must be strong for my baby."

Bjorn encircled the couple with his long arms and said, "I am with you in this outrage."

After some moments Bjorn checked on the grandfather. The curandera was wrapping a splint on his broken leg. Searching through the bushes, Bjorn found a suitable stick with a comfortable handle for a crutch. He trimmed the sharp edges and presented it to the grandfather.

Joaquín said to his uncle, "Bastón para ti."

"Gracías."

He comforted his friend, who held his sobbing wife and brother's body but trembling with impotent rage.

Using English, the distraught leader of the Murrieta Mine said, "Señor *Amigo*, what am I to do? My grandfather built that house many years ago. It is now ashes. They destroyed my mine and drank my tequila. Señor Brannan demands I return to Mexico, but Señor B'Horny, this is my home. I cannot leave."

"It's that god-damned Brannan again."

My family tried to resist but the soldiers were too strong. Mi *Amigo*, these bad men hurt my family. We run a mine here for ten years in Sonora before that. They are jealous because we are good miners.

"Brannan sent his henchmen to attack you. I'm next."

"Ride with me to get revenge."

Blazing fury consumed Bjorn's thoughts. Rumblings of resentment filled Joaquín Murrieta.

Bjorn pounded the nearest tree and exclaimed, "Brannan!"

Joaquín punched the air with his fist and said, "Si, Brannan, no."

Bjorn said, "He's a thief and a pirate."

"Un mal hombre. I have an idea. I know where is semillas de campanilla. You say morning glory seeds. The Aztecs used them. "

"What does that do?"

"You be much strong and muy brave. With tequila, you are a one-man army."

"We will stop Brannan."

"*El Grupo* will help."

"You have the Hatfields and me behind you."

18 - All is Lost

Boudicca jumped out of her bed with her ears pointed down the trail. She warned the camp with a low rumbling, grrrrrwrrrwrrr, wroof, wroof, and grrrrr."

It was midmorning the day after the Murietta massacre. Bjorn had shoveled gravel into the mining contraption since dawn while intently watching the path into his claim area. He did not speak to the twins, only shoveled them gravel. The only sounds were splashes of water, the crunch of the shovel, and the rattle of the gravel. He stepped to the bank of the river to see what agitated the dog who was his ears, eyes, and nose on the world.

A cloud of dust rose over the trail. "What is it, dog?" He ran to the edge of his claim and heard the clompety, clompety, clomp of horses. Barking furiously, Boudicca ran in front of Bjorn to defend him from the posse of sweaty horses that charged him.

They skidded to a halt at the cabin, and the leader said, "This is Sutter's land. Vacate the premises immediately or suffer the consequences."

Bjorn retorted, "It's my claim. I have the deed in my cabin." He shouted to the river, "Maverick, Jethro get up here. We have a problem."

The rider said, "Claims, clams, shit. It don't matter, you are trespassing and Sutter wants you gone." He pulled his Colt revolver.

Bjorn said, "No need for that. We are peaceable, but this mine is mine."

Looking down from high on his horse, the deputy waved his Colt. "You're an Indian lover and we're here to keep order against those savages—and that vicious beast. He pointed his gun at Bjorn and said, "Stifle that crossbreed mongrel or I'll make it dead meat."

With a flick of the reins, the horse loomed toward Bjorn. Boudicca clamped her jaws on his foot in a violent jerk. The horse bucked with an arched back and landed with its head low and forelegs stiff. The rider pitched out of his saddle and Boudicca pulled him to the ground.

She punched her fangs into his leg with the strength of a tiger. The instant raging pain took his breath away and killed his judgment. " . . . get it the hell off!"

Boudicca released his leg and crushed his arm with one crunch.

The screaming man pulled his revolver and fired point-blank into her chest. He fired again through her head.

Bjorn screamed at him, "You shot Boudicca."

"Had too. It was self defense and that vicious dog was killing me." Boudicca's falling body ripped long gashes down his arm.

"She was defending me from rats."

"I'm a rat?"

"Rat bastards, all of you."

The situation deteriorated after that.

One of the posse members said, "I ought to plug you right now except you haven't attacked us".

"I have now," yelled Bjorn as he threw the bleeding enforcer to the ground and pinned him with a knee to the chest. He pounded the face with both fists. Primal howls of anguish came from deep in his throat. Bjorn's wild punches mangled the face as is badly as the arm.

"Assaulting a lawman is against the law. You're under arrest."

"Arrest hell," he said as he picked up Boudicca and left the shooter groveling in the dirt.

He rubbed his beard against her furry body and pulled her upright, "Stand up for me, or sit, or anything." He raised her into a sitting position, but his work-scarred hands told him she was gone. He hugged the limp bundle of tan and black fur and rocked on the ground oblivious.

The three posse members and the lead soldier grabbed Bjorn's hair, beard, and body and tied his arms behind him. They wrapped a blindfold around his eyes and a rope around his neck. He made no resistance, even when they knocked him out with a club. He didn't care.

"Your all going to jail," the posse boss man yelled, "Squatters in the river, get your asses up here." He tied their hands behind them but left their eyes uncovered to see the way. The rope circled their necks as it did Bjorn's. The posse untied Bjorn's unconscious arms, least them through the upper arms of the twins for support, and retied them behind his back.

After loading their unconscious leader on a horse, one member climbed up to ride and support him. He towed his horse behind.

"Follow me," said the new leader as he dragged the chain gang, actually rope gang, toward town. He kicked Boudicca's corpse onto her mound of dirt.

After they left, Boudicca's three puppies nuzzled her body to see what happened. Their mother was gone.

In the holding cell of the jail, the jailer flattened a piece of paper on the table and handed Bjorn a quill pen. "Sign here," he said. "You can write your name can't you?"

Bjorn was confused and dizzy from sometimes walking and sometimes being dragged through the dirt to the jail. He mumbled, "What does this say?"

"It says you trespassed on Sutter's land grant and you are returning it to Mr. Brannan while requesting his mercy."

"Give me the damn pen." He signed his name which was the height of his literacy at the time.

"Get in there and shut up." Bjorn stumbled next to his friends.

Jethro said, "Back in Tennessee, I'd shoot every blasted one of them on sight. They're lucky I don't have my rifle handy."

Bjorn hung his head between his knees facing a corner. None could see him, but he sobbed in masculine grief for a long time.

"I will get revenge at any cost, no matter how long it takes. Goodbye, my faithful Boudicca." His clenched crooked fists showed his depths of resolve, but no one in the holding cell bothered to look.

"I've seen you before," Bjorn said to the soldiers guarding the main jail. "You tried to steal my mine."

The leader with the rattlesnake skin around his hat said with a lisp, "Shut up and get inside." He tried to kick Bjorn's backside through the bars but his boot was too big.

The other soldier, the one with a scar on his face and a missing little finger said, "I'll never forget the way you tied us up, poured honey on us, and fed us to the bears."

Bjorn retorted, "I was teaching you a lesson, you damn thief. You weren't going to die unless you acted like a bastard."

"I felt like I was." He raked his club over the bars in the door and locked it with a flourish.

Bjorn stared at the motley group of strange prisoners.

He sat with his back in a corner where he could see everybody but no one could sneak up on him. He said to himself, They fixed the wall we blew out last time. It looks a lot stronger now, but that was fun. I like using black powder.

Bjorn breathed deeply. He was nodding off to sleep when he heard a key click in the door. The soldier guards stuffed in a group of four Californios at the point of a gun.

"Get in there you dirty greasers. We're going to fix your gang of bandits once and for all." Noticing Bjorn he pointed his pistol and said, "You're in for it now. These ruffian bullies will work you over but good. They hate white men."

Bjorn stepped away from the corner to avoid being trapped. He confronted the desperados and recognized Joaquín Murrieta in front. When he was close to Joaquín and out of sight of the guards, he extended his index finger and winked. Murrieta whispered, "Tranquilo," to his men.

He grabbed Bjorn by the shoulders and gave them a strong shake. Bjorn exaggerated the gesture and fell to the side as though he had been tripped. The four bandits jumped on him and made like they were beating him to a pulp.

The guard with the snakeskin hat lisped, "Serves you right. Go get him."

The other guard with the scar said, "He's all yours. Hit him again." The guards laughed as they clanged the door shut and locked it.

Prisoners around the room were indifferent. If somebody was not being shot or beaten to death, they were bored and stayed out of other men's arguments.

The fake beating stopped as soon as the jailhouse door closed. Murrieta said, "You too?"

Bjorn looked at his bleeding friend and said, "What happened to you?"

"*Amigo*. My family was cleaning up our camp from yesterday when these men came. They tied me to a tree and beat me with sticks, yelling for me to take my filthy clan back to Mexico. They said, 'You didn't pay your miner's taxes this month, or last month, for the month before.'"

"I said, the tax was not passed then. He hit my mouth and beat my feet. When my cousins came to help, they arrested us, and here we are in jail with you."

Bjorn examined Joaquín's wounds. "They worked you over good."

Bjorn tore his shirt into strips and wrapped them around Murrieta's injuries to stop the bleeding. Somebody said, "That damned Sutter.

"Sutter hell, this is Brannan's doing."

Bjorn was all ears when another prisoner who looked Chilean said to a companion, "We are locked up at the orders of Sam Brannan. He wants to eliminate us small operators, especially if we make alcohol."

Bjorn remembered that earlier in the week Madam Pearl had warned him that Brannan was coming for his successful enterprises.

Back at the New Viking camp after signing away his ownership, although he didn't know it yet, Bjorn said to the twins, "How do you get revenge on a despicable thief?"

Jethro said, "I clean my rifle and mold four times as many bullets as I need."

Maverick said, "I get a jug and a club."

Bjorn said, "Here comes Murrieta with a bag of something. Hey there, come in. What are you carrying?"

Joaquín said, "You make brave with morning glory seeds. Big ideas, no pain."

"Morning glory seeds?"

"That's what the medicine man says."

Jethro said, "I always add 'shine," and Maverick said, "I made it."

Bjorn said, "Sounds like a plan. We'll prepare ourselves and visit Brannan's store. Get your men."

Joaquín brought two men from his extended family. He wanted to help Bjorn and the twins prepare for their anti-Brannan campaign.

Maverick passed the jug of his rescued moonshine around the group. Each man took a hefty swig. Bjorn said, "Is Sam Brannan a skunk?"

Everyone answered, "He stinks!"

"Are we going to get him?"

Joaquín said, "We will burn down his store. He cheats my family every time."

"I'll drink to that. Pass the jug please."

Joaquín opened the bag from his waist and said, "This makes us mucho strong and brave."

Bjorn said, "Tell me in English what that stuff is?"

"Power comes in seeds from the morning glory and fruit from the cactus. I add henbane for power. This is the strongest spell the curandera knows."

They each took a portion from the pouch and washed it down with spirits from the still."

"You are growing bigger."

"Let me at them," said Joaquín as he punched the air."

The little marker over Boudicca's grave rose up and its arms shouted to Bjorn, "Revenge, revenge, revenge."

The men hooted and hollered, banged their chests against each other, beat the ground, and declared themselves invincible.

Returning to their ex-mines, Bjorn and Joaquín outlined the plan to their corps of evicted followers.

Bjorn tied a keg of black powder to the saddle of his horse. He mounted and said, "Let's go."

Murietta's entire family gave themselves a spark of hope and followed Bjorn to the next pit, the Lucky Ducky Mine. He explained their mission in English to the Chinese engineer who spread the word in Chinese throughout the company.

Bjorn stared in awe at the variety of vicious fighting weapons they took up. There was the matched pair of hook swords with a sharp blade ending in a shepherd's crook. One man carried a kind of sword with the broad blade and weight forward used for decapitation. Two ex-warriors carried throwing stars from Japan. The rest carried normal mining implements sharpened to razor edges.

One wizened fellow missing two fingers carried a coil of fuse and a barrel of blasting powder.

Bjorn at the head of his growing group of men entered each encampment along the river with the same message. "Sharpen your tools and join us. We're going after Brannan." The workers joined with gusto.

News of their approach traveled through the grapevine ahead of them. Recruits from every wrecked claim site joined up.

Bjorn trembled with rage but understood the tactics of attack. Joaquín was clearheaded but not as strong a natural leader.

Bjorn halted the mob of thirty men to organize. He said, "What should we do first?"

"Burn down the store."

"Hard to do. The walls are adobe bricks."

"Clean out the overpriced shelves and donate the goods to those who Brannan evicted."

"That'd take too long."

"Shoot the son of a bitch."

Bjorn said, "I want to get even with Brannan. We'll see how it goes when we get there."

"He's a tyrant and a crook."

"And lower than dog shit."

Holding out his arms Bjorn said, "Listen to me. The American River runs in a channel fifteen feet below the store. We'll approach unseen and surprise them. Follow me, stay low, and keep quiet."

The motley hoard followed Bjorn more or less single file to the banks of the American River and turned in the direction of the

Brannan store. He whispered, "Stay down. We don't want them to know we're coming."

They walked through rushes that hid their line from direct view. The indirect view was something different.

The army of thirty wronged miners stopped in a grove of trees that concealed them. Every man was fearless but smart. Joaquín was an expert raider and held his finger to his lips for silence. They split up and sneaked from bush to bush until they faced Brannan Store through the open gates of Fort Sutter.

Bjorn whispered, "Wait here while I lay powder along the front and blast it off. Then we rush the store."

He muttered as he walked up the hill, "You're a thief, Brannan, and I'm coming to get you."

Bjorn and Jethro ducked behind the shrubbery framing the front door. Bjorn poured a line of blasting powder along the corner and Jethro inserted the fuse. As they ducked around the corner Bjorn hollered to the men, "Take cover."

They flopped to the ground just before the explosion. A huge noise and a gigantic cloud of smoke happened, but it only broke a nearby window and blasted the shrubs out of the ground. The store was undamaged.

Jethro said, "Dammit. We should have tamped it with dirt. They build these adobe walls like a fort,"

Bjorn said, "Imagine that. Brannan needs a fort."

The rumble echoed back and forth between nearby walls and faded. People poured from every structure in the fort to see what was happening.

The modest squatter's force raced from the riverbank to the front of Brannan's store. Carrying rifles, shotguns, blades, shovels, and revolvers too, the squatters swarmed the corner of the adobe store. They encircled the front door with an offensive line.

Jethro ran to the door. "It's locked." He motioned to the men to breach the door with their raised weapons. "We will never have a better chance than right now."

To the sounds of steel on wood, Brannan appeared at the small balcony over the door. He looked down on the rabble. Waving his revolver over the mob, he said, "I'll blow your brains out if you touch my store."

Three masked men appeared beside him on the balcony. Their masks were familiar to Joaquín and he cried, "You hanged my brother."

Brannan said, "You're loco. They've been here all week." He yelled to someone inside, "Get the sheriff and posse—now!"

Maverick said, "There he goes out the back. I'll get him."

Bjorn hollered, "Stay right here. We need all our hands on deck."

Out of sight of the attacking squatters, the aroused Sheriff and Mayor galloped on horseback in every direction to rally their friends to defend the store.

Old Four-Fingers said to Brannan, "I saw the rushes in the river swaying with no wind. I warned you when these trespassers crossed a bare area.

Brannan said, "I demand you retreat this instant."

Crash! The door that was under attack opened inward. Two men with axes stumbled into the wheels of a six-pound bronze cannon rolling out. Brannan said, "I'm giving you one last warning. There is a load of canister shot coming your way.

Joaquín's men were accustomed to using herbal courage and were somewhat coherent. Bjorn, Jethro, and Maverick were out of their minds.

With a roar of rage, Bjorn leaped onto the muzzle. The gunner panicked and detonated the charge. Bjorn's weight tilted the barrel toward the ground and the canister shot bounced off the hardpacked ground. The ricochet slowed the spikes and balls and injured the nearby attackers, but did not kill them.

In a cloud of dust, the Sheriff's posse charged the right flank of the miners. The sheriff leveled his rifle and shot over the heads of the crowd. Jethro turned his rifle toward the posse. With a deadly aim, he picked the best target and shot back. It was the mayor riding horseback. He was badly wounded by Jethro's bullet and would lose his arm. A deputy returned Jethro's fire. His bullet entered Jethro's chest and passed through his heart. The twin collapsed dead with his rifle gripped in his hands.

Bjorn used his enormous natural strength that was enhanced by the herbal courage to charge Brannan on the balcony. With a hellacious leap, he grabbed the railing in front of Brannan. But when he tensed to swing his body over the railing, the three masked guards pried his fingers off. He slipped backward one story to the ground and hit his head. He was groggy enough that five stout members of the posse could subdue and tie him faster than leashing a dog.

"Araah, rrroar, wrrouw," he yelled. "Let me go. I gotta get Brannan."

"Oh no, you don't." A pistol butt knocked Bjorn unconscious.

A stunned Bjorn came to tied across the back of a horse. Maverick limped after him to help but was too badly wounded from the canister shot to do anything.

Two platoons of the sheriff's posse poured around each side of the building in a pinchers movement.

Joaquín drew on his experience to roll on the ground and drop out of the line of fire of Brannan's revolver. Maverick didn't and the bullet caught him in the leg. His moonshine skills saved him since Brannan knew he had operated the still. His aim was only to wound.

Brannan shouted at Maverick, "I'm letting you go for now. You'll run my stills. You make the best moonshine in the country."

"Damn right I do."

After they were all restrained, Brannan stood on the second story balcony and said, "I figured something like this was in the works, Amundson. You're nothing but a squatter-lover, " He watched as Bjorn shook his head awake from being slung over the horse.

A combined shout from Brannan's defenders was intended to cause a stampede of the thirty, now twenty-nine. Yet they stood their ground, even when the pretend sheriff, covered with sweat and gore, arrested Bjorn hanging on the horse. Brannon said, "Lock him in the prison ship and throw away the key."

Brannan hurled curses at the squatters from the balcony and repeated his declaration of the ordinance that structures be removed from his land that was occupied by trespassers.

The posse, now numbering about a hundred armed men, surrounded the squatters. They fired several shots into the air.

Brannan called after the horse carrying Bjorn to the prison barge, *La Grange*, "You are going to pay for the damage to my store. You've disrupted this region for too long."

He pulled out a piece of paper and read, "I hereby convey to the Brannan Company my entire claim for the New Viking Gold Mine, the rights to minerals therein, and all such illegal improvements as are erected on the site. Signed, Bjorn Amundson."

"I never signed that. It is a fraud."

"This is a clear and proven title to that land on which you are squatting. You signed this confession when you were in jail last time. Let me show you."

"You tricked me. You knew I couldn't read and made me sign after dragging me through the dirt."

"Your signature is clear and is attested by the sheriff. The name of those workings is the New Brannan Gold Mine. It belongs to me and you owe me fifteen thousand dollars in back rent."

He waved the sheet in front of Bjorn hanging off the horse. Bjorn could tell the signature was his even though it was smudged and shaky. He spit on it.

"The same goes for your henchmen. They are seriously in arrears in their foreign miners' taxes and I, as a representative of the law, am hereby foreclosing on their mines."

He waved at the restrained miners and called to the Sergeant, "Lock this total bunch of malcontents in the *La Grange* prison. My lawyers will prepare the paperwork later."

The Sergeant pulled a clanking wagon from behind the store and threw the other prisoners in. Guards chained each man to a bar. The driver flicked the reins, said "Haw." His route to the prison barge somehow managed to hit every chuckhole, rock, and rut all the way to the prison. Each prisoner bounced clean off the wagon floor at each one. It was a relief to reach the Sacramento River in the prison barge.

Along the way, the magic potion wore off of Bjorn. His exhaustion was interrupted by severe indigestion and he vomited on the bed of the wagon.

Approaching the jailer at the entrance to the prison barge, *La Grange*, the guard riding shotgun said, "Here is a bunch of worthless pussycats. I have orders from Sam Brannan to lock these men up and never let them out. The final paperwork will be down tomorrow. Put this big ash-blonde bastard in solitary. You can bunch the others as you have room."

Bjorn groaned on the floor of his cell and said aloud, "Being a berserker is not everything it's cracked up to be."

Alva Dahl, privately known as the Madam of *Madam Pearl's Pleasure Palace*, walked down H Street to the waterfront at the Sacramento River. Bystanders were stunned to see her bright orange dress with a flowing skirt that was accented by real gold embroidery. Her white parasol kept the blazing sun from her creamy skin and completely concealed the pistol inside the shaft. She paid homage to the Paris fashions of the day with an elaborate hat and two flowing feathers. The brim was just wide enough for some lace trim and to give a touch of shade under the parasol. She carried two books in addition to a small purse.

The faces on the street stared as she strode up to the guard blocking the end of a gangplank. The other end rested in a doorway to a superstructure on the most unusual boat in the river. Alva read the name of the boat on the bow and said to the guard, "Is this the prison ship *La Grange*?"

The guard looked Alva Dahl up and down before answering, "Yes ma'am."

"I understand you are holding a man by the name of Bjorn Amundson."

"I'll have to check the current register," as he turned to go inside. Alva followed him but he said, "You can't come in here."

"I don't see why not."

"Regulations say that only prisoners may enter the jail."

"Young man, I have lived in Sacramento far longer than you. I know most of the men's names in here and they will vouch for my character. I must see Mr. Amundson."

The flustered guard opened the jail register and said, "We have several prisoners today. There's the crazy foreigner that bangs his head on the walls, a forger, a thief, and rioters from the ranks of the squatters."

"Mr. Amundson would be in the latter group. Show me to him"

"Ma'am, I have to check your person for weapons before I can let you proceed."

"Don't you dare touch me. I'll cut off more than your visits to my girls."

The guard put his hand over his crotch and said, "Follow me." They entered the interior of the jail barge and walked past several cells formed of stout oak bars. The guard stopped at the last cell and said, "I believe this is Mr. Amundson."

"Open the door. I need to talk to him."

"Are you sure, ma'am? He's a dangerous man."

"Are you going to unlock this door or not?"

The guard unlocked the door to let Alva Dahl in.

She looked down at Bjorn the bottom of a bunk bed. "You certainly get yourself into scrapes."

He looked up and said, "I was only protecting my property."

Alva said, "Now that you have free time, we will make great strides in your reading lessons. You can study all day by the sun instead of a dim lamp at night. It will save your eyes and grow your mind."

"My mind is fine but my body is crumbling in this stinking hole."

"I want to check your progress. Take this pencil and write the alphabet on these oak bars. I expect to see all of the big letters and little letters."

Bjorn wrote the following down on four oak posts in his jail cell.

Aa Bb Cc
Dd Ee Ff
Gg Hh Ii
Jj Kk Ll
Mm Nn Oo
Pp Qq Rr
Ss Tt Uu
Vv Ww Xx
Yy Zz
1 2 3
4 5 6
7 8 9

"Read them to me."

He read them all.

"You are missing something."

Bjorn thought and thought. "I am missing nothing, here is a zero." He added a zero on the last line."

"Here is a book by the greatest Norwegian poet we have, Henrik Wergeland."

"What the hell is a poet?"

"Watch your language. You are not on a ship. A poet writes words that flow and sound alike. When you can read this book, you can truly say you have learned to read."

"If you say so."

"Here is a verse I have always liked."

> *And only there where blue of day*
> *like spring so clear does now arise,*
> *grow violets in blue array*
> *as lovely as her pair of eyes.*

"Here is another sample from the sagas of our Viking ancestors. Remember where Odin gave a speech?"

> *"My father told me many times."*
> *Alva a verses fro Odin's famous speech,*
> *My garments in a field*
> *I gave away*
>
> *to two wooden men:*
> *heroes they seemed to be,*
> *when they got cloaks:*
> *exposed to insult is a naked man."*

"When you can read this, you will be an educated man who could talk to the King."

Bjorn said, "That is interesting, but I like my book Two Years Before the Mast because I have been to sea."

Alva said, "You will benefit from reading every book you can find. I expect an improvement next time. Before I go, do you have a message for anyone?"

"Please ask Sergio to care for Boudicca's puppies. He knows what to do, and he will not bring them to *Madam Pearl's Pleasure Palace*."

"One should hope not."

The student beamed inspiration after the teacher left. "Bjorn Amundson, himself, can address the King of Norway?

How about that?"

Amid his reading a few days later, the sounds of a commotion on the gangplank interrupted Bjorn's concentration. His tiny cell window looked out the river side of the barge and he couldn't see anything onshore. But he could hear the familiar voices of Joaquín Murrieta and several cohorts arguing with the guard about something. Bjorn could tell they were about five sheets to the wind drunk, but that was normal.

the vaqueros faded out of earshot after a brief exchange of pleasantries.

Jangling keys told Bjorn the jailer was coming his way. With the turn of the key in the lock, the jailer opened the cell door and let in Joaquín.

"Hola, *Amigo*."

"Joaquín, what are you doing here?"

"Señor B'Horny, it was an accident. I don't know what happened."

Bjorn said, "What do you mean an accident?"

"I don't know."

"Tell me about it."

"We were riding through the hills and accidentally saw three men and a hug of licor."

"You mean jug of moonshine

"That's what I said, a hug of moonshine."

"What happened?"

"We walked toward them to help."

"Help, like joined them"?

"They had five or six heavy hugs of moonshine."

"Damn, that sounds like you found Maverick's stash. He hid it before they trashed his still."

"It drank good. They wanted to gamble so I played Faro with them."

Murrieta was too drunk to describe how they played Faro, but Bjorn knew the rules from his days at sea aboard *Agilis*. He had tried a hand or two in the gambling halls and discovered it was easy to lose his money.

He could see Joaquín's smooth hands lay down thirteen spade cards with the King high and the Ace low. He would shuffle a full deck of cards and discard the top one to show he was not cheating. As the dealer, he would draw two cards that he laid down with the faces showing. The winner's card was to the players' right and the loser's card to the left.

Men, drunk or not, made their beds bets by putting their chips on the winner or the loser spade card.

The dealer drew the next card. If it matched the loser's card, the bets there went to the dealer. If it matched the winner's card, the bets on that doubled the money to the bettor. It was simple and fast.

Murrieta continued, "I put thirteen cards on the ground and passed out chips to them. Bjorn wondered how old and grubby the chips were. He had seen some that would actually stick together. "We took a drink and played a hand, and shared two drinks, and played two hands. It was fun."

"Lots of money moves around I think," said Bjorn.

"The first hug got empty, and we tested the next one. But the man with a scar on his face and four fingers cheat. He moved his chips from a loser card to a winner card when I look away. But Joaquín is smart and he notice," as he tapped his finger on his temple.

"I know that man. He is the stagecoach holdup man and claim jumper."

Joaquín said, "That bad hombre beat on me in jail. I catch him and say, 'You cheat.' I am a stranger to him because all of us Hispanics look the same."

He acts mad and says, 'Who are you calling a cheater?' He draw his revolver, but I shoot fast when I am drunk and he gets dead."

"One down. Go on," said Bjorn. He studied his drunken friend with mixed feelings and resolved never to drink with him.

"The man with black boot and hole in brown boot point his revolver at my men a lot and he has more holes in him."

"You are good but dangerous, Joaquín.

"The man with snake eye hat run behind a tree and shoot at me. My men circle him. Bang, bang, bang. His rattlesnake no buzz no more."

"I take the chips, the money, and the hugs, because you know I always leave a clean campsite. It is a heavy pack on my horse."

The jailer returned and said, "Times up. Your gang is back and waiting outside. You better hurry because every one of them is tipping a jug. They're higher than kites."

Bjorn said to Joaquín, "I am not sorry to lose those outlaws, but this gives the Murrieta name a bad reputation."

Bjorn could hear the riders holler up and down I Street and shoot their guns at every branch, squirrel, or rock that moved. It sounded like the local law enforcement was right on their tail.

The next day, copies of wanted posters appeared across the goldfields and throughout the town.

WANTED
DEAD OR ALIVE
JOAQUÍN MURRIETA
REWARD $5000
no questions asked

Bjorn divided his time on the slowly rocking barge between sounding out strange words in Norse poetry and watching boats on the Sacramento River through a crack in his cell wall. Throngs of goldseekers poured in every day. Rich men, poor men, families dragging bedraggled children, smartly dressed gamblers, sailors wobbling on their sea legs, and general humanity.

He could catch only glimpses of passersby on the shore, but he could hear their eager conversations.

"Someone to see you," said the jailer. He let a man into the cell. The man said, "Look at you."

Bjorn yelled, "I'll be damned if it isn't Richard Porter!"

"How are you?"

"How did you find me?"

They hugged each other tightly.

"All the rumors in the San Francisco newspapers are about the riots in Sacramento. They say the miners are being cheated and jailed. When I heard about a giant of a man with golden hair and a beard, it had to be Bjorn Amundson."

"How did you know I was here?"

"The papers talked about the attack on Brannan's Store and the arrest of the leader. It was easy to find your prison. You're famous."

Bjorn called to the jailer, "Hey Warden. I am a model prisoner and make no trouble for you. I want a furlough to have a drink with a friend. I promise not to run away with this damn ball and chain on my foot."

Richard Porter said, "In my capacity as master of the brig *Agilis* I can post a bond for his safe return." Looking at Bjorn he added, "How much are you worth anyway?"

The jailer looked around and rubbed his chin for a moment. "I think a bond is not necessary, but be back in an hour. It's my job if Brannan finds out I did this."

He unlocked the cell and Bjorn and Richard clanked across the gangplank to a local saloon. Bjorn carried his iron ball on a chain like a trophy of resistance.

Over a beer, Bjorn said, "How the hell are you? It's been a year."

"The position of the master on the ship is a lot harder than the second mate. I was excited when Alex MacIntyre, who now owns *Agilis*, promoted me to her master. I'm not sure he did me any favors, even though my first voyage went well. We carried a load of foodstuffs and hides to Canton and I just got back. We outsailed more than one pirate ship, but only raced to drop anchor in the Pearl River."

"How is Master MacIntyre?"

"His new home across the bay in Oakland is a fine structure. The wife and he are healthy and enjoying a good retirement."

Bjorn waxed nostalgic, "That was some trip we shared on *Agilis* from Boston to California around Cape Horn. I've missed you, even when you shot a hole in my gold pan."

Richard laughed uproariously, "Yeah, I was pretty pissed and tired out. It looks like you're doing well enough now."

"I was until that damned Brannan stole my mine. He made me sign something I couldn't read. It gave everything I had to him. What a crook."

"People can be cheats if they get a chance. What are you up to now?"

"I am learning to read like an educated man. My teacher is a woman from Norway."

"How did you meet her?"

Bjorn cleared his throat and glanced away a moment before answering, "It was in the course of business." He did not add that her business was a brothel.

"Listen. My family is under an ancient Viking curse. I lost the New Viking Gold Mine, and a soldier killed my dog Boudicca, the best friend I ever had. You are my second best friend. I'm sorry, but that's the way it is."

Richard laughed and said, "I know what you mean. My best friend was was with me on the *Agilis* until she ran off with the bosun. That black cat felt the sailor needed her worse than I did, and he was probably right."

"Where are you off to next?"

"I am preparing for a voyage to Bremerhaven with a stopover in Boston. Germany is where *Agilis* was launched back in 1841."

Bjorn got intensely interested. "Bremerhaven. That's only about four hundred miles south of Norway isn't it?"

"Right, but why?"

Bjorn thought for a while before saying, "Is there any chance I can accompany you to Bremerhaven? I haven't forgotten my sailor's skills and you'll find it harder than ever to sign a crew in San Francisco."

"I'll be glad to have you, but as a passenger not a sailor. What is your interest?"

Bjorn pulled on his beard for a while, scratched his head, and finally said, "I would like to petition the King of Norway to lift my curse."

"King of Norway! You're crazy, my friend."

"That is what I want to do. I can read and write a petition to present to him. The king's name is Oscar of Norway and Sweden."

"I can take you over, but I cannot help with any king of a country."

"I understand. But I have a connection who can help if I ever get out of prison."

"Okay. I need about six weeks to finish my preparations and sign a crew. We'll stay in contact. Good luck with your petition and tell me where I can help."

Bjorn was overwhelmed and said, "Thank you for remembering me."

Richard said, "Your furlough is about up. You want to stay on good terms with the jailer don't you?"

After Porter left, Bjorn sat alone on the bunk and stared at the rough timber walls that a past workman had thrown together on the *La Grange*. Occupants before him scratched their names on the oaken columns of the cell. He carved into the post below the alphabet, Bjorn Amundson '51. He stared at the wall and thought,

Four walls to hear me.

He peered down the grim hallway lined with oak bars and cells holding other despondent squatters.

Four walls to see

But instead, he saw visions of the fjord leading to his home in Drammen. Thick forests of stately conifers caressed the channel for twenty-five miles. Summers there are the warmest in all of Norway. Vivid images of colorful Viking longboats stood out against the deep green hills. He wondered if his exiled Viking ancestor Bjorn the Bold felt the same on his return to Tønsberg. The last cell of the *La Grange* was home to the new Bjorn.

Four walls too near me,

The vibrant green Norwegian forests were in striking contrast to the hot muddy wetlands where the San Joaquin and Sacramento rivers met.

Closing in on me.

(Song by Marvin J. Moore, 1941)

He resumed reading Two Years Before the Mast, the account of California Richard Dana wrote seventeen years earlier. "I'll be damned. Dana published this book at the same age I am. He could read and write, but I'm still working on it."

Musing to himself, How can I prepare a petition to the king of Norway from half a world away? What is a petition anyway? I'll ask Alva in my reading lesson this afternoon.

The jailer rattled the lock with his key and said, "Ma'am, he's all yours." To Bjorn, he said, "You have a visitor."

Alva Dahl sat down on a little stool the guard brought in for her. "How are your reading lessons progressing?"

Bjorn said, "Very well. I can read ancient sagas."

"Excellent. You are the smartest student ever."

Bjorn smiled at the unexpected compliment since his teacher was normally stern and strict.

He cleared his throat and stared at the floor for a moment. With a resolute face, he looked his teacher in the eye and said, "I want a make a petition to King Oscar of Norway."

Alva's eyebrows shot up in surprise as nothing shook his confidence usually. "What do you want with the King?"

"My family has suffered from a Viking curse for a thousand years. Only the ruler of Norway can remove it."

Alva was aghast. "That is an ambitious goal. I can try to help but you are asking a lot." She shuffled her books and a slate board. "We have to start somewhere, and today is as good as any."

"What do I do?"

Alva Dahl rubbed her chin and adjusted her hat, smoothed her hair, and raised her nose before answering. "I have never petitioned the king, but my sister teaches in Drammen. She has a better reputation than I do, and might have connections."

Bjorn said, "I'm leaving for Norway in six weeks on the *Agilis*."

She chalked a line near the top of Bjorn's slate and wrote under it,

Introduction

Grievance

Reason for Action

Conclusion

"These are the parts of your petition." Alva pointed above the line, "You must have a title."

Bjorn looked confused and muttered, "I don't know what a title is."

"Why are you petitioning the king of Norway?"

"I want to end my family curse."

"Just a curse?"

"My ancestor named Bjorn the Bold served the famous Viking leader, Rollo. Bjorn was a berserker when they attacked the fortress of Chartres in Francia. The year was 911."

"Those berserkers were fierce. What happened?"

The Vikings lost that battle. It was their first defeat in Francia. Rollo made my ancestor a scapegoat and cursed him and his family forever."

"Nobody believes in those pagan superstitions."

"I lost my New Viking Gold Mine, they killed my best friend, Boudicca, and Brannan's thugs killed Jethro. That feels like cursed to me."

"Go on."

"I want the King of Norway to lift the burden of the shaman's curse. Rollo founded Normandy and forgot the curse. It still endures."

Alva put her hands on her hips in feigned disgust, "Why would they let a commoner into the palace to see his Majesty? You might have a better chance with his son, Prince Oscar Fredrik. He is interested in education and economic development and has explored other lands such as Iceland and America."

Bjorn said, "I must see the king."

Alva sighed, "One of my clients met Frederik Stang, the Norwegian Minister for Cultural Progress when he visited California. He is searching for successful immigrants in California and other places. You qualify I should think."

"What department will accept my petition once I get to Norway?"

"You are an ambitious young man, Bjorn Amundson, but I think you can do this. Start with a title that says what you want to do. Tell his Majesty points he should consider in granting your petition. Emphasize benefits to the King and Norway. I expect to see these sections in our next lesson. We will refine them from there."

After she left, Bjorn sat on his bench and said to himself, "This is a big thing, but I can do big things now that I read and write. Where do I start?

On a blank piece of paper using a quill pen that Maverick brought he wrote, "Title," He thought a while and said, "This is hard. I'll write the title later."

From the cell across the way, the crazy foreigner banged his head on the wall several times and said, "What are you mumbling about?"

Bjorn ignored him and wrote, "Introduction." Under it, he scratched, "My name is Bjorn Amundson. I am descended from Bjorn the Bold who served Rollo."

He tried to imagine what the response of the King might be.

"His Majesty will say, 'Who was your ancestor again?' "

"I would say, 'I am descended from Bjorn the Bold, the Viking berserker,' and his majesty will say, 'Are you crazy like the berserkers?'"

"Oh no, sir, I think clearly. I have a gold mine in California and two men working for me. One distills spirits and the other hunts game for our table. Sometimes he sells meat to outsiders. We are paid in gold that we add to our nest egg."

"'Yours is the initiative I expect from a Norseman. We establish cities to trade with. It is our tradition.'"

I would agree with his Majesty and present a gift of gold from my claim. The monarch would smile gratefully and I would follow up, 'Should it please your imminence, there is a small request.'"

"State your question."

"Our esteemed ancestor, Rollo, Duke of Normandy, directed a shaman to curse my family. I humbly request you to remove it, sire."

Bjorn said aloud, "That should work." He basked in his brilliance."

Maverick Hatfield, although badly injured in the attack on Brannan's store, managed to evade the posse. He and Joaquín Murrieta roped a stray horse and rode double upstream to the ruins of the New Viking Gold Mine. Maverick's mind cleared by the time Joaquín helped him dismount in what was left of the camp. The mound of dirt was no longer a lookout for Boudicca. The Hatfield retrieved a little jug of moonshine from a secret hiding place. They sat to talk.

Maverick lit his pipe and Joaquín lit a cigarillo.

"What a blowout," said Maverick to Joaquín after a sip of spirit as they passed the jug back and forth. "Sam Brannan got my twin and killed your brother."

"He is a mucho bad man," said Joaquín.

"Yet Bjorn sits in prison, and Boudicca lies under a gravestone." They sighed and lapsed into their private thoughts.

Maverick said, "I miss that big blonde man."

"Señor B'Horny is a good leader. Adios to Jethro."

"Have you been in prison?"

"Jail in California, prison in Mexico."

"Bjorn shouldn't be there."

"No!"

"I want to break him out."

"Yes! But how?"

Maverick thought for a while and picked up a stick. He scratched a diagram of the *La Grange* barge in the dirt. On a pointed rectangle for the barge, he marked R for the river side. Front Street ran along the wharf in connection with the gangplank. H Street came down from the center of town.

He said, "The hull of the vessel is moored in the river. They constructed the jailhouse six feet wider than the deck on each side. There are two stories of cells for the squatters. It's a top-heavy son-of-a-bitch."

Joaquín said, "I get scared and look the other way when I see a jail."

"We've got to rescue Bjorn."

"*Si, señor.*"

"Prisoners constructed the jailhouse. I met one after he was released. He told me the walls are strong and the cells are oak beams, but the floor out over the river is not so sturdy. The project leader over the construction was never in jail himself and didn't think of escape out the bottom."

Maverick outlined his plan. The first hurdle was to find Bjorn's cell which they hoped was on the first floor. A group of volunteers makes a diversion on the wharf. A small rowboat loaded with Chinamen sneaks up on the river side, and with their ungodly knives and swords chop a hole in the floor of the cell. They drop the prisoner into their boat and disappear before the diversion ends.

The ringleader said, "Bjorn talked about a woman teaching him to read. She visits once a week and can show his cell."

Joaquín said, "He should talk to me. I can read it."

"He might prefer a person of the female persuasion. We need the Squatters Association with us."

"My Grupo comes too."

"You and your men notify all the association members you can by tomorrow afternoon. We will meet at Front and I Streets and march one block to the *La Grange*. We'll make so much noise they'll never hear the Chinese pirates with those hook swords hack a hole in Bjorn's little cell. We'll escape across the river before the Sheriff's posse knows what happened. I hope we get Bjorn out before they even get there."

"That is a good plan, Mr. Maverick."

Maverick said, "I will talk to Alva Dahl when I limp my way to town."

Joaquín walked on up to his destroyed family camp where his relatives and friends were sleeping on the open ground. It was fall and the beautiful weather made the nights glorious under the stars. The distant calls of the coyotes and hoot owls made for a peaceful slumber. He said to his family members, "Tomorrow night we rescue our friend B'Horny Amundson. We owe it to him for the times he got us out of jail. Go to Front and I Street tomorrow afternoon."

He got a good reception.

Joaquín, working his way to each mine upriver, encountered rising anger at every jumbled mass of debris. Each represented Brannon's destruction of a man's dreams by his raiders.

He approached the highest encampment of Nisenan Indians with loud yells. "Hello. Hello, I come in peace and have no weapons." Several elders emerged from their triangular cedar bark huts of brush and mud. They faced Joaquín silently with their arms folded but listened as he explained his mission. "I would be honored for you to join us."

After a long pause, one elder said, "the great Kuksu spirit has spoken to me. It is true your companion disturbed the bones of our ancestor, but it is also true he honored him and overcame his error. I pledge my braves to join you tomorrow."

Maverick and Joaquín entered the ruins of the Lucky Ducky Pit. The leader who spoke a little English mixed his words with the Spanish accented words of Joaquín. Somehow, they talked to each other. All the Asians felt hopeless amid the onslaught of discrimination and welcomed even a small chance to fight back. Maverick drew a picture in the sand of a hook sword. He pointed to the edge and said, "Cut, cut, cut." He pointed to the shepherd's crook near the tip and gave a big jerk. The Asians nodded. The drawing of the broad blade and heavy weight of the weapon brought the same reaction and Joaquín simulated the decapitation of a prisoner. Their leader said, "Most good. We chop. Our blades defeat the Mongols in old times. Still work today."

Out-of-work men from other wrecked encampments prepared for the assault on the *La Grange* with gusto by sharpening their mining tools to razor edges. They didn't have much else to do since Brannan's vigilantes were evicting them everywhere.

Richard Porter asked three unemployed miners in rocking chairs on a front porch to update news of the squatters' riots.

They knew Bjorn and complained about Brannan's tactics. One said to the other, "We have to rescue Amundson."

Richard agreed with them and said, "Let's organize the others."

Bjorn didn't know his friend Richard Porter was as outraged as he was at the treatment of the settlers. Fellow gold seekers were furious with Brannan up and down the American River because Bjorn always helped them out in any difficulty or did them favors. It's what a Norwegian did.

By that afternoon, Richard and a handful of ex-miners appealed to thirty-five or forty angry men to muster a force at the wharf. Their call was, "We have to spring him out."

For weapons, they were armed with everything from fists to revolvers, to axes, to bows and arrows. All were evicted from their livelihoods by Brannan's shyster vigilantes or his lawyers under the ruse of being squatters.

They had a bad attitude.

They were mad.

They were dangerous.

They met at Front and I Streets, one block away from the *La Grange*.

Since their objective was to divert attention, not attack, they raised the biggest fuss they could. A motley fife and drum corps shrieked martial tunes and marched around the mob of squatters. Several men staged mock sword fights with their mining tools, careful to keep the sharpened edges away from their opponents. One man in tattered clothes jumped on a barrel and yelled, "Bjorn yes, Brannan down."

Chants of "Bjorn yes, Brannan down," swept the crowd.

The noise had the desired effect and several spies ran to the Sheriff's office.

Maverick pushed the tattered man off the barrel as he climbed up. "Quiet! Listen to me. There is a small guard stationed at the barge by the governor. Against as many as we are, it is powerless. Here is the plan. And remember. We are making a diversion not mounting an action. No shooting or killing." He pointed to the English speaking Asian and said, "Signal when you have Bjorn. He bowed.

The fife and drum corps marched, agitators agitated from the top of the barrel, ringleaders straddled the horse trough. The assembled crowd rattled their weapons, waved them in the air, and became an angry menace, almost but not quite yet out-of-control.

The sheriff and his posse galloped down I Street shooting into the air. "I order you to disperse immediately. This assembly is not allowed."

"Give us our land back."

"You are trespassing."

"I'm warning you, break it up before Brannan's Raiders get here."

Maverick pointed in the direction of the barge and ordered, "For'ard, march."

The fife and drum corps led at a smart pace, followed by the Evicted Squatter Association's Memorial Members that packed the full width of Front Street. They forced the frustrated Sheriff's posse to detour a block over to third Street. The two groups drove forward a block apart and converged on the *La Grange* at the same time. The Sheriff yelled to the guards, "Raise the gangplank and prepare to receive an assault."

Watching from across the river was the anxious group of Richard Porter, Alva Dahl, and Indians from several tribes. Four fierce Asians sat in a rowboat holding the antique Chinese weapons of warfare that defeated the Mongol hordes at the Great Wall.

Richard ordered, "Go!" when he heard the clash of the squatters and posse on the other side of the prison. Unseen by either collection of rowdies on the wharf, Chinese men with chopping tools pushed away from the far bank and rowed to the back corner of the barge with a few sweeps of their oars. The rescue force crawled into the angled braces under the overhang of the prison cells. They attacked the boards above their heads with fearsome energy. Chips flew as though a family of frenzied Oriental beavers was at work.

The Miwok and Nisanan Indian warriors were stoked too. They tied whistles to their shafts and lit them on fire. Born to archery competition, each tribe strained to release more screaming arrows over the rowboat than the other. The fire they ignited on the roof of the barge was secondary to their archery competition.

The sheriff was beside himself between the screaming arrows and the blazing roof. "Drop your damn gangplank," he screamed at the guard. Several posse members jumped aboard to pass buckets up to the roof. A disorganized fire brigade using buckets raided from Brannan's store dipped water from the river, but barely held their own against the flaming terror from the sky.

Feints by the August Association of Evicted Memorial Miner Member Squatters terrorized the posse and degenerated into a free-for-all.

Nobody paid any attention to the hidden rowboat at the back of the barge. No one that is except the occupant of the cell just above the overhang.

Bjorn could tell something big was happening on the wharf but couldn't make it out. He smelled the smoke from on top and yelled, "Jailor, we're on fire. Let us out. We'll burn to death. "

The jailer was fighting the fire with the posse and never gave a thought to his prisoners. It took all the bucket brigade's efforts to control the fire with flaming arrows raining down. Bjorn heard one firefighter say to the other, "Give me the Mexican war any time. This is crazy."

Bjorn could not see the boat underneath his cell but figured out something was going on from the vibrations on his feet. He called out his window, "Hey! Give me an axe and I'll chop from here." A big knife appeared outside the tiny window. His hand on the floor felt where the vibrations were strongest and he stabbed the knife there.

A massive blade punctured the floor and just missed his foot. He jumped a little to the side and chopped next to the opening, glad to have all his toes in contrast to his ancient ancestor. He waved to the Asians through the hole. "Hello there."

Other prisoners saw what was happening in Bjorn's cell and yelled, "Don't forget us? We want out too."

Bjorn yelled back between chops, "Sorry, you're on your own. Brannon's out to get me, not you."

The wicked sharp blades in the hands of the skilled Orientals ate a hole in the floor. One of them motioned to Bjorn to come through. He dropped his feet through the hole but his butt was too big—far larger than the Chinese's. Pulling out, a few quick chops around the edge enlarged the opening to Bjorn's dimensions. Just before he dropped through, Bjorn tossed the knife into the next cell. "All yours, go for it." The occupant started chopping.

Bjorn held his iron ball at the end of the chain and slipped through the new hole too easily. The awkward ball and chain unbalanced him and he fell into the river missing the boat. He sank like a rock or like a ball and chain.

In terror he screamed, "I can't swim." He kept screaming as his feet hit the bottom of the river at five feet depth. "Help! I can't swim." He stood on the bottom.

He kept screaming even as the Chinese miners pulled him into their boat and rowed like hell to the opposite shore. Safely on the beach, the Chinese leader lit a rocket. The red star in the air and the explosion stopped the melee.

Bjorn heard the familiar voice of his moonshine helper across the river. "We have made our point. Time to go home."

Richard Porter and Bjorn bowed to the Chinese and said, "Thank you for your help." They shook hands with big smiles.

Alva Dahl interrupted and said, "We have to go before Brannan gets here.

They rode rapidly away from the column of smoke still rising from the roof of the *La Grange* and the fire brigade leading from the bank of the river to the same.

In a great hurry, Alva said, "The grapevine says Brannan will execute you if he can. You have to leave town. We will disguise you so well it would fool your mother."

Bjorn helped Alva into her sidesaddle on a beautiful palomino. Richard slammed a huge sombrero on Bjorn and they jumped double on a horse. The poor overloaded animal and the palomino galloped around the edge of town to *Madam Pearl's Pleasure Palace*. They hustled through a side door before anyone spotted them.

Bjorn had never seen the little room they entered. Alva said, "This is going to hurt but there's nothing we can do about it. Sit in the chair."

Bjorn's eyes got wide and he said, "What are you doing?"

It's your most distinguishing feature."

"Not my beard. The ladies love it.

Alva said, "Sit still." She began cutting Bjorn's beautiful ash-blonde beard with scissors. He sat mute but several of the girls from the entertainment wing of the palace stole clumps of trimmings from the floor as souvenirs.

Her client looked like a freak when his beard was gone. The lower part of his face had not seen sunshine in years and the top part was sunburned as dark as a Norwegian can get, which is not all that dark. Alva said, "Time for your hair."

"No! I refuse to be bald."

Richard and the barber laughed and said, "Just enough trim to make you look civilized," Richard said, "There will be plenty of hair left, but it will fit under a hat."

The haircut was less drastic than the shave.

Alva said, "I'm sorry to cover this up but it's for your own good and it is only temporary. You are getting the same beauty treatment I give my girls. You like them don't you?"

"Not that well."

They finished Bjorn's disguise with a darkening skin toner and a vegetable dye to turn his ash-blonde hair into a muddy brunette."

Richard stepped back and said, "We've got a stranger in our midst. Who are you?"

Alva admired her handiwork and said, "I cannot do anything about your size. Walk slouched over like an old man and get a shirt with horizontal stripes. It will make you look shorter.

The new Bjorn groaned with regret at the passing of the old Bjorn.

Richard said, "Let's visit a blacksmith shop and lose your iron ball and chain. They're a dead giveaway."

The blacksmith looked up as Bjorn clanked through the door with his friend. Richard said, "I have bought a ton of ship's hardware from you. You need to remove this ball and chain right now."

The blacksmith said, "You're one of those squatters I've heard about. I'll bet you're just escaped prison. Brannan will run me off if I aid the escape of a prisoner."

Bjorn grabbed him by the collar and said, "I want it off now. Brannan is the least of your worries. His huge bulk convinced the stout short blacksmith of the wisdom of compliance. A hammer and chisel and Bjorn was free. He said to the blacksmith, "Throw that thing in the river. A ball and chain is torture from the devil and no man should ever have one."

The blacksmith agreed to dispose of the ankle bracelet. The two friends left in unshackled comfort.

19 - Danger on the Way and Maria

A tall stranger bent and trimmed, joined Alva and Richard at supper around a table in the dining room of *Madam Pearl's Pleasure Palace*. Richard said, "How can we help this Norwegian misfit present his petition to the King of Norway?"

Alva explained, "Any petition to the king must be in the correct form."

Richard said, "Diplomats around the world offer a gift before asking for a favor."

Bjorn said, "Alright, you two. I have been working on the petition Alva gave me. I have the Introduction and Grievance so far. But, how can somebody like me offer someone like the King a gift? A handful of golden pebbles?"

Richard said, "Maybe. High up people like to live well and hold fine objects in their hands. Here in Sacramento, right here and right now, you have an opportunity unknown in the history of the world."

Alva and Bjorn looked at him with wonder. "Go on," they said together.

"The salacious yellow metal, to which we have sold our souls, infects high men with colossal greed. You were producing ninety ounces a week of yellow lust, I mean dust, from the New Viking Gold Mine. There is a goldsmith from the old country in Monterey, south of San Francisco. The rumors are he can fashion splendid vessels of silver from the Mexican mines in San Luis Potosí. Perhaps he could fashion a goblet from your gold. Fit for a king, even."

"Huzzah! It can be fancy with garnets from the mountain outcrops," said Bjorn.

The excitement rubbed off on Alva, "If your artist can do engraving, I have a picture of the coat of arms from the House of Bernadotte. His Highness, Oscar I, would be impressed."

Richard said, "I'm going down to San Francisco tomorrow. Why don't you join me? Bring about sixty ounces of gold and your garnets. It is a short hop over the hills to Monterey and the goldsmith shop. It will be interesting."

They ended the dinner agreeing to make a chalice to present to the King of Norway. Nobody called it a bribe, even though it might look like one to an outsider.

Two steamboats, their boilers full of steam, were open to passengers at the dock behind the Sacramento ticket terminal. When loaded, they were ready to leave for foggy San Francisco from the heat of Sacramento. Vertical plumes of smoke rose from the twin smokestacks on each vessel that mimicked the giant Sequoia trees that grew twenty or thirty miles away in the Sierra Nevada foothills.

The *La Grange* prison barge was still moored at the far end, but Bjorn looked the other way happy to be free. He approved of the continuing rain of flaming, whistling arrows from the Indians across the river. It was the best chance to get even that they had experienced in many a moon. They were just about out of arrows though.

Richard said to Bjorn as they walked into the ticket terminal, "Remember to slouch. You look entirely too vigorous for an old man."

Bjorn bent over and slowly shuffled his way toward the ticket window. Richard said walking at his side, "We'll have to take one of these steamboats, unpleasant as they are. Urgent business demands my attention in San Francisco before we can leave for Boston and points east." The stagecoach beats a schooner to the bay, but not a steamship. Besides, our luggage is too big to fit on a stage.

Richard said, "Pull your hat down and stoop like an old fart. Don't look at anyone, especially those two armed guards in the corner. They are Brannan's henchmen watching for some scoundrel named Bjorn Amundson to leave town, whoever that is."

Bjorn said, "I hate them."

Richard chuckled.

Behind them, the door to the terminal crashed open with a dramatic flourish. In flowed the most astonishing woman that Sacramento had seen in many a year.

Bjorn said, "What has happened to Madame Pearl? She is dressed like the dancers in a Paris Concert Café."

Richard said, "There's her name embroidered in pearls on her back."

"Oh my God."

With the freedom of impropriety and enthusiastic abandon, Alva Dahl twirled her gorgeous skirt into a wide circle that revealed a glimpse of her bloomers. For emphasis, she planted her highheeled shoes and stopped directly in front of Brannan's guards. She looked to the side, pulled her right arm across her chest, and pointed her hand outward.

She looked across her palm to her right, and looking back to the front slapped her thigh. Pointing the right hand down she rubbed her inner thigh and stood up on her high heels. Palms rotated and hips swung like a Hawaiian hula dancer when she twirled to the center of the room.

Bjorn panted like a dirty old man, Richard stared, and the two guards lost all interest in scoundrels and pretty much anything else.

Alva sashayed to a support pole in the center of the waiting room. She reached high with a hand, straddled the pole, and spun down.

The waiting passengers burst into wild applause, at least the men did. The women not so much.

Richard slapped Bjorn's shoulder and said, "Keep your head down, you're supposed to be an old man, remember. Let's get our tickets."

Bright colorful posters scattered around the terminal touted the safety, speed, and sumptuousness of eighteen competing steamboats and posted their fares. The extravagant fares took their breath away and Richard said, "It takes a gold mine to pay for passage." All the lines displayed equal fares.

Passengers Upstream - $25.00
Passengers Downstream - $30.00
Staterooms - $10.00
Meals - $2.00
Freight - $40 to $50 per ton
Discounts may apply.

One poster caught their eye and Bjorn showed off his brand-new reading skills by reciting the contents.

Marianna Bell

The famed Marianna Bell is the finest steamboat in California. The new paint and gilding make her as trim as the day she was launched. The main saloon is one hundred and thirty by twenty-six feet. Ladies enjoy a saloon thirty-five by twenty feet.

This beautiful vessel is a sidewheeler equipped with an engine and boiler brought in pieces from Boston on a three-masted windjammer. The firm's best mechanics assembled her at Benicia. Success crowned her maiden run on August fifteenth.

Her boiler and the steam engine, the most powerful on the river at two hundred and fifty horsepower, enable the swiftest passage to your destination.

Bjorn slapped the brochure with the back of his hand, "I'd like those horses in the *New Viking Mine*. Would have except Brannan's got it now." Richard laughed and they shook hands.

That sounded pretty good, but then what company would advertise their vessel as second finest? A competing vessel offered other inducements to travelers. Richard read the poster.

Colonel Frémont

Named after the famed military leader, the Colonel Frémont is the newest and most modern steamboat plying the waters of the Sacramento River. The grand salon is as luxurious as any river boat on the Mississippi. Her chefs serve gourmet dishes at every meal in the sumptuous dining room.

The swiftest passage to San Francisco is guaranteed by the high pressure boilers of the latest design. They are rated for one hundred and seventy-five pounds.

The Colonel Frémont is destined, without a doubt, to be the premier steamboat on the Sacramento. She is worthy of the regard of all Californians.

That sounded pretty good too, but Richard the Cautious was in a hurry and said, "I prefer the proven performance of the low pressure boilers on the Marianna Bell. Limiting the boiler pressure to ninety pounds is safer."

The waiting room echoed with a great round of applause when Alva Dahl's impromptu burlesque show was over.

But the applause was interrupted by a violent argument between two captains, each of whom was accustomed to being obeyed explicitly.

"You are destroying the livelihood on the river with your ridiculous rates," said the tall one.

"Ridiculous?" said the short one. "You can't compete with your floating, aging derelict. Your old, low pressure boilers consume wood like a fire-breathing dragon which you have to feed from every wood yard along the river."

"Bullshit. Your secret is out. My pilot did one turn on the *Colonel Frémont*. He maintains she was the most out-of-control boat he ever suffered on."

"You stole my pilot, Kidd Morrison."

"He runs the best steamboat on the river."

"Not even close."

"He was lucky to survive the Colonel Fraudmont."

"We will see about that," said the short captain as he stomped out the door.

Bjorn's eyes followed the short captain down the wharf to the *Colonel Frémont*. His ears could hear the exhortations to the roustabouts. "Lively now. Snatch that firewood aboard. Don't you hear me? Move those logs down the hatch, now! My dear grandmother, may her bones rest in peace, was faster than you."

Richard said, "Let's go with the tall Captain and his courageous pilot." They bought tickets on the *Marianna Bell*.

The ticket agent commented the Bell had ample storage for firewood and only stopped twice on the run to San Francisco. "Under normal conditions, her boilers burn about a cord of wood an hour. I'm sure you know that a cord of firewood is four by four by eight feet."

Richard said, "That is a prodigious pile of wood, the size of the one we burned at the squatter's meeting. No wonder the tickets are so expensive."

The former shipmates strolled up and down the wharf admiring the assorted brigs, schooners, and other craft with their gleaming sails and disapproving of the smoking steamboats. "Now there is glory on the waves," said Richard.

Bjorn watched as the porter wheeled their luggage marked with distinctive marks over the gangplank to the *Marianna Bell*. He made sure that his locked trunk containing two hundred ounces of gold dust was safely handled. The stout wooden trunk disappeared into the maw below deck.

The Bell was berthed at the downstream end of the waterfront. Across the gangplank's, the stevedores toted aboard the last cords of firewood. She was ready to depart.

The *Colonel Frémont* was running behind despite the frenzied activity to load fuel for her boilers.

Bjorn said, "I'm glad you found me on the prison barge. I look forward to seeing Norway. I'm not so sure about meeting King Oscar."

Richard said, "The quickest leg of our trip is downstream. I have to secure a secret cargo for a Boston bank."

Bjorn thought about his request to King Oscar and wondered what was going to happen.

"It feels strange to have you as a passenger, Bjorn. I can't order you around, even as the master of the *Agilis*. It's been a busy year and a half since we jumped ship together."

Bjorn commented, "Look at this thing. The deck of the *Marianna Bell* is twice as long as the *Agilis*."

Indeed, the appearance of the vessel was imposing. The side wheels rose two men high and were even larger than those on the *Colonel Frémont* that was moored in the next berth upstream.

Two serious looking men chatted within an earshot of Bjorn and Richard on the wharf. They listened in.

One, with a demeanor of absolute confidence, said to the other who matched his appearance that the Sacramento River was more difficult to navigate than the Mississippi. His companion agreed as he described the early days in California as rough and dangerous. He noted the delta, where the San Joaquin river joined the Sacramento, was a maze of marshes and islands, and that there were no charts available. It was worse in the winter because fog obscured the visibility from the pilothouse.

The first said, "I couldn't make it without those echo boards along the river that reflect the sounds of our whistle. That's how I find the main channel."

A deafening scream from steamboat's whistle startled Bjorn and Richard. The conductor called out, "All ashore who aren't leaving."

They hastened to the railing and waved at the people who wished them bon voyage from the wharf. The scowling guards, they ignored until the ship was out of sight of the wharf.

Despite his revulsion to stinking noisy machinery, Richard was fascinated by the steam engine. He dragged Bjorn to the midship area to inspect the apparatus. The engineer gave them the thirty-second tour before he resumed his activities. He pointed out the pressure gauges on the boilers and how the steam moved pistons back and forth to drive the pair of sidewheels.

Bjorn examined the maze of pipes and said, "This looks like our moonshine still before Brannan's goons destroyed it. Both had pipes, vessels, and fire. I could run this, but I don't want to."

Richard said, "I hope she doesn't explode like New World did last week racing Wilson G. Hunt. Serves them right for rushing down this narrow river, especially during low water in the fall."

Black smoke from the twin stacks on each boat rose like pillars to the sky. Clouds of steam hissed from the safety valves on the boilers and circled the smoke shafts like a fog in the forest.

Bjorn heard one of the firemen below decks say, "Shovel that pine resin on the fire. The captain wants the blackest smoke we can get to impress the passengers."

"Explode?" Bjorn said as he looked at a column of pitchblack smoke pouring out of the *Marianna Bell's* smokestacks like a shaft to overhead hell.

Burning embers rained onto the deck, but the deck crew stomped them out before they ignited the wood.

"They go several weeks between explosions but be ready to swim. Oh—I forgot you can't swim. That might be a skill to pick up."

"Maybe after I learn to read."

Richard said, "I hope we won't need to swim."

They could hear the Captain speaking down the tube to the engine room. "What's the boiler pressure?"

"A full ninety pounds, sir."

"Very well. Carry on."

He rang the bell once and the engineer opened the valves to the steam engines. To the peals of the ship's bell, the gangplank rose and the stevedores loosened the mooring ropes. The *Marianna Bell* floated free to cheers on the deck and shouts from the wharf. The giant sidewheels turned backward with creaks and groans and a massive scream of escaping steam. Passengers and wellwishers ashore were impressed as the gorgeous hundred and eighty-foot boat backed into the main channel. The steam engines shook the deck, black sooty smoke belched from the chimneys, sparks fell all around, and the passengers on board chattered with excitement.

The captain rang the bell twice and shouted through the speaking tube, "Reverse engines. Quarter speed ahead."

The huge paddle wheels on each side shuddered to a stop and rotated in the opposite direction. Several passengers stumbled. The stately *Marianna Bell* turned her proud bow down the main channel to the fragrance of burning pine resin.

The first mate pulled the cord on the ship's whistle as she passed the schooner *Swiftness* preparing to embark. Since she was only a small sailing brig, she could not compete for a berth with the large and profitable steamboats.

"You're so slow by the time you raise 'Frisco you'll forget what year you left," hollered Bjorn as they passed. The gaggle of rowdy gamblers mixed with wine and brandy drinkers on the schooner's deck paid no attention to him. Neither did those on the *Marianna Bell.*

Richard and Bjorn stood near the open window to the pilothouse and eavesdropped on pilot and captain conversing with the engine room. Pilot Morrison said to the captain, "You, Sir, are the captain of the boat but I am the master on the water."

"True enough, but I will feel free to offer my opinion from time to time."

The pilot said, "This journey is burned into my brain. I know every bar, every shoal, every bluff, every slough, every bend, every sunken vessel, every beached vessel, every shoot, and every tree trunk. I know the easy water, the deep channels, the willows on the shore, high waters, low waters, night waters, the drift, and the trees that fall when the bank collapses. I have an instinct gained on the Mississippi and the Missouri rivers."

The captain said, "Fair enough. I yield to your experience."

A musician of questionable talents approached the keys of the primitive musical calliope. He roared out the strains of *Oh California* to the tune of *Oh Susanna*. The passengers celebrated by singing through the ending verse,

> *I soon shall be in 'Frisco*
> *And there I'll look around,*
> *And when I see the golden lumps there,*
> *I'll pick them off the ground.*

> *I'll scrape the mountains clean,*
> *My boys, I'll drain the rivers dry,*
> *A pocketful of rocks bring home,*
> *So brothers, don't you cry.*

> *Oh, California, that's the land for me,*

I'm bound for San Francisco,
With my gold pan on my knee.

Back at the wharf, the short captain was beside himself with fury at the delay in loading his firewood. Still, in good time the fuel got stashed aboard and her twin stacks posted their own giant poles of black smoke as tall as the sequoia forest.

Marked by three blasts on the whistle, the beautiful *Colonel Frémont* with creaks, groans, clanging and her calliope screaming, backed into the current and chased after the *Marianna Bell*. The Colonel was behind by twelve minutes and a mile and a half.

Richard was nervous about the floating trees in the river that could snag the hull of a passing vessel. He stared at the shallow bottom in places that were tricky to navigate or the mud that accumulated on the inside of a bend.

There were many bends. Flowing water eroded the outside of the river bends and moved the channel to compensate.

Every trip on the mighty Sacramento was a new adventure.

To embark even on a short voyage was a busy time for the Captain. But on the *Marianna Bell*, Bjorn noticed the pilot did more actual work than the Captain. He said to Richard, "That's different. How come?"

"On these river hulls, the Old Man's main duties are social. He entertains important passengers, lends his presence to the dining saloon, and upholds the pride and dignity of the steamboat. It is different from *Agilis* where I'm responsible for everything."

"Hmmm."

The air filled with a growing rumble and a chuf-chuf-chuf. "What's that?" said Bjorn.

Richard said, "The *Colonel Frémont* from behind us is impatient. I believe the Short Captain wants to race. I'll see if the Tall Captain wants my help."

The rival tried to pass, but the *Marianna Bell* caught her suction and forced her crab fashion onto a mud bank, where she hung up. Her captain managed to get her off in a few minutes with a blue string of profanity and a few nautical commands. She charged even harder in pursuit of Bjorn's vessel with both smokestacks erupting like volcanoes. The passengers on deck began pulling their six-shooters and made ready for a fight, but the short captain assured them he had a better idea. His chance came at the next sweeping bend in the river.

The *Frémont's* high pressure boilers had propelled the vessel to a high speed. As the *Marianna Bell* followed the main current of the river around a sweeping bend to the right, the sawed-off captain plowed the *Frémont* across the narrow muddy shortcut where she scraped bottom but forced her way through with momentum. Despite the two furious short rings of the bell on the Bell signifying, 'I intend to pass you on my starboard side', the *Frémont* jammed her bow into the front quarter of the Bell.

The Bell's captain rang three clangs for full speed astern, hoping to slide off and rake the *Frémont's* side and carry away one of her paddle wheels. But the impatient steamship was churning full power ahead, and in that position, the *Colonel Frémont* pushed the *Marianna Bell* sideways down the river for half a mile before the captains called it quits, or at least enough to separate. The encounter did not lead to open gunfire this time but it was a close call. The Bell was still ahead by a length.

A wave of excitement ran over her deck when a little portable table appeared at the railing carried by the Irish gambler. "Step right up, gentlemen, and place your bets. Will we reach San Francisco before they do?" A mob of betting men took form in front of the table with money and bluster. Thousands of dollars soon overwhelmed the table. The guard behind the gambler was Josh the gunfighter. He kept each hand poised over a Colt revolver to stop any trouble. His guard's black eyes scrutinized every man and woman in sight from under a low hat.

The Irishman said over his shoulder to Josh, "These chance encounters often lead to a race on the river. I love the excited passengers egging the captains to cram fuel into the boilers and beat the other boat. Gamblers are always itching to wager the *boat* they are on. They're addicted to the thrill of uncertainty."

Bjorn said, "I've heard stories of deliberate ramming, but this is a new experience."

Richard commented that escaping steam on the other boat suggested more pressure than was safe. "The whistle is higher pitched."

By this time the two ships were apart. The *Marianna Bell* surged ahead because of the superior skills of Pilot Morrison at navigating the hazards.

The *Colonel Frémont*, with her more powerful steam engines, gained on the Marianna Bell until they neared the shortcut to Steamboat Slough.

The Tall Captain on the *Marianna Bell* explained to is passengers that the pilot was in charge of the boat, and gave him time to engage the passengers. "You will notice Pilot Morrison is reducing our speed for safety as we approach the turnoff to Steamboat Slough. It's a shortcut."

The pilot yelled to the engine room and the *Marianna Bell* slowed. A waiter in the saloon stumbled and dropped a tray of expensive glassware. The Bell circled wide and entered the channel of Steamboat Slough. Several landings along the b text anks of the four-mile shortcut featured firewood for hungry boilers or a mooring to offload goods.

The Bell swung wide in the main channel. In her haste, the *Frémont* attempted a short cut across the inside. She scraped a new bar of silt that had accumulated overnight. The silt was held together by tangled brush from the trees the lumberjacks had felled to make firewood. The grasping grubby mess robbed the momentum from the Fremont. Her rival increased the lead by an eighth of a mile.

Bjorn and Richard on the deck could see the twin plumes over the trees behind them as they continued around the bend. Bjorn and Richard alongside the tall captain climbed on top of the pilothouse for a better view of the race. The captain hollered down to the pilot, "That fireman on the *Frémont* is a busy fellow tossing logs into her boilers. Her stacks look like volcanoes belching showers of burning embers."

The pilot said, "That happens when you overfire the boilers."

Born pointed to a hilltop and said, "Look at the farmer shaking his fist at the brush fire his embers started."

The Captain turned to Bjorn and Richard with a strange glint in his eyes and said, "I enjoy steamboat races. Our two red-hot river boats raging neck-and-neck, straining every rivet in the boilers gives me a thrill. The challengers groan from stem to stern and spout steam from innumerable pipes. The bows slice the river into long breaks of hissing foam. A horserace might be well enough, but nobody is ever killed, at least while I have been there."

The village of Rio Vista where the Steamboat Slough rejoined the main river was their next destination. It was the normal landing to take on a new supply of firewood.

Because the Bell had slowed to enter the slough, the *Frémont* was close behind because she proceeded at full speed. She came huffing and puffing. At the last minute, the Short Captain pushed the pilot aside and spun the wheel to starboard to aim her into Steamboat Slough. Of course, the vessel tilted to the outside and sent the passengers sliding across the deck to the port railing. The mass against the railing leaned the boat even more.

The *Marianna Bell's* pilot looked at the tilted smokestacks, "That is dangerous. With that list, she will be sloshing water in the boilers to one side and uncovering the flue pipes. They'll overheat and burst. I am glad to be well away from her."

Even worse, the *Frémont* hit a snag which twisted her about into the sloppiest turn possible. The water gauges showed low on the boilers, and the engineer sped up the water pumps. This flooded the boilers with cold muddy river water.

The Short Captain bellowed down the speaking tube, "What is your pressure?"

"One hundred and eighty-five pounds," replied the engineer.

At that instant, cold water cracked the overheated flue pipes in the boiler. The superheated steam blasted off the glowing red door to the firebox and threw burning logs onto the wooden floor of the engine room.

The deafened engineer shut the steam valve from the ruptured boiler to maintain the steam pressure to the other three boilers. In the twinkling of an eye, overheated flues in the other boilers expanded their length and pushed out the ends of two more boilers.

An unimaginable blast of superheated steam destroyed the engine room and the main deck. The destruction continued forward and severed the bow section which crashed into the river. A thousandth of a second later the pilothouse flew into the air. The occupants of the *Marianna Bell* watched in horror.

The Short Captain, the pilot, and several other people in the pilothouse and superstructure fell into the muddy water. The falling pilothouse crushed the swimmers when it crashed down on top of them.

Almost like a flying carpet, a sleeping man rode his mattress from his exploding stateroom to the water. The magic mattress landed flat with a massive splash. He woke up in confusion and said, "I did not do it," followed by, "Where am I?"

Exploding steam from the massive blast created waves on the water. The waves struck the *Marianna Bell* just before the cloud of superheated steam arrived. A sinister vision arose from the back half of the Colonel. It was wood smoke but not from the boilers. A fire dragon began eating the wrecked wooden superstructure of the late steamboat. The burning firebox contents blasted through the length of the grand ballroom and down the hallway to the promenade deck at the stern. Fancy lace curtains caught fire and ignited the ceiling, which sent flames racing across the outside decks. Stunned but uninjured passengers screamed and ran to what was left of the burning railings. Most of them jumped.

Debris that was hurled hundreds of feet into the air rained down on the unfortunate survivors and injured many more. The chaos was complete.

The Tall Captain shook his head and said, "We've had our differences, God rest his soul. He was doing what we attempt every single run."

The spectators aboard the *Marianna Bell* stared in silence at the burning Colonel Fremónt. None had ever seen a more dramatic moment.

Standing outside the pilothouse, Bjorn heard the Tall Captain order the pilot to turn the boat around, but the pilot refused to say, "If we turn broadside our momentum will create a tidal wave that swamps the survivors and the remains of the steamer. We best navigate by our stern upstream and render aid."

The pilot rang the bell three times and said down the speaking tube, "Dead stop. Stand by for dead slow astern."

The massive steamboat shuddered to a stop and began easing her stern toward the explosion. To ease the potential panic, the pilot said to the captain, "Thank God we have a sidewheeler. The rudder is near useless but I can guide her with the side paddles. "

Richard shouted at the men standing motionless on the main deck, "Follow me to the stern," and leaped down the stairs in two jumps. Bjorn tripped over seven more men. Anxious rescuers ran to the railing at the stern.

Bjorn said, "Everybody pick a section of the river and watch for survivors. Porter, stay in contact with the pilothouse."

The *Marianna Bell* closed the distance to the debris field on the water. Richard hollered to the pilot, "Dead stop."

Richard was the first to spot several survivors struggling in the water. He ordered the men to ditch their boots and coats and rescue the survivors. As he removed his boots, he looked at Bjorn.

"You too."

"But I can't swim."

"Off with the boots. It's time to learn." He pushed the terrified Bjorn over the railing as he dove after him.

Bjorn sank straight to the bottom, but instinctively propelled himself back to the surface with a mighty kick and began dog paddling.

Between involuntary slaps on the water, he saw a woman nearby calling for help. He splashed through the water to her. She flung an ivory-colored arm over his shoulder. He grabbed the other arm and at that moment learned to swim, to swim for two.

She screamed in hysteria. "Help me, I am drowning, help!" she screamed as she seized his long hair and pulled herself onto his broad shoulders. They sank beneath the surface but Bjorn thrashed them up. It took all his newfound swimming strength to keep their heads above the water. His injured party screamed all the way to the bank. Bjorn stumbled out of the water on his hands and knees with her on his back and deaf. They collapsed into the grass. Bjorn panted like a racehorse.

Several bystanders ran to help and lifted the woman passenger off of him. She turned to her rescuer and cried, "Oh my God, Bjorn Amundson. You saved my life." She hugged his dripping heaving body and rubbed his brown hair coloring off on her dress.

Despite his condition, Bjorn turned red with embarrassment. "Maria, I had no idea. Are you all right?"

"Oh . . . , oh . . . , oh . . . , I think so. I don't know what happened. I was standing at the railing admiring the other boat when I flew through the water. I was so surprised. I never flew before "

Bjorn said to the bystanders, "Please watch Maria. Others need my help. I'll pen you a letter at the Hacienda." He dove in to rescue more victims."

That evening, Richard and Bjorn sat exhausted at the bar as their trip continued. They enjoyed many shots of whiskey offered by grateful passengers.

Richard said to Bjorn, "Look on the good side. Maria's last image of you is washed clean of the mud, blood, and manure of the rodeo ring."

"Who told you about that?"

"You're the famous champion. The shortest bull ride known to man."

"María looked better then than she does now. I'll always remember her as a beautiful dripping kitten."

Richard laughed and said, "My friend, you rescued the kitten today. Eight other survivors call you a hero. And you said you couldn't swim."

"I did what I had to but I'm no hero. Folks did the same for me at the barge. I'm so sorry I couldn't save the bartender. The burning whiskey from the bottles overhead got him."

The patrons of the bar hung their heads in a moment of silence for the lost bartender.

"He poured a fine shot I must say."

"That he did."

Bjorn took a few moments to savor a shot of whiskey before asking Richard, "How long before we reach San Francisco?"

"The pilot estimated fifteen hours if we don't get hung up on a sandbar or encounter other delays. Fifteen hours and we can abandon this infernal contraption. I knew I didn't like steamships."

It was an uneventful trip for the rest of the down river passage but at a more sedate pace. On the way, Bjorn leaned against the bulkhead, and said, "After today, the King of Norway is not so intimidating. He is far across the pond and up the fjord. We'll see what he's like when we get there."

They docked at the new wharf in San Francisco alongside *Agilis*, which was being loaded for the departure to Boston.

Master Richard Porter took his leave. "I must see to the preparations for our departure. We'll visit Monterey tomorrow, where I believe you have business."

20 - Preparation

Bjorn and Richard asked about metalworkers upon their arrival in Monterey. A jeweler directed them to the shop of a famous artisan. "He is a master silversmith I worked alongside in the old country. He fashions the most amazing drinking cups you ever saw."

Bjorn and Richard made their way to the shop with a sign over the door written in peculiar medieval letters,

Johann Diefenbach
Goldarbeiter.

They encountered a wizened man seated at a workbench who was ham-mering a bar of silver. His shop was arrayed with an assortment of tools, in-cluding mallets, hammers, vises, files, pliers, punches, specialized anvils, and shaping forms. There were silver cups, dishes, and vessels in all stages of completion around the shop. They were amazed.

"Sprich Englisch?" questioned Richard.

"I speak English very well," said the hunched fellow who ignored their presence and continued to hammer the silver bar.

Bjorn watched the bar become flat and curl into a drinking cup. The skillful metalworker held up the vessel and grunted in satisfaction.

"What do you want?"

"Can you work in gold as well as silver?"

"No one ever requests a gold item."

Bjorn said, "Sir, I am asking."

"Gold is easier but too valuable."

"I have the gold."

"I ask you again, what is it you want?"

"I need a chalice."

"Why does a dummkopf like you want with a chalice? How can you pay for it?"

"I have a bag of gold from my New Viking Gold Mine." He placed his bag on the counter.

The reluctant goldsmith picked it up, looked inside, and gasped. "These hands never held so much gold in their life. You did not steal it?"

Bjorn got mad and said, "By God, I wrenched those nuggets from my claim with two bent hands as good as yours." He made a fist, but Richard stepped between the German and the Norwegian. Bjorn relaxed, a little.

The master artisan emptied the bag into a pan on a balance scale and almost overloaded it with the weight. "This is forty-eight ounces of gold." He took a nugget to a little anvil and tapped it with one of his hammers. The more he tapped, the larger the disc became. He tapped and tapped and the disc grew and grew.

He rested his mallet and said, "This nugget is the purest sample of gold I have seen. I estimate the purity at ninety-eight percent from its malleability. It is extremely rare."

Richard said, "I've seen the mine and I can vouch the contents of this bag are as pure as the nugget under your hammer."

The artisan said, "Gold works more easily than other metals but is uncommon because of its value."

Richard said, "it is not rare in Sacramento. Gold is so common it is worth less than food."

The artisan said, "I should not be surprised at what you are showing me, but I am."

Bjorn cleared his throat and said, "I want you to make a drinking cup. I have garnet stones to inlay around the rim." He poured a handful of ruby-red stones on the counter alongside the pan of gold.

"Humph, why do you want a gold cup? Is it to boast about your luck?

"It is a gift to his highness, the King of Norway."

"*Mein Gott im Himmel, der König von Norwegen!* No, I cannot do it." He slammed down his tools and glared at Bjorn.

Richard said, "Your reputation is the finest worker of gold in California. This will be your crowning accomplishment and make you famous."

"No."

"Your skill is renowned in the goldfields. Your fame will attract students to start a school of metalsmithing. Think of the apprentices you will have."

"All idiots without a doubt."

"Johann Diefenbach will leave a legacy as the master Goldarbeiter."

The craftsman relaxed a tiny bit.

"What would the outside look like?"

Bjorn thought a few minutes and said, "I am leaving for Norway in six weeks so a simple design is the best. I think garnets would be beautiful. And on the back, I would like to engrave a coat of arms." He pulled out the copy of the Norwegian coat of arms that Alva Dahl had given him."

"It is not possible. Fine craftsmen must have time to do the job right. You do not want a mistake, do you?"

Bjorn said, "My goblet must not be too heavy. Thirty-two ounces is about right, and the rest of the gold is your fee."

The goldsmith thought, lifted the gold, tapped his fingers on the workbench, walked around the room, muttered to himself, and sat with his head between his hands.

"It is not possible to fashion this in six weeks, but I cannot give you a guarantee. I know a jeweler down the street who will polish your garnets. My cup might be good enough for the Prince of Norway, but it will not be an appropriate gift for the king. I see black forces arrayed against you."

Bjorn was overwhelmed at the size of his request but persisted, "I want to thank you for your generosity, sir. I am staying at the home of Master Alex MacIntyre in Oakland. He is a retired ship's master at this address."

He wrote out Alex MacIntyre's mailing address of his new home in Oakland, across from San Francisco. "He owns *Agilis*, the ship that will carry your chalice to Norway. Let me introduce the Master of *Agilis*. Richard Porter. We sailed together and I expect this will be a good trip."

"Leave me alone. I am busy."

"How do you sculpt this cup?"

"Cannot you leave me in peace?"

"We are interested in your skills. These are beautiful examples around your shop."

"I forge the nuggets into an ingot. I hammer a section into a six-inch circle and tap the middle to curve it into a cup. The flat base and stem, I fuse on to finish a vessel." He waved his arms nonchalantly at works in progress.

"What is on the base?"

Richard said, "Let me speak for Bjorn since I saw one in a museum. Your hallmark of authentication is required. We also want NVGM for the New Viking Gold Mine."

Bjorn said, "I want the head of a cougar and a BA for Bjorn Amundson. Is there room?"

"It takes a lot of space but I'll see what I can do. And the coat of arms on the side?"

"Absolutely."

"Very good. I have forty years of forming beautiful objects. I am sure you will be pleased with my work."

Richard and Bjorn shook hands outside the little shop. "What a master you found. Did you see those fabulous things around his shop?"

"Glad to be of service, my friend."

Bjorn made the rounds of his old haunts in San Francisco and marveled at the changes in a year and a half. The surrounding tent city carpeted more hills and new buildings had sprouted up in competition. He bought a sea portmanteau with a lock and supplies for the journey. New was his razor since he no longer wore a beard. Also new were three books he could now read, a pipe, a pencil, and sundries. There was barely room for his cougar fur coat. He released his rented room and arranged to store the bear rug. He wrapped and rewrapped the chalice in his cougar fur coat, and placed it in the center of his new chest. The porter stowed it in the new stateroom on the *Agilis*. His room was tiny but had been carved out for him as an honored passenger.

Bright the next morning, Bjorn mounted the gangplank in high style, far different than his desertion from the same ship the year before. Dame Fortune smiled on him in the goldfields, even as she frowned on ninety-nine percent of the other forty-niners, but even she could not protect him from Brannan's malfeasance.

Master Richard Porter welcomed him aboard with his hand outstretched. Bjorn's old habits from his days as a sailor took over and he said, "Master Porter, sir, at your service."

Porter, which was his customary name at sea, laughed and said, "You're my passenger, Bjorn, not a seaman. I wish you a bon voyage with us." They shook hands.

"You have the run of the ship, but I do have one rule."

"What's that?"

"Passengers keep their hands off my sails."

They hugged each other, roared, and pounded their backs as they recalled their first trip up the Sacramento River. Impatient at the slow progress of the schooner, they had retrimmed the sails for more speed. She was faster all right, just before she plowed into a new sandbar. They were delayed twelve hours waiting for the rising tide to free her.

Bjorn said, "I didn't think a riverboat captain could get so angry over an honest mistake."

"You haven't seen me. If your hands itch to pull a line, I'll arrange a tug-of-war between you and your choice of three ablebodied sailors."

"Duly warned, sir."

"Richard please, not sir."

Bjorn kept an eagle eye on his locked trunk as a deckhand wheeled it up the gangplank. He followed it to his stateroom, where it took half of the floor space. He knew Master Porter's quarters were not much roomier because *Agilis* was not a large vessel.

Bjorn surveyed the frenetic preparations to embark and thought, I used to be part of that. I can't say I miss it, but I know what it means.

Porter said, "Meet the first mate, Oscar Jones," as he introduced the man next to him. They shook hands.

Jones got a wide grin on his face and said, "Bjorn Amundson. It's a small world and I'll never forget you rescuing me."

Bjorn said, "I'll be damned. The last time I saw you, you were lashed to a broken spar and abandoned overboard. How are you?"

"I am the mate and doing well."

"Glad to see you."

Master Porter said, "The tide flows, Mr. Jones. Please set the sails."

Jones was the officer of the deck and bellowed, "Prepare to set sail."

The crew snapped to attention and several tars erupted from the forecastle.

"Lay aloft."

Eight sailors scrambled up the shrouds to the yardarms.

"Loose topsails. Loose topgallants."

The men aloft untied the gaskets that wrapped the sails to the yardarms.

"Sheet home topsails. Sheet home topgallants."

The sails fell into magnificent white clouds hanging from the yardarms.

"Brace around. Lay on deck "

The sailors braced the sails to catch the breeze and the *Agilis* tugged against her anchor. Sailors lying aloft descended to the capstan.

"Weigh anchor."

"Wait! Wait! I want to come with you." A man frantically rushed down the wharf.

Porter said, "What's this?"

Bjorn said, "Maverick. Where have you been? I lost track of you."

"Please, sir. I'll sweep the decks, I'll do anything you want but take me with you."

Porter said, "Avast weigh anchor." The *Agilis* with her filled sails dragged her anchor along the seafloor.

"You know this man?"

"He worked for me. He's a good man and a whale of a cook."

"A sea cook was the one hand I couldn't sign. If you say so, I'll bring him on as cook."

"Thank you, Mr. Porter."

"Come aboard."

Maverick threw his ditty box to the deck and leaped over the widening gap. Willing hungry arms pulled him aboard and slapped him on the back. Somebody said, "I'm hungry already. I remember that famous barbecue you made for our Squatter's meeting. Damn, that was good."

"Weigh anchor."

Willing hands rotated the capstan and raised the dripping anchor amid loud creaking and clunking. They lashed it to the railing.

Bjorn saw the edge of the wharf smoothly slip away and realized he was at sea again. It felt good.

He said to Porter, "We Vikings traveled the blue oceans farther than anyone else. You can thank me when you please."

Porter said, "That's true. Modern ships are bigger and faster but those Norse mariners had real balls."

Bjorn was astonished at the change in Master Porter's demeanor. He became a tyrant barking instructions to the man at the helm. "Watch those redwood trees on the eastern shore. Line up those tallest trees with the tip of Yerba Buena Island coming up. You will avoid a collision with Blossom Rock."

He pointed out the conspicuous trees several miles off.

"I had a tragedy on Blossom Rock and killed my best friend as a result."

The good ship *Agilis* that exited the San Francisco Bay was manned by a fine crew. Porter's reputation as a good master to sail under encouraged the few hands willing to leave the goldfields to sign on. Richard said, "I finally signed a good crew, but I had to provide references from previous sailors before anybody would join me."

"Remember me?" A gaunt man with a spring in his step shook hands with maverick and Bjorn. "I sold you the equipment from my failed diggings. I hope they worked out."

Maverick said enthusiastically, "They worked out real good. You should have seen the still we built in the moonshine we made. We found a farmer to buy corn from and had a thriving enterprise until Brannon got jealous and destroyed our operation. I want to thank you for your help."

Bjorn said, "Welcome aboard my friend. We'll grow no corn here. I'm glad to see you're back on your feet."

"I'm an ordinary seaman these days, and glad of it. You will be happy to know I still have your nuggets as souvenirs and I did not buy a revolver to rob the banks."

Bjorn slapped him on the shoulder and said, "Good man."

Bjorn and Porter savored the breeze as they rounded the point of Lands End and sailed into the open waters of the Pacific.

Porter said, "I relish the air of the sea without that smoke and noise. The winds look good for our trip down the coast. The current from Alaska and Russia helps."

Bjorn stumbled against the railing and said, "I've lost my sea legs. I'll find them and a day or two, but it feels good to be back on the water. I am looking forward to our jaunt to Boston and my old home in Drammen, Norway."

The voyage past San Diego and south to Valparaiso, Chile, was uneventful for Bjorn as a passenger. There were times, though, when he got bored and couldn't help himself. He clambered up the rigging as a lookout for what lay ahead.

What they met was an endless armada of sails. There were brigs, brigantines, schooners, clippers, hermaphrodites, and anything that floated or mostly floated. Belching steamers were in the mix, as were a few rowboats. The fleet was streaming north to join the gold rush insanity in Sacramento. Bjorn waved and shouted from the rigging a hundred feet up, "Good luck. I left plenty for you."

He did not mention that Brannan was ejecting squatters from every claim he could, and harassing or jailing those that he could not.

The nights got warmer and the days got hotter as the *Agilis* worked her way south. Some five weeks later, Jones made an announcement after taking a reading with his sextant. "We can't see them, but the Galapagos islands are about three hundred miles to our starboard."

Bjorn looked at Porter who looked at Jones who looked at the tars on deck. All but one had a big grin. Maverick Hatfield said, "What?"

Jones cleared his throat and stood tall with his nose in the air as he said, "Mr. Hatfield. We have entered the realm of King Neptune."

"Who?"

"He has informed me we have a scurvy pollywog on board and may not cross his equator."

"So?"

"Have you met the God of the Sea?"

"I don't know anybody named Neptune."

Jones looked at the assembled company and said in a loud voice, "You are hereby called to the court of King Neptune, attended by Davy Jones and her Highness, Amphitrite. But first, you must dress for the occasion." Several tars pulled Maverick's clothes off and redressed him backward. Maverick looked up to see his Majesty King Neptune sitting on the capstan.

Maverick was bewildered to see the sailors had donned the most outlandish costumes. Most astonishing of all was the giant King Neptune with his long flowing muddy blonde hair. He wore a dramatic white robe and carried a trident in his right hand. The brass crown with pointy teeth was polished to a brilliant shine.

Lecherous pirates tied Maverick's wrists with a rope looped through the knots to lead him around the ship like a prisoner. Crew members cracked raw eggs on his head, spread mustard on his face, and dumped flour on top.

"Look, a ghost. Wash him off." A bucket of foul bilge water did the deed with glee.

Pulling on the rope, a deck cadet led the stinking pollywog into the presence of his Majesty.

Maverick put on a brave face as the charges were read. Porter dressed as a clerk of the deep spoke first, with all the seriousness of a vaudeville clown.

"You have maliciously violated King Neptune's realm." An attendant alongside was dressed in the cheapest drag imaginable as King Neptune's wife.

The crimes were read aloud and included spying for Brannan, poisoning the population with moonshine, and slaughtering God's sweet and lovable creatures known as wild hogs, to say nothing of blistering fish from the deep in a large frying pan.

"His August Majesty of the Deep is offended by your odor. Wash him off."

A net fell over the prisoner and drew tight. The thing was hoisted aloft like a cured ham so that the flesh in the net swung free. Buckets of seawater drawn from the railing washed the crud from the accused. More buckets of rinse water were still required, and the net spun round and round. The rotating ball was lowered to the deck and a very green Maverick was unwrapped. The assembled crew gave a great cheer and he wobbled to his feet.

Now that you are decent, you may kiss the Royal Baby's belly and rescue the royal olive. A fat sailor coated with grease exposed an olive glued in his naval. They pushed Maverick to retrieve it, while buckets of water continued to douse him as well as the entire crew. On his hands and knees, he managed to flip the olive overboard with his tongue but his face was still covered in grease.

King Neptune held up his hand to conclude the ceremony. His crown was slipping off and the very last of his brown hair dye marked streaks down his white robe. The Royal baby was soaked. The Queen was a mess. Everybody was soaked.

With a dramatic flourish, King Neptune handed Maverick a certificate he had written by hand in an elaborate script. It read:

Ancient Order of the Deep

This Certifies That
Ordinary Seaman Maverick Hatfield
having crossed the equator in the Agilis, Richard Porter Master,
on January 12, 1851, 00° 00' 00' Latitude and 87° 43' 22" W.
Longitude, and having been initiated, then and there, into the
solemn mysteries of the realm of the raging main, is and should be
recognized as a
TRUSTY SHELLBACK
DAVY JONES by order of NEPTUNUS REX
His Majesty's Scribe Ruler of the Raging Main

"Don't lose this or you'll be initiated again."

Maverick took the ceremony in good spirits. "Never has this Tennessean heard of such an initiation. I'm proud to be one of you." The men crowded around to slap his shoulders and give him hugs of brotherhood.

Bjorn that is King Neptune, said, "This ritual dates from far before Christ. Welcome to the Order of Shellbacks.

The following twenty-eight days south were not eventful. Pushing south from Valparaiso, Porter and Bjorn discussed the Drake passage south of Cape Horn. Bjorn said, "I have seen the Drake passage like the Drake Lake occasionally and often raging in the Drake Shake of man-killing, ship-eating storms."

"I plan to round the official cape on the Island of Horns as closely as possible. Let's pray for good weather."

The Drake Passage past the white lighthouse on Cape Horn was beautiful. Prevailing winds flowed west to the east and carried the *Agilis* from the Pacific Ocean to the Atlantic Ocean amidst sightings of whales, dolphins, petrels, albatrosses, and penguins.

Porter said in a low voice, "An albatross carries the spirit of my friend, Kawai, who drowned between Hawaii and San Francisco. That may be him up there now." He waved, "Go with God."

After over a year in the hot Sacramento desert, Bjorn was cold and wrapped up in his serape that showed off to good advantage his flowing hair.

Porter reminded the crew, "Remember, in this weather, one hand for you, one hand for the ship."

Porter guided the *Agilis* through the Drake Passage around Tierra del Fuego and northeast toward Rio de Janeiro. He said to Bjorn, "Thank God we have no damage needing repair. We can bypass the expensive Falkland Islands."

The leg to Rio took forty-three stormy but uneventful days. Bjorn welcomed the warming temperatures and a chance to see the beautiful harbor of Rio de Janeiro. With the luxury of time cruising north along the coast of Argentina, the passenger wrote letters to María Rojas and Alva Dahl. He was proud of his literary skills and wrote in a large script with a set of new quill pens, describing the experience with every big word he could think of. He addressed the envelopes and entrusted the precious documents to the steward on the *Surprise* to deliver them in California. She was the swiftest vessel destined for San Francisco and was famous for her gilded eagle figurehead.

Porter released Amundson to visit Rio for two days while he focused on replenishing his food and water supplies. The massive bureaucratic paperwork took a day.

That evening, a collection of sea captains gathered in the grand salon to swap stories and catch up on the latest news. One experienced mariner cleared his throat and said, "The law is an ass. I'm here to tell you the tobacco that fills our hulls requires the diligent labor of slaves to grow. It is the same in the States where cotton replaces tobacco. Back in 1794 President Washington signed a law prohibiting Americans from outfitting a slave ship, but the custom continues unabated. Brazil started the practice a long time ago."

Porter said, "that is news to me. That must be why the *Agilis* was launched in Bremerhaven, Germany."

A ruddy sea captain, with silver whiskers looked at him askance and said, "She looks fast enough to outrun a slave patrol boat from the United States navy of England."

"She is fast for sure. Last year I won a race between San Francisco and Honolulu against the *Zebra*. My *Agilis* can outrun anything except a school of dolphins."

"The *Zebra* you say? You mean Hornigold's Hellship? You were lucky the ruthless bastard didn't ram you."

"He did and tried to board us to boot. We still won."

"As I was saying, the sea lanes of Charleston are getting tense. Cargoes of cotton trade to England by day. Despite the ban of 1831, slave merchants manage to smuggle African unfortunates into the same ports in the darkness. I've seen pitched battles between patrol sloops from the northern states and slave ships from the south. I mention this for the benefit of Captain . . . , what did you say your name was?"

"Master Richard Porter."

"All yes, Mr. Porter. The visage of *Agilis* is quite that of a slave-carrying ship, and her speed reinforces that impression."

Porter said, "My command was converted to a merchantman in 1845. I only trade goods from California in my hold." That the ballast of the *Agilis* was several tons of gold didn't need to be mentioned.

"My advice to you, sir, is to stay far offshore from Cuba to Philadelphia. Watch for USS *Perry* or USS *Germantown*. They are aggressive in chasing suspected slavers and they will give you grief if they succeed.

I would point out that Lieutenant Davis on the *Perry* captured the *Martha* with slave paraphernalia on board but no actual Africans. Nevertheless, he sailed her as a prize to New York. The authorities condemned the vessel and demanded a bribe of 3000 dollars to let the captain escape prison. The law is an ass today."

Another Captain joined in. "Common decency induced me to rescue two negroes thrown overboard, doubtless from a slaver. I had a hot time with those same authorities, I want to tell you, to explain I was carrying them as free men not slaves."

Porter to change the subject said, "On the whole, Rio de Janeiro is not a bad port to replenish supplies. The harbor is safe and commodious. There are unlimited fruits. Fresh Beef (though first cousin to shoe leather and bad) is plentiful and jerked beef the same. Rum, sugar, and molasses are good and cheap. Tobacco is cheap, but not good.

Their mines yield gold but at a high cost of lives. Forty thousand Africans are imported each year on the king's account. Still, the darkies died so fast that twenty thousand more were drafted from Rio.

Precious stones are so abundant they limit collection. The Viceroy sends a troop into the deposits to collect the quota. It takes a month. After that it is death for anyone in the gem country until the next year."

Porter excitedly said, "Wait till I tell Bjorn. His problems in Norway were trifling compared to Brazil."

The impromptu tour guide continued, "The entrance is narrow but the sea breeze which blows in every morning makes it easy to reach a mooring. Any number of ships can tie up in five or six fathoms of water.

The river and the whole coast abound with a greater variety of fish than I have ever seen. The sea is home to mackerel that bites any hook dangling in the water.

In short, this country with little industry of produced unlimited necessities and luxuries prospers, even under the direction of the Portugese. I take them to be the laziest and the most ignorant race in the whole world."

Porter said, "Tell us your real opinion."

The ruddy Captain's parting advice was, "In the hands of a competent crew, the . . . what was your ship's name again?"

"*Agilis.*"

"Ahem, the *Agilis*, in the hands of a competent crew can outrun a war sloop except straight into the wind. The brig is better to maneuver. You best keep a sharpeyed watch aloft at all times."

Porter said, "I have just the man."

Master Porter and passenger Amundson turned their brig and thoughts north leaving the port of Rio de Janeiro. Porter ached to see Becky Revere in Boston. He hoped she remembered him after she prepared a getaway pack three years ago when he ran away to sea. It seemed like a lifetime since his first roundtrip from Boston to Charleston.

The dangers of Cape Hatteras remained clear in his mind. He remembered how the first mate described the navigational hazards of the Diamond Shoals just off the Cape. "It is more difficult to escape them than to recognize them. Those barrier islands have sunk hundreds of ships. They call this the graveyard of the Atlantic."

Amundson added his thoughts. "The *Agilis* looks like a slave ship because she was. Her profile remained after the changeover to a merchantman, and we can be accused of engaging in that vile trade."

From the latitude of Charleston and about fifty-eight miles offshore, Porter prepared to run the gauntlet of Hatteras. His first command was unusual but made sense. "Mr. Amundson, I know you are a passenger but I also know you are a superb seaman. If you would be so inclined, the *Agilis* would be grateful for you to stand the lookout through these treacherous waters."

"It would be my honor, sir, if I can help."

"Please come to my cabin." He laid out a series of charts extending from the Florida strait between Cuba and Florida north past the Bahamas to Cape Hatteras. On a separate sheet of paper, Porter sketched the coastline and the location of the Gulf Stream. "It is about sixty-five miles wide depth unknown and flows at four knots. If we find the western edge, it will double our speed to Boston. The danger is the Diamond Shoals that extend eight miles east from the Cape. They shift bottom with every storm."

Amundson said, "I was through that area twice and saw stranded vessels both times."

Porter continued, "I need you to guide us into the Gulf Stream by watching the whales, measuring the water temperature, and noting changes in the water color. It is your responsibility to grasp the benefit of the Gulf Stream and reduce the chance of grounding on the shoals."

Amundson added, "I can see changes in the depth from aloft as well."

"I expect you to keep the navigator Mr. Jones and myself well informed, is that clear?"

"Yes sir. With the full moon, I can watch through the night. I suggest the *Agilis* drop to half speed after dark. If we are beset by scudding clouds it would be prudent to heave to."

"I agree on heaving to. This period of perils will persist for a day and a half or two days. We are in your hands."

Porter mulled over the words of the captains from the salon in Rio. "Mariners must pay attention to shifts in depth that can occur at random spots in the sound."

"If it were me I would be 25-45 miles off Hatteras to catch the stream north since your next stop is Boston."

"The flat islands provide no natural landmarks, and you can run aground in storms before spotting land and realizing your predicament."

"Most war sloops chasing slavers are armed with carronades for the economy of manpower."

They were making good progress toward Cape Hatteras under moderate winds that morning when low scudding clouds decorated on the horizon. Amundson lay aloft and shouted updates about the occasional whale, water colors, and ocean depth. He noted changes between pilot whales and longfin whales who prefer different waters.

The enthusiasm of the day evaporated when Amundson spotted a tall sail approaching from Cape Lookout.

"Ship ahoy, stern to port."

Porter ordered, "Raise the Norwegian flag."

First Mate Jones ordered the Stars & Stripes lowered and the Norwegian flag raised that displayed a red cross with a black accent. Maverick Hatfield, the cook, heard the commotion and left the galley to observe the action from the bow. It was a new exciting experience.

Porter ordered to set all sails and outrun the approaching vessel. The two ships were relatively matched as the sails off their stern gained slowly.

Amundson called from atop the mainmast, "Incoming att . . . .," but the whistle of the cannonball over the bow cut short the announcement. Hatfield gave a loud cry and fell bleeding the deck. The cannonball had ricocheted off the anchor that was lashed to the railing and broken his thigh bone on the way to splashing to starboard. Jones ran to the fallen man, "Not our cook! He's the most important man on board."

Porter hollered, "The shot across the bow is their warning. The patrol must have mistaken our Norwegian flag for the Danish flag since the only difference is their flag has no black accents. But

Denmark was active in the slave trade to the West Indies until two years ago."

A second whistling cannonball punctured a hole in the forward jib sail, but it did not slow the *Agilis*. Porter ordered, "Mount every foot of canvas we have."

Oscar Jones said, "All sail mates and it quick."

Amundson from the top rigging had excellent eyesight and said, "Her captain is enraged. He must be behind his quota of capturing slavers this year."

Indeed, the captain of the sloop was so intent on capturing a slaver for a prize that he forgot his seamanship. The peal of two bells signaled he would pass the *Agilis* on his starboard side. The intent was to deliver a broadside as he passed.

Amundson called out, "Shallow water off port."

Porter ordered, "Alter course two points to port."

From above, "Shoals approaching."

Jones said, "With respect, sir, we are in danger of running aground."

Because the war sloop altered course to cut off *Agilis* and gain ground, the third cannonball missed entirely.

Amundson called out, "Nigh onto Diamond Shoals."

Porter said, "Five points to starboard."

The *Agilis* made a sharp right turn into deeper water and demonstrated her superior maneuverability. It was the war sloop who did not turn in time. Her distracted Captain couldn't believe it. His command shuddered to a stop aground on a Diamond Shoal. His wild firing of the carronades on deck missed the *Agilis* by hundreds of yards.

Amundson said, "Back into the Gulf Stream. Well done, sir."

Porter commented to Jones and the crew, "That was a close call. They tried to intimidate us into surrender. They don't want to damage the ship for fears there are slaves aboard, but they do want to capture our vessel as a war prize. Hoist the Stars & Stripes. There's a double ration of grog for everyone tonight."

"Begging your pardon, sir, might I have a moment," said Bjorn when they passed Nantucket on the way to Cape Cod.

"Yes?"

"I would like to call on the Norwegian Embassy in Boston if there will be time."

"It would need to be quick. Why?"

"My countrymen help harvest ice from Spy Pond just outside Boston. They work for the Tudor Ice Company to bring ice into Boston. Frederic Tudor started this company when he was twenty-two years old, younger than I am now. He ships ice to the Caribbean, and India. Ice from Norway cools London in the same way ice from spy pond cools New York. I want to see how they do it."

Agilis rounded Cape Cod and anchored in Boston. Porter discharged a load of gold bars for Boston banks, and a moderate cargo of hides, tallow, and goods from California. But the value of the other cargo barely equaled the value of a single gold bar—a far cry from its value in California.

Richard Porter was not lucky with his love. He asked people from the Concord area if they knew of his girlfriend, Becky Revere, but they didn't know her. They said that after old man Podwinkle drank himself to death, his family dismissed his indentured servants and sold the Podwinkle farm. Richard addressed a letter to the general delivery, Concord Massachusetts, still hopeful.

He opened the lid to his old sailor's ditty box where he carved her image from memory. A companion sailor and an extraordinary master woodcarver on his first trip, who was an escaped African slave, taught him how. Porter sealed his letter with a long, lonesome sigh.

Leaving a message for Bjorn, Porter rented a horse for two days. The half-a-day's ride to the site of the Podwinkle farm was disappointing. The current owners knew almost nothing about Podwinkle and had never heard of Becky Revere. That night at the Colonial Inn in Concord, he composed a long letter to Becky and dropped it off at general delivery in the Concord post office the next morning. He returned to Boston a dispirited man.

Bjorn and Porter turned their attention to his petition.

Porter said, "I have experience with bureaucrats from around the world. They're all the same."

Bjorn objected, "King Oscar of Norway is not a bureaucrat. He is the big bear in the forest."

"You can't believe the enemies that hound him. We need an entrée to even enter the court. You are a commoner asking to see the king."

"What's an entree?"

"A person to guide us through the bureaucracy and into the presence of the King. The mountains surrounding the New Viking are nothing compared to the obstacles lurking in the procedures of the Norwegian government."

Bjorn did not say anything.

"I met the son of King Oscar at a trade conference in London. He had Norway's Minister of the Interior Frederik Stang with him."

"What does my petition have to do with the interior?"

"Stang is founding a school of agriculture and has agents gather information about Norwegian immigrants dispersed around the world. His motto is to serve the "People's Prosperity, Health, and Formation," at home and abroad."

Bjorn said, "Norwegians are leaving Norway because of the book Ole Rynning wrote in 1838 called A True Report on America for the Enlightenment and Benefit of Farmers and the Common Man.

It encouraged Norwegians to come to the United States. That man wrote the oldest piece of poetry by a Norwegian immigrant.

Beyond the surge of the vast salt waves
Deep hid lies Norway' rocky shore.

But longing yearns the sea to brave
For dim oak forests known of yore.

The whistling spruce and glacier's boom
Are harmonies to Norway's son.

Though destiny, as Leif and Bjorn,
Call northern son to alien West,

Yet will his heart in mem'ry turn
To native mountains loved the best,

As longs the heart of a lone son
To his loved home once more to come.

Bjorn said, "I saw him give a lecture that Miss Dahl dragged me to. He might make an example of my prosperity when I present the goblet to the king. Maybe he will take my petition."

Bjorn skimmed over his rough petition.

"Frederik Stang made an impression after the lecture when he pounded the lectern in frustration. 'There are so many Norwegians coming to America that it damages my country at home. I try to meet personally with as many Norwegians in foreign lands as I can, even in California.' "

Richard said, "Start with a gift to the sovereign. You will catch his attention with thirty-two ounces of gold and a ring of garnets.

Bjorn said, "I love my gems from the hills. The biggest came out of the Indian war club in my side. It was the color of my blood running out and as big as my thumb. I'm saving it for Maria if I ever see her again. The others are good enough for the King."

"Enemy Indians or wildlife, you get into trouble when you're alone."

"It happens without friends or enemies."

Richard laughed, "You've got more friends than you know."

"I've got more enemies than you know and his name starts with B." He scowled but then brightened. "I recovered forty-eight ounces of gold in two weeks and I had the garnets."

"Capital. Keep a nugget for Mr. Stang, and a bigger one and a jewel for the Prince. You are ready for the King?"

Bjorn gulped and said, "Yes, sir. I have a contact from Norway. She is a local businesswoman with a wellplaced sister in Drammen. I have a letter of introduction" He did not say what her business was.

"I will be ready."

A frontal Viking attack on the massed bureaucratic forces of Scandinavia was nothing compared to the plan of Amundson's assault on the kingdom of Norway. At least to all appearances.

Bjorn was desperate to present a petition that would remove the legendary curse on the Amundson family. Alva Dahl had said his Majesty held weekly public audiences and Bjorn wanted one.

But no one on *Agilis* had ever enjoyed a status above a commoner.

Richard had seen important people in parades on the Fourth of July but had never dealt with an official higher than a Harbormaster. At the receptions in foreign ports where he was invited as the Master of *Agilis*, the high muckety-mucks kept to their exclusive circles. They surrounded themselves with an escort that shunned contact with the great unwashed, especially sailors, and avoided any Scandinavian with crooked hands.

Richard looked at Bjorn's contracted fingers and said, "Where did those come from?"

"These are common in descendants of Vikings. Some Frenchman named it Dupuytren's Contracture but his assistant called it the Viking Disease. It afflicts my trouser snake down below too."

"Damn it, keep your pants on and cover your hands with gloves. We'll get you white leather handhiders when we get to Christiana."

"And then?"

"You might be a lion inside, but you must appear like a gentleman on the outside. We have to work on that shaggy mane of yours. You can keep your new beard after it's trimmed like a gentleman's."

"My beard hides my scar."

"We will find a creative barber. And you'll need a jacket, vest, and trousers."

"I've never worn a suit in my life."

"About your petition."

Bjorn pulled out the draft covered with changes and blobs of ink. The sections were,

Introduction

Grievance

Benefits for the King

Conclusion

"What is your title?"

"I don't know. How about, 'Clear Viking Curse'?"

"Try 'Correct Injustice.'"

Bjorn wrote Correct an Injustice and moved to Introduction. He read in a proud firm voice,

"My name is Bjorn Amundson. I am descended from Bjorn the Bold who served Rollo the great Viking in many campaigns. He was famous as the most ferocious warrior in Chartres."

"That's a good start. Your Grievance section?"

"Bjorn the Bold was the scapegoat when the siege failed. Rollo directed the shaman to outlaw my ancestor and put a curse on his offspring for the ages. Rollo became the Duke of Normandy and forgot the curse. I am jinxed a thousand years later."

"Clear enough, but what can the King do?"

"His Majesty's action is next."

Bjorn said in a public speaking voice, "As part of your Majesty's crusade for justice, a review of this pagan ritual is appropriate. I request his Majesty enable a shaman to lift this curse. Such an honorable gesture would increase the fame of his Majesty at no cost to the treasury. Thank you, sire."

Richard thought for a while. "Okay," but there are important tasks that come first in Christiana.

1. Hire a mentor to help us with the bureaucracy.

2. Visit the Bird Room in the Royal Palace where we wait.

3. Buy a suit of clothes and shoes.

4. Meet the clerk of the court who makes his Majesty's schedule.

5. Practice royal etiquette in the presence of the King.

6. Practice the speech.

"That is a lot."

"You have to do it."

The calm passage in the English Channel made up for the tumultuous North Atlantic. Bjorn was overjoyed to be nearing his home several hundred miles away. The air smelled different and the days got longer as they sailed north.

Porter said to Bjorn and Maverick, "We are in Europe. Plymouth England is forty miles off the port railing and Brest France is forty miles to starboard. Waves of the English Channel undulate ahead."

Bjorn said, "All I see is the haze but it feels good to be back."

Maverick said, "I'm in England. I never expected to see it. Family legends say my people came from here a long time ago."

Porter said, "About this time tomorrow, we'll be a hundred miles northwest of Chartres, France. That's where your ancestor the Bold Berserker got his curse."

Bjorn shuddered and gazed away out to sea.

Porter chuckled and said, you must be brokenhearted that we don't have time to sail past Le Havre and up the Seine River to your site of fame."

"That's all right."

"*Agilis* was a frequent visitor to Le Havre during the slave trade. You know she was built as a slave transport ship?"

Maverick said, "I knew some slaves but they came from Africa, not Europe."

"We are passing the cliffs of Dover and the mouth of the Thames, but we can't visit London yet. *Agilis* has to unload her cargo at Bremerhaven. Our first landfall in Europe will be in four days."

Docking at Bremerhaven, Richard turned Bjorn and Maverick loose for the day to explore the city.

Maverick reveled in his first steps on European soil and Bjorn revisited the taverns along the waterfront. He ducked into one saying to Maverick, "Come on in. I tipped many a glass here."

Maverick declined. "I'm going to check out Bremerhaven since I've never been here."

"See you back here midafternoon."

Maverick wandered the streets of Bremerhaven in delight. His only money was American gold dollars but the merchants were overjoyed to trade their mere goods for real gold coins. They bit down on them to judge the purity of the gold.

After a quick lunch bought with sign language and beer, Maverick took a shortcut through an alley. The odor in his nostrils was unmistakable. Somebody was brewing beer and he was an alcohol nut. Equipment was rattling inside a door under a sign in German that read, *Die Einreise ist verboten. Kein Zutritt*

He didn't know what the sign said, but he did know the other side of the door would be interesting. He went in.

It was to all appearances a normal brewing operation. However, the portly manager did not feel visitors were normal. He charged Maverick in a bear hug. Stumbling outside, the manager hollered, "*Polizei. Polizei. verhaften diesen Mann.*" (Police. Police. Arrest this man.)

Efficient German policemen appeared as though from thin air and grabbed Maverick.

"*Komm mit mir ins Gefängnis*, (Come with me to jail.)"

A policeman roughly prodded him several blocks to the police station and locked him in. Maverick's southern accent was baffling to their German ears that were accustomed to careful proper English.

By late in the afternoon, Porter had waited and waited but Maverick did not show up. Bjorn returned and didn't know what happened to Maverick either.

With a passing familiarity with German, he asked the local tavern owner about Maverick. The owner suggested a visit to the nearest police station.

Porter followed Bjorn in. Using a mixture of sign language, pigeon German, and intuition they asked if they had seen anyone looking like Maverick.

The police chief said, *Ja. Er ist hier.* (Yes, He is here.)"

"Can we see him?"

Communicating with a mixture of spoken and body languages, the police chief led Richard to a very unhappy Maverick.

"Mr. Hatfield. I can't let you out of my sight without you getting in trouble. What happened?" said Richard.

"I followed my nose to the smell of mash. I wanted to expand into beer. I guess that sign on the door meant 'keep your ass out' but I couldn't read it."

Bjorn said, "How did you get locked up?"

"I don't know. I was looking at a brewhouse when they got all excited."

Bjorn said, "They take their beer making seriously and guard their secrets like a treasure. You're lucky we found you."

Richard said, "Can you understand these people, Bjorn?"

"A little."

They walked back to the huge wooden desk in front of the police chief. Bjorn cleared his throat and the chief looked up. "*Ja.*"

Flustered, Bjorn asked the chief if he understood the Norse language.

Replying in Norwegian, the policeman beamed and said, "Yes I do. The brewer and I have partnered with the Aass brewery in Drammen to construct a brewhouse. I learned Norwegian in the process."

"That is a coincidence. The man in jail is also interested in a joint brewing venture. He is from the famous state of California. Have you heard of it?"

"Of course I have heard of it? Just this month, my entire family left from the port of Le Havre. They will get rich in the gold rush."

Richard said, "They could have been part of that armada sailing north to San Francisco."

"Why didn't you say your associate is a brewmeister? I have to give him a small fine for the record, but he can go." Opening the cell door to release Maverick, he said, "Please stay in touch. Here is my address."

They negotiated a small fine that dropped by half at the sight of the gold nuggets. They shook hands.

"What is the name of your operation?"

Maverick thought a bit and had an inspiration, The Sonoma - Sacramento Brewing Company, a Genuine German Beer.

"Sonoma? My cousin is destined for a vineyard near Petaluma. Maybe you will meet."

Richard said, "There is a good chance. Amundson and I own a vineyard there. Maverick doesn't know it yet, but he will be offered the position of head brewmeister and winemaker."

Maverick was shocked, but overjoyed to get out of jail."

Bjorn said, "Let's board the ship before they change their mind."

"Let's go to Drammen."

"Let's go to Drammen."

The two *Agilis* hands, Master and passenger, wrote and revised the petition on the sail from Bremerhaven to Christiana one last time. They followed the advice of Alva who edited the working draft but left out the looming menace of the curse. Her background included an amazing span of humanity and beliefs but she did not necessarily accept all of it.

Bjorn remembered her words, "Write down your beliefs about the curse"

"My ancestor received a spell and I suffer the effects."

Alva continued, "Poke holes in those beliefs."

"The curse caused me to lose my *New Viking Gold Mine*."

"What do you mean, could have caused that?"

"I could not read the confession."

"Can you really think the shaman lost your workings?"

"I don't know."

"Debunk these misfortunes, cleanse yourself, and go home. Get new beliefs to replace the bad ones."

"I can read."

"I can speak."

"I can persuade."

"I can lead."

The philosopher woman said, "Use these new beliefs in your life."

'I will visit King Oscar, but I am still marked.

Richard said, "You are superstitious."

"No, I am not, just realistic."

Richard said, "We will print your final appeal in Norway. Are you ready?"

"I will be ready."

21 - HM Oscar I of Norway

The mentor's office overlooked downtown Christiana. In his hands was the handwritten petition. "Your first line must say, 'Unto his Majesty, the King of Norway and Sweden.'"

Bjorn nodded his approval and Richard smiled.

"Address the envelope with royal titles or it will show disrespect. He wrote with a firm hand, 'His Majesty, Oscar I, King of Norway and Sweden.'" The engraved card he placed in front of Bjorn said, Never Touch the Royals.

"Always wear your gloves. If the monarch breaks tradition, your grip must be light and fast. Never remove your gloves.

Later, they found a recommended tailor who was skilled at dressing Norwegian men. Bjorn left the shop in a fine new suit. Under the Bernadotte coat of arms, the warrant in the window of the barber read, "By Appointment to the Royal Court of Norway." That was good enough for Bjorn and he submitted to a proper haircut and beard trim.

Richard looked at him and said, "Aren't you a handsome specimen. The King won't know what hit him"

At the end of that week, Bjorn Amundson and Richard Porter stood facing the entrance to the gleaming new royal palace in Christiana, Norway. A line of carriages stopped to drop off ladies in furs and men in cummerbunds to attend the King's weekly audience.

Bjorn and Richard walked through the entrance showing that they belonged in the palace. After sign-in formalities, they were ushered into the Bird Room to await his Majesty. The room had been filled with chairs since their tour the previous day.

Beautiful murals covered the walls and the ceiling with scenes from Norway. Scaffolding in the center of the room supported an artist rushing to touch up the tail feathers on a bird on the ceiling before the public poured in. The soaring white bird looked complete to a casual observer or even a careful one.

They were dismayed to see at least seventy-five people ahead of them. The mentor shook hands with the clerk and said, "Thank you for the appointment." The clerk checked the Amundson name on a list. It petition was seventy-five out of seventy-five. The mentor said, "This is the best I could arrange at the last minute, and it's not a good one. There is a chance the King will not finish the list. You will need to reapply for next week.

Born's cleared his throat and quietly rehearsed his Norse poem one last time.

Valiant were the Norsemen all
Led by Bjorn the Bold
Fierce the walls of Chartres
Strong the warriors from within

The painter looked down from the top of the scaffolding and commented through his oil paints, "You sound as Norwegian as I am. The king loves ancient sagas and poetry and he will like yours."

Bjorn reviewed the previous days' activities. They were lucky to get the last appointment on the royal schedule. The court clerk said the petitioners could reach a hundred people and cautioned them to listen closely for their name. "They don't ask twice."

Bjorn rubbed his sleeve over the carved mahogany box with the gold nameplate engraved with HM Oscar I. The gold cup inside was polished to a mirror finish.

The mentor explained, "The officer will announce your name and the reason for your visit. He will introduce me. I know his highness and will present your case. Approach his Majesty with respect and never speak until spoken to."

Bjorn whispered, "I hope I can remember that. Life on a ship is not so formal."

"I will inform his Majesty that you wish to present a gift. Hand the case to the sergeant-at-arms who will give it to the King. I must warn you, King Oscar may accept it and he may not. You could be dismissed. It is his pleasure at all times."

An announcer opened the doors to the throne room and called loudly, "Attention, petitioners to his Majesty, King Oscar of Norway for September twenty-second in the year of our Lord eighteen hundred and fifty-two. His Majesty is prepared to receive you."

The room of petitioners stood and bowed including the mariners from *Agilis*." You may be seated."

Some held gifts, some came with papers, and some with attorneys. The the King could be seen through the open doorway sitting on a fancy chair. Some might say a throne, but Norway had a constitutional monarchy and the royal formalities were reduced.

The announcer called the first name. In a short three minutes, the petitioner was led from the throne room in chains and surrounded by policemen. The mentor said, "I wonder what he said to his Majesty?"

The day dragged on with petitioner after petitioner. In some cases, the King refused to hear the matter. In others, he made a direct ruling. Some he explored. No one could predict his reaction.

The pendulum inside the tall case clock in the corner swung slower and slower. The stream of petitioners lengthened and lengthened.

Bjorn was hungry and asked about lunch. The mentor was horrified and said, "We Norwegians do not eat lunch, although a few have an afterbreakfast we call lunsj. You will have to wait until dinner."

The afternoon dragged on and on except for the excitement when a second fortunate was dragged in chains out the doors. The mentor said, "That man was accused of stealing his Majesty's time. Oscar must be in a foul mood."

By the end of the day, Bjorn lost all hope he would be presented or ever escape his curse. It was a surprise through the slightly cracked open doors to the throne room when they heard the secretary say, "Your Majesty, do you have time for one more?" His Majesty said, "The last one if you would."

The secretary said, "Please have the mentor and Bjorn Amundson approach the throne." An official looking stranger sat to one side but said nothing until Bjorn bowed to the king.

The stranger began, "Sire, as Minister of the Interior, I have a program to foster the agricultural and mining interests of our fair country of Norway. Many Norwegians carry their talents around the world, even as the Vikings did. These efforts have borne fruit in the remote land called California."

The King grunted and said, "I know of California. Russia is competing with England and France for influence there. Spain and Mexico's influence is waning, but America's is increasing. Norway has growing interests in California."

"My client wishes to offer your Eminence a token of his love for Norway. Mr. Bjorn Amundson, a capable and courageous Norwegian gentleman, operates a mining enterprise in California. He begs you to accept this small gift of his success. It is pure gold from his mine near a town called San Francisco in the New World."

The king made an offhand gesture to the Sergeant at Arms who took the mahogany case from Bjorn and extended it to the royal hands.

Raising his eyebrows at his name on the lid, he opened the lid and smiled at the name repeated in the embroidery on the lining. In his hands, he hefted the weight. No other royal cup in the palace was heavier. Courtiers strained to see as he turned it round and round with his gnarled hands. The garnets brought sparkles to his eyes. Those closest saw the bit of grin at the Bernadotte coat of arms on the back, his family crest."

"What a marvelous object from our countrymen abroad. They represent our Viking ancestors well. Your gift to the people of your homeland, Mr. Amundson is appreciated. It shall be presented to the Church of Norway for its high celebrations. I am sure they will treasure this chalice."

The mentor said, "We are honored by your gracious approval, your Grace."

After the King raised the chalice for the room to admire, the mentor looked at Bjorn and quietly continued, "If your Eminence would spare us one moment more, we have a minor petition."

The king looked distracted, but he was pleased enough with the gift to say, "You may continue. What is it?" The sigh showed the fatigue of a long tedious day of tedious requests.

"My client offers a short poem for your pleasure, Sire."

"You may proceed."

Bjorn called on every shred of courage and selfcontrol he had ever imagined. The time was now. The blond Norwegian stood tall and man to man faced his Majesty, King Oscar I of Norway and Sweden, Knight and Commander of the Order of the Seraphim, Founder and Master of the Royal Norwegian Order of St. Olav, Knight of the Order of the Golden Fleece.

With a clear calm voice, he envisioned the fjords, the mountains, the Viking stories of his father, the gods of the Norsemen, the spirit of Rollo and his great-great-great-grandson, William the conqueror.

> *Valiant were the Norsemen all*
> *Led by Bjorn the Bold*
> *Fierce the walls of Chartres*
> *Strong the warriors from within*

"Enough." His Majesty looked tired.

The mentor stepped into the moment, "As you remember Sire in the year nine eleven our Viking ancestor, Rollo, advanced across the ocean to Upper Normandy. Our ancestors were valiant."

The King closed his eyes for a moment.

"Yet in this harsh environment, we Norsemen succeeded. Of course, your highness remembers the campaign Rollo conducted in Normandy. Due to unforeseen circumstances, the partial victory at Chartres resulted in the treaty of *Saint-Clair-sur-Epte*.

Rollo blamed Bjorn the Bold at random for the partial victory. The return to camp was delayed to vanquish three Turkish mercenaries, and a sentence of cowardice was pronounced and he was outlawed. A shaman planted a rune stone with the curse. The Bold was disgraced and banished from Norway. The Amundson family has lived with that stigma for generations.

We petition the court to examine Amundson's family history. They have honored Norway from then to now. We respectfully request that this curse be erased. The malediction was placed by a shaman and only such can remove it."

The King stood in a towering rage. "You are requesting that we the King of Norway embrace paganism? As the leader of the Christian Lutheran Church of Norway, we reject the dark forces of the pagans. We deny this request. I am insulted."

He signaled the guards, "Take him away."

The King stomped out of the room.

The Sergeant at arms called to the soldiers standing outside, "Another one."

They seized Bjorn and escorted him to the Bird Room.

"Wait here for the police."

The exit door from the throne room opened and the secretary announced, "His Highness, King Oscar I of Norway and Sweden, has concluded today's audiences."

The late-arriving petitioners folded their paperwork and plodded out. Beautiful Norwegian landscapes painted on the walls by Johan Christian Dahl, a distant relative of Alva Dahl, escaped their consciousness. Norwegian birds and butterflies were no solace to Bjorn.

Collapsing in a chair at the back of the room he mumbled, "I am lost. All I accomplished was to anger the King of Norway and Sweden too." He spit on the royal coat of arms on the wall.

Richard said, "You're not a failure and don't spit on the floor."

"Ejected from the presence of the King and arrested? That's nothing."

The mentor had a benign point of view and said, "There are times a petition is successful and times it is not. By the way, you are not going anywhere and certainly not to prison. His Majesty can get irritable at the end of the day but he will recover. The counselors see to that."

Bjorn leaned back against the wall and closed his eyes defeated, down, and disappointed. The bailiff said, "All of you must leave so we can prepare the Bird Room for a state visit tonight."

Bjorn's opened his eyes to stare at the ceiling. The scaffolding was gone and the image was complete.

"What kind of bird is that? I see a whitetailed eagle on the ceiling, brave and undefeated. I wish I was like him."

Richard followed his gaze upward and saw the same heroic bird. "That is the type of eagle that flew over the American River and guided us to our first gold strike. He inspired you then and gives you hope now. Bjorn, you are that heroic eagle."

The guard spread his arms to push the group from the waiting room but he was stopped by an official looking sentry who called loudly, "Is there a Mr. Bjorn Amundson present?"

He said to Richard, "This is it. Thank you for helping me but I will never escape the curse."

He stood up, "I am he."

"His Royal Highness, Prince Oscar Fredrik, commands your presence. Come with me."

Bjorn looked at Richard at the mentor and back to the guard. "What did I do now? Spit on the floor?"

22 - HRH Prince of Norway

The petitioner questioned the escort, saying "I am supposed to go to jail, not to see the Prince."

"Hurry. He is waiting."

The company followed the escort down a long hallway. He stopped in a vestibule where a clerk sat behind a desk. The escort said, "Bjorn Amundson and company to see his Royal Highness Prince Fredrik."

The clerk said, "Prince Fredrik will see you now," and opened the door. At the far end of the room, Prince Fredrik sat on a chair smaller than the King's but nearly as ornate.

The secretary announced, "Your Royal highness, Knight and Commander of the Seraphim, Knight of Charles XIII, Commander Grand Cross, Order of the Sword, Commander Grand Cross, Order of the Polar Star, Commander Grand Cross, Order of Vasa, Grand Cross with Collar, Order of St. Olav, if it is your pleasure I present Mr. Bjorn Amundson and company."

Bjorn and Richard bowed slightly to the prince.

The Prince said, "Welcome Mr. Amundson back to our country. May I call you Bjorn?"

Bjorn nodded, "Certainly sir."

"My father, his Majesty King Oscar, has many burdens and cares deeply in his position as leader of the Church of Norway. The church rejects the slightest hint of pagan worship as the evil temptations of Satan. Their doctrine preaches that no such thing as a curse exists, especially one that endures through the ages. A shaman is considered to be a charlatan."

Bjorn's heart sank. He thought I am doomed.

The prince continued, "I am studying the sagas from Norway and Iceland. The Vikings displayed the height of heroism, courage, and ambition. Their poetry is the most beautiful in Norse literature. You have clearly studied the sagas as well. "

Bjorn agreed, "Your Highness, that is true. I especially enjoy the saga of Egil Skallagrimsson."

"Your command of the Norse poetry recited to his Majesty was masterful though short. I commend you."

"Thank you, sir."

"I am studying the dark arts of the Völva Seer from the ages of the Vikings. I understand the nature of the curse Rollo put on your family. Whether a curse is real or superstition is for others to say. I am open minded."

"With respect, sir, it is real to me."

The prince cleared his throat and grunted slightly. "I do not pass judgment on such matters, but there is a contemporary Völva who is instructing me in the practice of the dark arts. She believes herself to have influence in the world of benevolent and malevolent spirits." He dictated a royal command to the secretary and sealed it with wax.

"I hereby direct that the burden of the Amundson curse, whether true or false, be lifted in its entirety."

Bjorn froze.

The voice in his mind said, What was that?

His heart skipped a beat.

His mouth refused to speak.

Time stopped.

"Entirety?" as he stared at the prince.

"That is the content of the order."

Bjorn's wide eyes begin to blink again, and he said quietly when he could speak again, "My gratitude knows no bounds, your Royal Highness." He bowed to the prince.

"I desire for you as a noble Norwegian to prosper. That is all."

An important looking man seated next to Prince Fredrik walked to them. He said, "This audience with his Royal highness is concluded. Please come with me."

The gentleman led Bjorn and Richard to the vestibule. "Allow me to introduce myself. I am Frederik Stang, the Minister of the Interior. I encourage cultural and mining activities everywhere to feature Norwegians. Your activities in the insane state of California have come to my attention as an outstanding example of the Viking qualities. You showed courage in addressing the king of Norway, and handled yourself well."

Bjorn said, "Do you really think so? I feel I failed miserably."

"Thank you, sir"

"On this day when my countrymen are immigrating for this infernal gold in California, his Majesty's government desires a representative in the area.

He said, "My emissaries report on Norwegians abroad. I love your initiative, courage, judgment, and yes, even your exploits. I like your leadership with organizing the squatters. Your stand for justice has not gone unnoticed by his Majesty's government.

Stang continued, "You are brave and honest, well prepared, and speak well."

You are the man to assume this role. Will you accept the role of contact for his Majesty's government in San Francisco? You would report to Christiana on the issues of interest to Norway."

Bjorn couldn't say anything for several moments. When he recovered his voice, he said, "I . . . I . . . don't know what to say. This is an honor, Mr. Stang."

As the representative of my father's government and all of Norway in San Francisco. I encourage you to open relations with the Norwegian community in Seattle and secure the future of our immigrants in the Western United States. Go now and good luck.

"You are our best man in the New World. I wish you good luck. My budget is severely restricted by parliament and I can only provide modest resources. Meet with my purser before you leave and present them a list of resources that you need. Together plan for your reports. We look forward to working with you, Mr. Amundson."

Prince Fredrik motioned to the attendant who approached, "Conduct this pair without delay to the royal shaman in the cave of spells and healing. Wait there for my instructions. He shook hands with Bjorn and Richard.

Please follow Vidar Johansson to the cave of healing.

Vidar said, "Please follow me." He led them from the Royal Palace, "We will walk to the cave, but it is some distance off. Would you like some coffee and . . . ," he coughed, "and a Danish pastry? They were stolen from Austria by Danish bakers and that name has stuck, even here in Christiana."

Bjorn said, "No. I must lose this family curse."

They walked through the town uphill from the fjord. The trail led through Norway spruce trees dripping with moisture, ancient and gnarled. Bjorn was too excited to notice, but Richard Porter noted they would make magnificent masts for sailing ships, at least those growing straight in the depths of the forest. Trees in front grew twisted and tortured in ways that reminded him of strolling spirits and ancient gods from stories told by sailors on his ship.

The forest grew dense, dark, and deathly quiet. Only the faintest trail pointed to a stag with huge antlers. The magnificent creature strode ahead to herald that an important person was arriving. He halted before an ancient runestone guarding the mouth of a deep grotto from which wisps of fragrant smoke wafted. Dank moisture dripped from every surface onto the illdefined path.

Vidar Johansson said, "You will find the shaman in the cave of spirits and healing. My Christian faith forbids me to enter." He retreated down the path.

Bjorn trembled with anticipation. His new life might come from this grotto. He plunged into the dim cave. Richard followed.

A surprising line of seven glowing torches placed in natural niches stretched far into the mountainside. Pungent odors of ancient ferns rose from the soft spongy mat underfoot with every step. Transparent ghosts appeared to fly around in overlapping multitudes and jostle them in eerie silence.

A distant gong announced their presence.

Sitting under the dim light of the seventh torch behind a small fire sat an ancient woman. She wore a shawl against the dampness of the cave, her hair was black and long and well cared for. Long slim fingers were twisted with arthritis but her voice was beautiful and functional.

She called out as the cursed Amundson approached. "By the spirits of the gods and the lords of the underworld, the goblins of the forest I asked for you to come. We have important business."

The rhythmic voice of the drum brought the shaman through the threshold from the physical to the spiritual world. The acoustics of the animal skin stretched over a bent wooden hoop echoed through the cave.

She threw a handful of powder into the flames that exploded with bitter smoke. She waved to Bjorn and Richard to partake of the smoke. Bjorn took a breath and coughed violently. He took another and another.

"I feel the presences entering my body."

Richard breathed more lightly and only coughed Mr. Big a time or two.

The Shaman with gestures motioned Bjorn to stand on a stone warmed by the fire and began a low chant.

She said as she reacted to his yearning, "For what purpose do you summon our ancient spirits?"

Bjorn stammered, "It concerns my ancestor, Bjorn the Bold who served the Viking leader Rollo."

"A very powerful man must have been your ancestor to serve a lord of Sir Rollo's stature. That Rollo founded the empire of Normandy? What is your business with him?"

Bjorn said, "He cursed my ancestor and family unjustly."

"Unjustly! You accuse the great Rollo of injustice?"

Bjorn summoned more courage than before the King, before Brannan, in the Squatter's Meeting—all the courage from every corner of his being. From his full six-foot and one-inch height he pronounced . . . , "Yes! I challenge the great Sir Rollo, Duke of Normandy, to end my injustice."

Encouraged that the world and séance did not end, he said, "My family does not deserve the Nídstang Curse."

"Ah, the Nídstang curse is most powerful. It can only be lifted with supreme sacrifice."

Bjorn said, "How much sacrifice?"

"Gold, much gold."

Bjorn handed his pouch to the shaman. "Yours."

She hefted it in her crazy knotted fingers and chanted to the ghosts in the dark of the cave, "A good man requests freedom. Spirits, can this powerful curse be stopped?"

From the blackest depths through shimmering incandescent fingers of flames he heard a voice of throbbing strangeness. "The Nidstang curse has stood for a thousand years. Why end it now?"

"May the curse be fulfilled forevermore," shrieked the shaman.

The disembodied voice said, "Thirty-two generations of Amundsons have lived under this curse without a fault. It is surely fulfilled."

Bjorn did not notice that the shaman was an accomplished ventriloquist and was throwing her voice to the back of the cave. No matter because the waves of redemption transformed his body into a new man.

The seer said, "Your pursuit of the supernatural beasts of the dead across the sky in the wild hunt is successful. You are free!"

Bjorn Amundson stood tall and said, "My father burdened me to conquer the curse and I have. No more will we Amundsons be plagued by misfortune."

The shaman said, "Go in peace and build on the shoulders of your ancestors. I see a fertile future in your endeavors." She gave a long chant, "The ancient gods have joined the spirits of the forest and our Savior Jesus Christ to bid you strong powers and good fortune."

Taking Bjorn's left hand, she rubbed her hands along his crooked fingers. "You have the curled hands of the Viking disease. Your curse is gone and so are these."

The old hag retrieved a bottle of oil. "This oil from the heart of grains has magic healing power. Take a small amount every day. Tie a splint to the fingers and straighten them a little every day."

"There is a curve in another place."

The shaman knew instantly that he was referring to the manhood between his legs. She had worked with many men and knew it was an exceedingly sensitive subject. "A surgeon has proven this oil heals that member with stretching."

When in a loud voice, she shouted, "You are whole!"

She faded out through the entrance.

A steady rhythm of ching, ching, thud guided them out of the cave of healing. The hunched figure of the Völva could be seen in the fog chipping away the lowermost runes from the ancient stone guarding the entrance.

Bjorn stood tall and said, "You were here and saw. I am a new man in all ways."

They returned to Christiana.

Over a beer that night in the Carlsberg brewery, Richard said, "I have a load of ice for London and an introduction to the East India Company. Bjorn, my friend, I got you to Norway. Will you join me to Canton, China? It is time to pursue your new fortune."

"I am honored but I must visit Stang in the Department of the Interior first to arrange my new duties."

23 -Am I Really Free?

Ice Masters at the Regent's Canal Dock in east London regaled Bjorn with stories of selling ice around the world. "Why, that Frederick Tudor fellow from Boston even delivered a load of ice to Calcutta in 1833. The crystal clear New England ice caused such a sensation that residents immediately constructed an icehouse. Your ice from Norway is popular in London as well. It would be good in steamy Calcutta too."

Bjorn said, "We Norsemen are enterprising. If people want ice, we will sell ice."

###

Acknowledgement

Maya Stefansdottir, an Icelander for generations, provided immense help with the Norse culture and the culture and history of the Vikings. You are a true *skjaldmær* (shield maiden) who contributed immensely to this tale. Thank you.

My personal gold panning experience (unsuccessful) was the basis for the gold placer mining difficulties.

Writing this book has been a whale of an adventure. Thanks to those I have met along the way

About the Author

Drawing on his life as a cowboy, farmer, engineer, and author, Clifford Farris brings gripping stories about real folks to his novels—always with a touch of humor. He has penned and published writings on woodworking, gardening, and meat smokers. Other credits include short stories, a musical melodrama, and a hundred and fifty technical writings. He and his wife, Ann, live in the Denver Metro area of Littleton, Colorado.

Request for Reviews

Thank you for reading my book. If you enjoyed Bjorn Amundeon's adventures, other readers would appreciate your honest review at the bookseller where you bought the book. You can contact me directly at

cliffordfarris@Desertcoyotepress.com

or visit the website

www.Desertcoyotepress.com

CPSIA information can be obtained
at www.ICGtesting.com
Printed in the USA
BVHW071206071221
623418BV00003B/23